Catcher

)

Kalyn Nicholson

koze.

Koze Publishing | Toronto

Copyright @ 2018 by Kalyn Nicholson

koze.

info@kalynnicholson.com
Visit the author on the web: www.kalynnicholson.com

Summary: Eighteen-year-old Carson finds her dream world and real world colliding as she unearths a nationwide conspiracy and fights to stay alive.

ISBN 978-1-9994151-0-5 (paperback)—ISBN 978-1-9994151-1-2 (e-book) [1. Action & Adventure–Fiction. 2. Coming of Age–Fiction. 3. Dystopian–Fiction. 4. Fairy Tales, Folk Tales, Legends & Mythology–Fiction. 5. Magical Realism–Fiction. 6. Occult & Supernatural. 7. Romance, New Adult–Fiction. 8. Visionary & Metaphysical–Fiction.] I. Title.

The text of this book is set in 11.5-point Minion Pro Regular.

Cover photo by Tung: www.instagram.com/iamtongue
Cover design by Zoe Alexandriah: www.instagram.com/zoealexandriah
Book design by Katherine MacKenett: www.kmghostwriter.com

First Edition

To my sister, Kyra, for being here for the journey since high school, when this book was called *Dreamcatcher* and the story was only just planted seeds. To my best friend, Maggie, for fertilizing the idea and being the push I needed to rewrite it years later. To my dad, Kent, for constantly believing in me whenever my confidence drifted, bringing me back to the keyboard and growing the clouds to new heights.

And finally, to caffeine and music, for keeping me floating amongst the clouds no matter the late-night hour.

All My Life - Texada

PROLOGUE
quiet – EXES

BLACK MIDNIGHT AIR painted the backdrop of that late second-state night. Every star seemed to shine visibly in the sky, like a blanket of string lights across a silky black curtain.

The final hours of my fourth birthday were just winding down. I sat on the squeaky, pleather seat of our air lift as it navigated up and down the same comforting streets of Vancity we'd driven through all my life: familiar corners and doorways . . . parks we played in on seventh-day afternoons. We had just left my birthday celebration, hosted at my Uncle Char's. There, my small family had gathered together and sung the birthday song while I blew out the fake candle flames, hoping to land a new portal update that had extended colour codes and games, with virtual furry creatures they used to keep in old-world zoos.

Now, as I leaned my head against the cool sheet of glass that divided me from the crisp air outside, staring at all the twinkling white specks sparkling back at me, I felt a peaceful sense of joy from what it meant to be another year older. Social schools would begin next week, and I couldn't wait to join the other four-year-olds of Vancity. I glanced forward, catching the subtle shift of my parents' hands as they laced fingers over the middle console. To my left, my baby brother Axel snoozed, sound asleep in his toddler seat.

We were one quiet, happy family—until a sudden pair of

1

headlights glaring through the front panel of our lift lit up our world of bliss.

It all happened so fast. The piercing sounds of colliding metal cut through the air with a shattering screech. My body lurched forward from the impact like a rag doll. The lift belt yanked tight across my chest and neck in a burning grip, and the horrified screams of my mother clashed against the sound of shattering glass like thunder against lightning.

In a flash, we had slammed through the guardrail of the road leading into our neighbourhood. I felt gravity pull our weight over the edge of the road with a sick lurch—and in seconds, we were plunging toward the dark river below.

A loud *smack* shattered the air when we punctured its surface. My head snapped against the side of the thick door, and my entire world turned into a flashing, dizzy haze of white spots and blurred lines. The lightning-fast moments ticking by suddenly ebbed back into an unnaturally slow rhythm . . . and the dark river welcomed us, chillingly, as it began to swallow us whole.

I blinked fast, struggling to process what had just happened. Around me, the bodies of the people I loved sat limp and motionless. The sight of them made my heart jump into my throat, and adrenaline surged through my veins. Instinctively, my hands shot toward my lift belt. I pulled at it frantically with shaking fingers, struggling to unravel the strap cementing me in place. I glanced again at everyone else, all of them unconscious, and the sudden horror of being alone in our sinking lift gripped my heart with an iron fist.

Then, piercing needles of icy water started to sting my feet. Water was beginning to pour inside.

I screamed for my parents as it rose, cutting into my skin like slow-growing, icy ivy. When it got to my neck, I gulped in a few last breaths, trying to swallow as much air as possible before the water took me with it.

Finally, after one last gasp, the water rose past my head—and the cold pierced the last of my skin like mini shards of glass.

My mouth opened in a panicked scream, my arms flailing slowly through the viscosity of the freezing water, thrashing desperately in search of some way to freedom. Then the water filled my lungs, and my vision began to cloud, dulling the edges of the unmoving bodies that surrounded me with it . . .

It was in that state of stupor that I first came face to face with him.

The first thing I remember seeing was white light, my consciousness slowly becoming aware of a new space around me. I could see it . . . yet, somehow, I felt as though I were the light itself, even as I was looking right at it.

This must be the doorway to death, I thought. That quiet moment of bright light I had heard about, meant to ease your pain and suffering before purifying your soul for whatever lay in wait on the other side. It welcomed me, and I felt myself pulled toward it like a moth to a flame.

Only, in the next moment, the light began to flicker, flashing in and out of countless vertical lines that seemed to come to life all around me now.

As the light faded to a backdrop yellow, I caught beams of its warmth through the cracks in the vertical lines around me—and realized that the lines were trees. Looking down, I became aware of the glowing image of my body. My feet seemed lighter, and my hands appeared to be my own, only softer. I turned my palms over, feeling the air not only between my fingers but also through my skin. A weightlessness lifted me to my feet, which was when I noticed the damp grass below me. I dug my toes into its lush soil, feeling the earth as though I were made of it.

Slowly, each of my senses returned to me, until I heard the sound of a bubbling stream nearby, its song luring me toward it with a sense of curiosity that danced to life in my mind.

I headed toward it. With each weightless step, I traced and

3

laced through the bodies of warm willows and old oak trees until, gradually, they thinned and gave way onto a vast field.

The warm energy pulsing through me kept me moving in the direction of the water, like an invitation, as my eyes took in the surrounding world of colours and textures with hunger. Everything smelled richer and beamed with a soft vibrancy, pulsing with subtle waves of energy that only became visible when I trained my eyes on a specific place.

As I walked, staring up at the cotton-pink clouds, a movement from up ahead caught my attention.

I stopped dead in my tracks—and saw him for the first time.

He was younger then, kneeling over a crystal-blue stream. The stream sat at the edge of a thick forest that mirrored the one behind me, every branch coated in buttery golden sunlight.

Our eyes locked with curiosity, and the warm energy nudged me forward again.

I made my way toward him through the long grass with slow movements, feeling the cool, damp earth beneath my feet as I closed the distance between us. Our eyes never moved from each other. I felt my tentative, four-year-old thoughts begin to race, wondering what was going on . . . yet my body kept moving forward with a confidence that was all its own.

When I finally got close enough, the boy stood, stopping me in my tracks with kind, charcoal-grey eyes that stood out against his soft, childlike features. He stared at me for a moment, looking me over with uncertainty before turning his gaze back to the other side of the stream.

I followed suit, curious to know what he might be looking for, yet seeing nothing but trees. When I looked back to him, he was searching my face, assessing me before locking eyes with mine again.

We stayed in that moment, lingering in the confusion that seemed to fold around us both, before the boy began shaking his head from side to side, an expression of determination coming over his face.

4

Finally, he opened his mouth, and the first breath of words between us filled the air, piercing the silence of the forest and the sound of the stream.

"Wake up."

Bolting up, I woke in a bed covered in sheets that matched the colour of the eyes I had just been staring into.

It wasn't long after waking up in the hospital that I found out Axel had died in the crash.

His loss shattered our family. Afternoons that had once been filled with evening strolls to the park and cartoon flicks on our family portal turned into family-member drop-ins veiled in whispers and weeping between the adults. Soft sobs and raised voices laced the air between my bedroom and the one that belonged to my parents, next to mine.

Each night, I waited patiently on the edge of my bed for them to walk through my door, tuck me into bed, and tell me everything was going to be all right. That Axel was just sick and needed to get better. That nothing terrible had truly happened and it was all just a bad dream.

But the door never opened. No explanation of why he was gone comforted my sorry heart, and the nights spent on the edge of my bed turned into mornings waking up on top of the covers, still wearing the same tracksuit from the day before.

I never understood what was going on, and my parents never truly seemed to recover from the loss. The week after Axel's death, over portal-food leftovers, my dad explained that I was no longer going to be attending social school. In order to ensure my safety, they had decided I would be a "home social," which meant I would be taught from the safety of our home by my dad.

The world wasn't safe, and bad things could happen if my parents weren't around. So, to them, the idea made sense.

From that day forward, they spent every moment trying to

control all outside occurrences that surrounded the only child they had left. They made me wear safety sensors anytime I rode my bike farther than the front drive. Whenever strangers approached, they shielded me like a human wall. We were never able to afford another lift, which meant long, awkward walks to supreme stores and family events. They even rewired our home portal to only serve natural foods, leaving the days of popped candies and chocolate turnovers to become a sugar-dusted daydream of the earlier years.

The thing was, it didn't help. No matter how hard they fought to protect me, our family limped along in a constant state of defection.

I prayed that, with time, the aching feeling of loss would subside, and we would become accustomed to a life without Axel. That eventually our dinner table could be sprinkled with laughter and play again, or that I'd at least be allowed to go back to the park for visits, even if it had to be with their surveillance. That life would find its way back to some kind of normal.

But it never did.

That's the thing about death: the flowers die, the people slowly stop coming by to check on you, and eventually the world moves on in its natural pace and everyone goes back to their regular lives. Everyone, that is, except for those who lost someone.

Days turned into weeks, which drifted into months, and eventually I let go of the idea that life would ever feel the same again. While my mother's crying gradually hushed into quiet stress and my father's anger muffled itself into mindless submission to his own day-to-day routine, I learned to deal with the loss of my brother in my own way.

A few short weeks after Axel's death, I started pulling out my own pyjamas and tucking myself into bed. I had grown tired of waiting for my parents, only to wake up with a kinked neck and tingling limbs in awkward positions.

The first night, I pulled on my favourite crescent moon sweater and patterned, cotton shorts, climbed under the covers, and let out a puff of air. I lay there, feeling the hard knot of confusion and frustration burn its way through my throat, and let my quiet sobs fall onto my baby brother's teddy until my eyes grew so heavy that they finally pulled me under.

Not long after they closed, a white light like the one from the accident cast itself across my field of vision, only to fade fast into an outstretched cloud that cushioned my trembling limbs. Tears still stained my cheeks, and the heavy sobs that had carried me off to sleep still lingered, following me into my dream.

"Are you okay?" a soft voice asked from above me.

Rolling onto my back, I stared straight up at another thick cloud hovering above me. Familiar grey eyes peeked over the edge of it. One look at them up there on the cloud—at the tousled dark hair topping the boy they belonged to—and somehow my sobs turned into hysterical giggling. He looked so silly, all concerned about a girl crying in the clouds. I wondered if he knew his hair was shooting out in all directions, like one of the wild animals I often saw on portal screens.

At the sound of my laughter, the boy's serious eyes turned up in a smile I couldn't quite see from where I was. When I blinked, he appeared beside me, sitting cross-legged a few feet away. I pushed myself up, marvelling at the feel of the soft cloud-wisps beneath me, and how they could somehow carry the weight of my small body.

"Who are you?" I asked him.

"I'm your friend," the boy replied with a soft certainty.

"What's your name?" I asked next, my childlike mind naturally curious to know someone new who was close to my own age.

Puzzlement instantly came over his face. "I . . . I don't know," he admitted. He looked to the sky, pulling at memories he seemed to be struggling to remember. Cascades of pale grey clouds filtered the warm sun shining down on his face, weaving through the shades of his eyes.

"You don't have a name?" I pressed, my attention still trained on their unusual colour: a mix of silver and dark grey that I had never seen before.

"I don't think so," he replied, looking embarrassed as he stared down at his hands.

"Grey. Let's call you Grey," I said happily, getting to my feet so I could walk closer to him. Standing above him, I held out a hand, wanting to make this boy feel better the same way he had done for me.

He looked up and smiled before taking my hand and getting to his feet.

"Want to go cloud surfing?" he asked, a wild look sneaking into his youthful eyes. Before I could answer, he pulled my hand forward, and jumped from the cloud we stood on.

I tumbled after him. As the wind rushed past my ears, we fell to the cloud below, landing with a graceful roll on the bouncy surface of its sponge-like vapour. More giggles filled the air, and for the first time in weeks, I found myself laughing.

We spent what felt like days bouncing from cloud to cloud, wrapped up in twists and flips until the sky faded from blue, to black, and then to white again.

The following morning, I sat at the kitchen table, munching down the tasteless buckwheat cereal that sat in front of me. My mother's face was still pale, and my dad's tired eyes scanned over portal messages about upcoming school lessons. I, however, felt a faint flicker of warmth—like happiness—return to my blotchy red cheeks.

From then on, I continued to dream of the boy with grey eyes. He slipped back into my unconscious mind every time I laid my head down to rest at night. With the uneasy state of my family and lack of friends, thanks to my new homeschooling, I didn't question it, let alone mind.

After our tenth battle of dragons and countless rounds of cloud bouncing, I found myself drawing simulations of our dreams during homeschool portal time. I'd scribble down our storylines of defeating bizarre monsters, or what the world looked like as we flew above the compounds of towns I had never heard of . . . until one late afternoon, when my father caught me in a daze-filled doodle.

"This is my friend Grey," I told him, motioning to the second stick figure in the photo.

"That's nice, honey. Can you show me blue and yellow, too?"

I could tell he didn't understand what I meant, so a few days later, I brought it up with him again.

"Dad, last night I had a dream that Grey and I turned into monkeys from those old-world zoos. We escaped our cages to a jungle full of trees! He told me bananas should come from trees instead of portals. Is that true?"

My dad gave me a puzzled look, collecting an answer as he scratched his bobbing chin.

"Yes, bananas once came from trees. Did one of your social-school books tell you that?" he inquired.

"No. Grey did," I beamed back at him.

"Grey, hey? Sounds like a pretty smart imaginary friend, kiddo." Chuckling, he patted my head and turned his concentration back to whatever was beaming back at him from his portal screen as he paced aimlessly back across the loft room.

At dinnertime, to break the silence, I'd often blurt out uninvited stories about my dreams with Grey. With time, the amused chuckles from my parents turned into humming nods and distant looks, as if everything I was saying was just another tale from a child that didn't quite amuse them like it used to. Instead of inquiring more about my new friend, they decided it was best to start arranging play days with Mina, the golden-haired girl who lived across the street. She was also social-schooled from home, which made it convenient for our parents to drop us off at one house or another so that we could start doing our lessons together as our parents grew closer.

Being an only child, Mina clung to me like the sister she never got, and I began to enjoy my evenings spent learning lessons from her soft-spoken mother, despite Mina's constant complaints.

As time moved forward, I slowly began to keep the tales and triumphs of my dreams with Grey to myself. Even with Mina, despite how close she and I became over time, any mention of his name resulted in hunched-over giggles or hand-on-hip judgments for being too old to still have imaginary friends.

I loved Mina, especially since she often saved me from ghostly moments spent in a house that no longer felt like home, but nothing compared to the friendship I built with the boy who only ever existed in my mind. And the weird part was that, as I got older, so did he.

As the years passed and he didn't disappear with them, I stopped mentioning him altogether. Although my parents were overprotective, they didn't seem to notice much past my general well-being, leaving it easy for me to live in the world inside my mind.

Even I had to admit, a part of me knew how odd it was that the one and only person who seemed to truly know me was a made-up character in my dreams. Yet at the same time, be it from denial or truth, I felt as though it wasn't as crazy as it might have seemed.

My dreams with Grey were my own little secret—my escape from an emotionless home and a confined world. From the minute I learned to write on a portal screen and received my first gift of one from my Uncle Char, I started sneaking old-fashioned notebooks out of my dad's office, tracing the words that documented every detail of my imaginary adventures. I feared that if I left them on my school-portal, my parents might embarrassingly stumble into a story that wasn't theirs to know about, so keeping the secret between sheets of old-world paper became my morning routine. Every sunrise, I'd jump from my bed and race for my dream journals, afraid that the edges of the moments Grey and I spent together would fade from my memory with each passing second. I wrote down every expedition, dream, and moment in those lined booklets, which I kept hidden away in the back of my closet.

By the time I turned eighteen, I had stacks of journals listing etails from all of the crazy adventures, fun excursions, and most of all, the story of how madly in love I had become with a figment of my imagination.

I fell in love with the boy of my dreams . . . literally.

CHAPTER 1
about you – kasbo

I CLOSED MY EYES *and leaned back, arms stretched high as the wind whipped and twirled, pulling at my hair like a hurricane. Shades of midnight blues cascaded through the night sky, the stars twinkling and dancing above me like someone had spilled glitter in the air. We tore down the empty streets at a speed that would definitely result in the loss of your lift privileges in the real world . . . but that was the beauty of this clouded reality.*

I screamed, howling like a wolf to the cratered full moon as I stood, towering over the topless lift with half of my body lurching in the air. A laugh melted into the scene from the driver's seat, and I looked down to lock eyes with its source. Adjusting myself to hold my balance, I stretched out my left foot, kicking the side of Grey's arm.

He latched on to my flailing limb to pull me down, and my body fell back into the passenger seat beside him with a thud. A warm feeling stretched its way across my stomach, then ran its way up my spine and out of my mouth in the form of uncontrollable giggles. I was high on life.

Well . . . sort of.

"You are absolutely nuts," Grey said, shaking his head in disapproval despite the devilish grin painted across his face. It should be illegal to look that enticing. My brain had really matured his features over the years. It took nothing but a simple flick of the corner of his perfect grin and a flash of those dimples to send my heart into a frenzy.

"I am absolutely adorable and you know it," I cracked back, and he responded with a wicked flash of his eyes, stretching his arm across the middle console until his palm found its way to my upper leg. I waited for the tingling sensation that often followed anytime we touched. Like a phantom limb, I could feel it like the echo of a whisper. There, but not quite.

"You are without a doubt adorable. Where to next?" His stormy eyes flashed back to the road ahead and mine followed. The headlights ricocheted off the painted yellow lines below, making the cracks in the pavement strike like lightning bolts across the asphalt.

I flipped through a few ideas in my head but couldn't come up with anywhere else I would rather be than right here. There was something about the cascade of street lamps and the vibe of the quiet night, speeding through the streets of an unknown ghost town, that made everything feel just so . . . right.

"To be honest, right here is perfect," I told him.

I reached forward, turning the knob on the stereo up full blast, and a downtempo beat bled into the air like smoke from the speakers. I looked over at Grey, taking him in as he bobbed his head to the song. The smile was still etched into his face despite the fact that he was hitting all the wrong notes as he attempted to sing the words. I racked my brain to remember what he looked like before his razor-sharp jawline became peppered with day-old scruff and his cheeks hadn't lost all their baby fat. When he noticed me watching, he commanded the lift off to the side of the road and turned off the headlights. Leaning in, his eyes held mine for only a moment before tracing a slow line up to the sky, mine following their lead.

Without the roar of the lift and the lights on the ground, even more galaxies appeared in the skies, glistening in shades of pink and purple. I felt the tingling whisper of his hand on my chin as he lowered my gaze back to his, only now the galaxies were in his eyes. Deep seas of stars outlined by the charcoal grey I had come to love over the years. He was beautiful, but not just for his looks; he was beautiful for the *radiant energy behind those smoky eyes, and for the genuine happiness that beamed from his ghostly smile.*

He was more alive than anyone I knew, in all ways but one.

Leaning in closer, I felt the tingling touch of his lips against mine, pins and needles exploding into sparks of electricity. We lingered there for a moment, letting this pocket of time—lost in space—embrace us as we slipped between cracks of consciousness.

"Shall we, darling?" Another wicked smile melted over his lips.

A moment later, the headlights struck the pavement again and we were off, returning to our blissful lift-concert-like state. My eyes travelled along the road ahead as we began belting the words to the song together, throwing hands and fists in the air at all the high notes. With each sharp note he missed and each dance move I attempted, laughs ruptured from the lift and my stomach cramped up in knots of euphoria.

This was my life. I never wanted to wake up.

☾

My eyes shot open to the obnoxious sound of a twinkling chime bouncing off the walls of my sunlit bedroom.

I groaned, despising the sharp contrast of reality against my dream as I settled into my conscious state. I could so easily let my heavy eyelids fall closed again, and drift back to the lift I was in just seconds ago with Grey . . .

A knock sounded at the door, closing the last inch of my entrance back into that world.

I groaned and buried my face in my pillow. On the other side of the thick, metal frame that closed off my bedroom loft, the echo of my father's voice muttered something about birthday waffles. Then his footsteps sauntered off in a hurry, without waiting for confirmation that I had heard a word.

I had barely made out anything he said, but my attention piqued at the word "waffles." Taking a deep breath, the smell of rich, buttery dough filled my nose, its hues of cinnamon and maple syrup tickling their way down my throat and making my mouth water.

For a brief moment, I had forgotten what day it was. My birthday. Great.

I sat up, pulling the fluffy white duvet from my legs before planting my feet firmly on the cool panelled floor. My hand smacked the top of my bedside portal, turning off the twinkling sounds with a little more aggression than I had intended, so that the swat left a tingling sensation on my palm.

"Good morning Miss Wallace! It is day 2-1-3. The temperature outside is a cool seven degrees; harvest is here. The time is currently 0700. Breakfast is warming in the kitchen portal."

I rolled my eyes, double-tapping my left temple to initiate the response speaker.

"Hey Port, once again, you can call me Carson. Also, yet another year you've forgotten my birthday," I groaned, tapping off the speaker button and opening the virtual home screen of the day in front of my tired, blurry vision. "Not that I care . . . " I muttered under my breath.

"Good morning Miss Wallace. It is day 2-1-3. The temperature outside is a cool seven degrees; harvest is here. The time is currently 0700. Breakfast is warming in the kitchen portal."

Useless. Checking the calendar in the far left corner of my vision, I confirmed the date before double-tapping once on my temple again to collapse the screen frame.

All of my temple portals had been dysfunctional for years now. When my dad decided to stay home to implement my homeschooling, our family took a bit of a financial hit, making up-to-date portal systems a luxury we couldn't afford. Instead, Uncle Char gifted me with hand-me-downs from my cousin Sasher each time she upgraded her software. He always synced the individual coding to my temple plate, but for some reason, whether it was the old software or just sheer bad luck, I had yet to receive one that didn't malfunction in one way or another.

I didn't care that much. It felt like irony in the purest form to start my day as a barely there shadow to what was meant to be my own personalized portal, only to go downstairs and mimic that same barely there presence as I joined my parents.

Only today was my birthday, which meant more attention than usual. Birthday waffles and quite possibly a personal question or two.

I braced myself for the awkward encounter. I absolutely hated my birthday. Not because getting older bothered me or because I was one of those people who couldn't stand the constant attention, given there weren't many people around to notice my birthday anyway. It was because of one reason in particular that this day always left me dazed in a cloud of pain, absence, and remorse.

My birthday also marked the anniversary of Axel's death.

Today commemorated fourteen years since he died. And without fail, my birthday always put the already detached energy of our family home on an even more distorted scale of awkwardness. Every year, I could tell my parents did the best they could to keep the focus of the day on me. In fact, during the fourteen rotations we'd taken around our solar source since the accident, they hadn't once even mentioned Axel's name. I'm sure they let his name drop from our dinner table "conversation" and his face disappear from our family portraits in order to help me—to help all of us—move on. But what I wished I could have told them was that all I ever wanted to do was ask questions about the brother I once had. To at least acknowledge his position in our family tree, or his toddler seat that was once tucked into the chair to my left every morning at breakfast. I wanted to understand where he had gone and why he wouldn't be coming back. But the topic was always out of the question, and I hated the way it made my mother cry when I brought it up.

It had been like that since he died.

His funeral was small and quiet, and the second his ashes were laid to rest, they both acted as if he had never even existed.

On my fifteenth birthday, I summoned the courage to ask to see his burial site as my only gift that year. After a few moments of blank stares from my parents across the table, I saw the water begin to swell in my mother's eyes and my father's mouth fall into a defeated yet firm frown. That was when I realized how broken they still were—how broken they would always be. They were my protectors, the parents who created the life within me and used all their power to protect it, but at the end of the day, they were still just afraid. Afraid to face their own pain and confusion, and unsure of how to handle mine.

They weren't angry with me when they said no. In their fragility, they were unable to even discuss the option. As though, if they let the slightest bit of remorse or remembrance through the cracks in their armour, the walls of strength and self-assurance they had built around the one thing they couldn't bear to face would crumble.

They were painfully human, and at such an early age, I struggled to process that.

I was only four when he died, Axel being two. But the feeling of being a protective older sister somehow never faded as time progressed, and while I tried to understand and accept my parents' way of handling their loss, I made a promise to myself never to forget him, no matter how much they felt they needed to.

I made my way to the kitchen loft, dropping into my usual chair before taking in the view of the three thick stacks of apple-cinnamon waffles waiting for me there. Their sinfully sugary scents infused the air with enough promise of comfort that the annoyance of waking from my dream began to drift away to the back of my mind. In the chair across from me, my mother sat silently sipping her coffee as she read what I assumed to be the latest updates of Thalia news on her embedded screen. I could see the small blue light just above her left temple flashing as she blinked and tapped away pages of details, navigating to some random headline. Then she shifted gears and commanded her portal first to move her 1400-hour client up a slot, and then to adjust the temperature in the room up three degrees. She always complained it was too cold.

Picking up the utensils beside my plate, I began to cut slowly into my breakfast, keeping my eyes away from her face.

I wasn't sure if I was waiting for a happy birthday, a good morning, or anything at all, but as I forked the first piece of syrupy goodness into my mouth, my mother's words broke into the cool air.

"Happy Birthday, hun," she said, giving me a quick sideways glance before shifting her attention back to the portal screen that only she could see, and taking another sip from her cup.

I stood and made my way to the kitchen portal, where I punched in an order for an almond-hazelnut latte before turning back toward her and replying, "Thanks!"

With a tight smile, she lifted her mug in my direction, signifying that her cup was now empty.

"Mind punching in another for me too?" she asked.

"Sure!" Spinning around again, I opened the door to find my favourite mug filled to the brim, a birthday candle etched into the foam that sat on top.

"Morning kiddo! How do you like the latte?" My dad's voice entered the main loft before he did. Placing my latte on the side counter, I shut the portal door again and punched in my mother's usual cappuccino before spinning to hug my dad.

"Great Dad, thanks! How did you manage to craft up the latte design?" I asked, watching him move over to our composter, where he punched in instructions for the usual morning cleaning. He must have made sure my favourite mug had been cleaned too, since I'd drunk some turmeric tea from it just last night before going to bed.

"Your uncle Char has been teaching me a few portal hacks," he said, making his way to the food portal to pull up the stock list of its contents. Punching away at the screen, he ordered a gateway delivery of the foods we were running low on and took Mom's cappuccino out of the portal before shutting it down for cleaning, forgetting to punch in a breakfast for himself first.

I sat back down at the table, taking another bite of my waffles and adding a few sips of my latte to turn them into a sponge. Then I closed my eyes and let the sweet concoction melt its way down my throat.

I had to give my dad credit: Despite the fact that our conversations didn't extend much past our homeschooling lessons and the latest upcoming simulation and portal devices, he was the glue that held our shaky house together. And, seeing as how we had spent almost every day together since I was four, I had grown to appreciate his subtle ways of showing that he cared. I took another swig from my mug, watching the thin foam lines of the birthday candle morphing away with every sip.

As my dad placed my mother's cappuccino in front of her, he kissed the top of my head, squeezing my arm briefly as he wished me a happy birthday, too.

"Thanks," I replied, cutting another chunk out of my waffles. I tried my best to chew slowly, knowing that I wanted to go for a morning run shortly after my meal. Eating fast might break me free from the shared space, but it would also leave me doubled over mid-run, and that was the only other headspace I enjoyed occupying, aside from being asleep.

My dad sat at the table, tapping his own temple screen on before flicking his fingers away in the air, blinking now and then as he maneuvered around the screen in front of him. My father always left his screen on public, saying it felt rude to be on private screening in front of others. I watched as the day's weather flashed alive in the air in front of his face, cool temperatures across the board promising an early harvest year, just like my bedside portal had said.

For the next fifteen minutes, the only sounds puncturing the air were my fork and butter knife scraping against my plate, along with occasional sips from coffee mugs. Glancing up now and then, I caught the faraway gazes of my parents eyes locked onto screens. Finally, I stood and took my empty dishes to the cleaning portal, where I placed them on top.

"Don't worry about those, hun, I've got it," my dad said, still staring straight ahead at his screen, one hand waving in the air.

Back in my room, I closed the door, sliding the lock into place as I made my way to the bed. Tapping my temple portal, I flicked through times and calendars until I found my playlist simulator. It was one of the only programs that seemed to sync properly to my bedside portal, which was good, because if any "real world" thing could take the edge off of dealing with my family, this was it. Mixed genres of music filled the screen in front of me, and I flicked through them with a few waves of my hand before settling on my "fire" mix. At the top of the screen, I set the sound option to play from both my bed and temple ports and my before I bent down, extending an arm beneath my bed.

From underneath, I pulled out a large box encased in a sealer bag that Mina and I had stolen from her parents at a sleepover years ago. She said it was a good way to keep secrets, and she was right: the only way to unseal it was by using the pulse from your own synced temple portal as a key.

Once synced, I tapped the side brim of the sealer and commanded it to unlock. "Opening your sealer bag now," the monotone voice replied from my portal hub. A second later, the pouch opened with a soft puff of air.

From the bag, I pulled out the box filled with my private contents: my current dream journal, some crystallized rocks I had found on different jogs around the city, friendship bracelets Mina and I had made when we were six and, finally, my running sneakers.

Pulling them from their hidden home, I tucked the box back inside the sealer bag and pushed it back under my bed. Then I stood and made my way to my closet portal screen to type in my usual jogger set. Opening the closet door, I retrieved the black, dry wick gear from its hanger before stripping my pyjamas from my skin in one swift movement.

As I slipped into my suit, I crept to my bedroom door and listened closely for any movement outside in the hall. As usual, it sounded as though neither of my parents had moved from their usual morning spots.

Walking back, I slipped into my bathroom, turned on the shower screen, and set the timer. Then I unlatched the lock of my bathroom window before climbing outside onto the soft, artificial grass on the ground below.

The sound of the music pulsing into my ears from my temple port blended with the morning birds chirping on the damp air, bringing instant comfort to my bones and space to my lungs, the way it always did. Ducking low, I made my way through our small back lot, then opened the white vinyl gate that led to the adjacent lot belonging to our neighbours.

Following around the back of their home, I continued to keep low as I passed the usual windows, turning the corner at the far end of their house and jogging left to avoid the street that passed in front of my family home. Taking another fast left, my feet pounded the dark road, carrying me away from view.

I had exactly twenty minutes. Best make the most of it.

I jogged down the slate, solar-panelled sheets of sidewalk slick with morning condensation, breathing in the subtle fog that lingered in the crisp, early harvest air. It was cool out for a second-state morning— perfect for a run. First-state days, being all days that began with 1, the air was always so hot at any hour that it made running feel as though you were pushing your way through thick, hot smog. Now that we had made our way into the second state of the year, however, the leaves on the few trees in Vancity cascaded to the ground in different hues of red and blood orange, and the air was growing thinner each day. Soon social schools would start back up, and then it wouldn't be long until the third state of the year, when ice fell from the sky.

I weaved through the city lift streets, trying to navigate which route I wanted to take to the harbour front that day. Running had become my only means of tapping into a high in the world of the awake, and it was the only time I really felt any sort of connection to Vancity. I had been born and raised here, but while the city was beautiful—cradled by a jagged wall of mountains covered with dark green vegetation on one side, and the pale, flat grey ocean on the other—it never quite felt like home to me. Or at least, it hadn't since the first short years of my life. After losing Axel, everywhere I went, I couldn't help but see the trails we once walked down as a family, or the river that we now avoided at all costs, effectively keeping us prisoners to the left side of town.

I turned a curve and jogged toward the path that I knew wound its way to the shore. There, my feet trudged through the damp sand, the backs of my calves burning with each lunge, but the energy and lightness of the morning falling away with every step kept me going. I charged forward, my lungs stinging as they gasped for air until, finally, I passed the abandoned lighthouse, tapping its side as I did so. I whooped in solo celebration as my portal screen flashed a new record time. Using the bottom of my shirt to wipe the sweat from my forehead, I bent over to catch my breath.

My heart thudded against my chest and I began to slow my breathing. I watched the heartbeat dial slowly crawl back to a high resting pace before tapping away my portal screen.

After a few moments, I rose, taking in the view from my new mental state. The cool ocean's hues and the whispers of sound it created as it rushed to and from the shore never failed to pull me out of my own head and into the present, if only for a moment.

I wanted to take a mental snapshot so I could somehow show Grey. Better yet, I wanted him to just be here with me. To slide his hand into mine as we sat in the sand, legs stretched in front of us, my head on his shoulder. He'd tell me some ridiculous story about the history of the oceans, or tales of wars fought on large ships out at sea, while I spun circles on the back of his hand with my sandy thumbs, a warm grin stretched across my face.

I kicked the sand in front of me at the thought, trying to rid myself of the torturous idea so I could get back to enjoying the view. If only I had fake flames to blow out now, that would be my only wish.

As the mirage of Grey faded and the beach sprinkled back into place, my eyes caught the corner of a white square standing in the space of sand that I had just kicked.

I bent down to examine it closer. Carefully, I plucked it from its spot and turned the foreign object over in my hand. As I peeled back the paper cover, I saw what appeared to be a pack of matches sitting in my palm, staring back at me.

Repelled, my first reaction was to throw them back—to get rid of the contact between myself and these tools of such destruction. Matches or fire starters of any kind were banned and illegal, punishable in ways I knew could result in portal blocks or, worse, portal prison.

But, even as I thought about the consequences, I couldn't help but feel a sudden flicker of curiosity and awe at the alien object in my hand.

I glanced up, looking left and then right, suddenly fearful— between the adrenaline of my run and my new discovery—that someone might be watching. I had heard of kids getting ahold of these things in order to start fire pits in the abandoned early cities that sat just outside of Vancity. During our homeschooling sessions, my dad had briefed me on them: the history of those early cities, collapsing into nothing but ash and atoms after fire starters in the form of bombs exploded over them, thanks to miscommunications and unfair trades. It always baffled me that the common public had access to such dangerous contraband back then. Even something as simple as a pack of matches or a gun in the hands of a common fellow could leave families broken, or towns in despair. Such things were banned when my parents' parents were only children. In the short time my dad and I had spent going over Thalia's history, he told me about how the first royals had collected the surviving population into what was then the small town of Terigon; how they had built civilization back up with new ground rules and regulations. From then on, anything deemed harmful to the public was only to be used by "Catchers"—those chosen by the original royals to catch any waking-world nightmare before it got out of hand.

I had seen photos of matches and knives so sharp they could puncture skin without much pressure, but the sudden thrill of holding one of these forbidden objects in the flesh felt like some sort of birthday karma. Such a curious coincidence that, I thought, tossing such a rare find back into the sand and simply being on my way would somehow always leave me wondering *what if?*

Not to mention that Mina would lose it if she got her hands on these. Neither of us had ever seen fire before, aside from the fake flames made by holographic candles, or the images on the portal news when whole forests sometimes disintegrated over the span of a few days from something as small as the fatal kiss of a lightning bolt.

No one had ever seen or made any real fire for more than thirty years, or so I had been told. As the newfound Thalia continued to survive and thrive, new inventions and technology came along to take the place of any human need for it or any other dangerous tool, leaving the Catchers with not much to do aside from ensuring that such weapons continued to remain weeded out of the hands of common folk efficiently and permanently.

Which made me wonder . . . why on earth was a pack of matches nestled here in the sand?

I sighed and shook the question off. Some delinquent must have lost them on the way to one of the abandoned cities. What other explanation could there be?

I shoved the matches inside the pocket of my running leggings and zipped it shut to conceal them before I could change my mind. My breath caught in my chest as I glanced around once more, making sure that there were no witnesses to my devious act. Keeping the matches tucked away in my sealer bag as a keepsake wouldn't quite make me a criminal, right? And showing them to Mina before adding them to my collection of cool keepsakes couldn't hurt, either.

Taking off again, I felt a dangerous current ripple through my body, making my legs feel light and my skin tingle with nerves as I traced the same route I had come down back toward home, the boxy corners of the pack of matches poking my leg with every stride.

By noon, I was sitting in the worn, black pleather chair of the Cove, sipping from a massive mug decorated with whipped cream and multicoloured sprinkles.

This ritual had become a tradition ever since Mina's fourteenth birthday, when we passed by the Cove and spotted some older girls with loud voices and vibrantly painted nails sipping from the same large white mugs. As we passed the open storefront, Mina stopped dead, her lanky legs pivoting toward the group of girls as she tossed her curly golden hair ever-so-boastfully over her shoulder. Reaching for my wrist, she kept me from moving on past the shop, turning my attention to the high-pitched *"no-way-he-said-what's?!"* coming from inside.

"Today, we are both officially women. We no longer drink hot chocolates like the thirteen-year-olds we once were. We drink coffees with pretty painted nails and loud squeals of womanhood. Come on!"

And with that, she pulled my resistant limb into the Cove for the first time, neither of us having any idea of the memories its walls would hold for us over the following years. As we approached the order portal, Mina tapped away at the screen of coffee orders until she landed on the prettiest photo. It didn't look very adult to me, but I knew Mina well enough to understand that any protest would only result in more hair-flipping declarations. Minutes later, two birthday specials consisting of overly sugared vanilla-flavoured coffees topped with massive dollops of whipped almond cream and sprinkles in every colour of the rainbow arrived in front of us.

Just like that, we were addicted.

Normally these days, Mina and I came to the Cove to sip on soy lattes and vent about our troubling issues of overbearing parents and restrictive portal firewalls. But, today being my birthday, we prepped our guts for the sugar overdose that awaited us.

"I can't believe we're finally eighteen," Mina gushed, leaning forward to squeeze my arm before rocking back again with her signature hair flip. "Well, you're eighteen. But two months doesn't count, especially when we both know I am not only wiser, but more worldly than my bestest friend," she added, sticking her tongue out at me and taking a long swig from her coffee cup. "Next stop, specialty schools!"

"Yeah, I guess," I replied, waiting patiently to bring up the matches I had found this morning as passersby continued to walk in and out of the Cove. My hand rested over the front pocket of the knapsack that held them. Still, what Mina was talking about seemed almost as big. I stared blankly out the window, trying to picture my life in just two weeks' time.

I had been homeschooled my entire life, so trying to pull together an image of hallways, portal screen lectures, and existing among fellow students hurt my brain. It just felt completely foreign to me.

It also didn't help that I wasn't all that excited to go to Kings Court Specialty. Don't get me wrong, it would be nice to attend a real school with Mina for the first time in our entire lives. But my dream had always been to go to Yorker—a school that specialized in brain simulations and virtual realities. I could still remember the day my father told me about Yorker and the types of studies and test work they did there to improve brain activity and creativity. Most of the specialty schools in Thalia catered more toward the improvement of technology, ethical advancements, and the conservation of the small, habitable pieces of the planet we had left, among many other scientific and mathematical backgrounds. When my father explained the brain-simulation tests healers did on inpatients to alleviate pain, or the virtual reality systems they worked on to improve brain training or practical talents for those who had the financial means to undergo the tests, all I could think about was how alike those simulations sounded to the dreams I had with Grey. From dying patients lying in clouds for their final moments to Catcher training schools that created virtual obstacle courses of flames and fury to test the ambitious minds of those who felt they could defend our state, I knew it was the only field I could really see myself getting into.

"I want to go *there!*" I'd said, my finger pointing to a picture of the thick black doors that led to the front entrance of what I now knew to be Yorker. As I flipped the portal page, my eyes gleaned at the sight of the tall buildings and lit-up streets of a place that seemed to be quadruple the size of Vancity. I could feel the magical energy of its thriving atmosphere pulsing from the pages. Even at the age of thirteen, I knew it was where I wanted to be.

Finding out that it was on the other side of Thalia had only heightened my attachment to my new waking dream. Dismissing my dad's chuckle at my newfound passion, I had never let the dream of Yorker die during my conscious hours. I thought about it nearly every day from that point on.

That said, as my last year of homeschooling drew to a close, I was forced to face reality. Even if my parents had the funds to send me to Yorker, there was no way they had the trust to leave my life in my own hands halfway across the state. With Yorker being located in Terigon, a place littered with people of all kinds climbing in and out of mountainous towers in the most central part of Thalia, I knew there was no way I could ever go. Vancity was on the far west side of Thalia, making it a full day's trip to Yorker by air train.

So, reluctantly, I let the dream of Yorker die out in the back of my mind, settling instead to explore the gridded streets and busy sounds of Terigon in my dreams with Grey. Though I knew it wasn't real, it took the sting out of another disappointment that came with knowing my life could never be that which I dreamed it to be.

"Carson, can you please cheer up? I know you'd much rather be packing up your things and heading off to Yorker, leaving your best—and might I add only—friend behind, but you're stuck with me. So you'd better get on my level because I will not have you raining all over my parade, mmkay?"

I shook myself out of the trance I had fallen into, and cocked an eyebrow in Mina's direction.

"How many late-night screener shows are you watching?" I asked, laughing at how ridiculous she sounded. I took a sip from my mug, having been so lost in thought that I hadn't yet embraced the sweet aroma of its liquid goodness. The sugary coffee took to my tongue like icing to a cake, and I could feel its warmth as it made its way down my throat, making me want more. Another customer entered the shop, and with shifty eyes I watched him walk behind my chair before turning my attention back to Mina.

"Honestly, not enough," she sighed. "I started watching this new show called Greenville's Richest, and the main guy, Bourbon, he is to die for. I swear we're meant to be." Mina took another sip from her cup before placing it back on the table between us.

Her eggshell-blue nails tapped against her left temple, lighting up a screen in front of her as she motioned me over to her chair. Squishing in beside her, I watched as the words "Bourbon Forres" appeared in the Syncher search-engine box, and his profile came to life in front of our eyes. Adjusting her position, Mina tapped her temple port again and adjusted the screen privacy settings so that only she and I could see the screen.

The newest portal updates allowed a share screen like this from separate locations, but being that my own port had many upgrades to go along with numerous restrictions for sites like Syncher, I was stuck doing an old-school temple-to-temple watch with Mina as people gave us sidelong glances in distaste. As if I were of a much lower class based on the visual proof of my low-grade portal.

I wondered how they would look at me if they knew about the pack of matches in my bag.

Meanwhile, Mina had already started scrolling through topless photos and the occasional picture of a muscular man covered in tattoos holding on to his dog. This close to her, I could hear her oogling over the photos as if they hadn't been completely staged or curated. With every sigh of adoration that escaped her, my eyes rolled.

Pulling myself away from Mina's screen, I plopped back into the chair across from her and laughed.

"You do realize that isn't who this guy really is, right? It's just who he's imaged to be on Syncher. An illusion that you, my friend, are buying into just like he and his screener-show producers want you to." Mina had always been obsessed with portal screen shows, hopelessly quick to fall for the forged personas and orchestrated drama between people who apparently lived "real lives" in the bigger cities of Thalia.

"You know Carson, you're lucky it's your birthday because you're about as friendly as a damp sponge today," Mina clucked as she gave me a disapproving and sarcastic once-over.

"Sorry. I'm just a little on edge today," I responded, my eyes darting back to the front of my pack. I wondered if there were a way I could show Mina the matches on our way home since, as I was slowly beginning to realize, there didn't seem to be much in the way of a pocket of opportunity to show her here at the Cove.

Mina nodded, mulling over her own thoughts before speaking again.

"Did your parents say anything about Axel this year?" she asked, guessing that would be the topic that was weighing on my mind. And I was surprised to realize that, after finding the matches, I hadn't thought about Axel or the morning with my parents at all.

"No, but I didn't expect them too. Speaking of which, I'd better leave soon. You know how crazy they get if I'm even triple 0-2 past when I said I would be home," I said as I took another large swig from my mug.

Now it was Mina's turn to roll her eyes. I watched their deep blue irises returning to centre as she threw her stringy arms in the air in exasperation.

"Parents. Can't live with them, can't live without them. How did it turn out that the two most interesting and highly attractive young females in Vancity ended up with two sets of the most rigid and strict parents in the history of Thalia?" She threw another classic Mina hair flip before reaching for her mug again.

"I ask myself that question every day. You would think that now that I'm eighteen they would grant me a little more freedom," I huffed back.

"Seriously though. I mean, I can't even complain that much. At least my parents let me have more portal power after finishing social schooling. You have no idea what you're missing out on. It's like a whole other world on here," Mina gushed, tapping just above her temple for emphasis.

I hated to admit how incredibly jealous I was the day Mina's parents upgraded the software of her portal. My hands balled into tight fists as she rattled off all the new things she could do and see, including being allowed to finally have a Syncher file. Even now, getting the tiniest glimpse at whoever the hell Bourbon was on Syncher left my bones aching. Despite the fact that specialty school would start soon, I felt like a current was pulling me into even more isolation, dragging me away even from the best friend I'd ever known—the person who had been by my side throughout all of our sheltered childhoods.

A tightness caught in my chest at the fear that her newfound freedom might put distance between us. I couldn't let it happen.

If only I could talk my parents into lifting some of my own portal restrictions. It wasn't like I was asking for an overall upgrade, just access to more screen shows, or even just Syncher. They'd always made it clear that such things were only made for melting brains, not nourishing them, and insisted on bookmarking portal news articles into my own system that they deemed to be "much more interesting than the crap other kids are doing."

Most times I didn't mind, being too caught up in getting as much sleep as possible to really push the issue. Not to mention, the enduring layer of overprotection felt like the only proof I had that, somewhere inside of them, they really did care and have my best interests at heart. They wanted to do right by the one child they had left, and I chose to believe this was the only way they had to pay tribute to the son they'd lost.

At the same time, the constant supervision, vast restrictions, and insane curfews were a total drag for someone my age. Not that I had any friends besides Mina to go out with anyway, but that was beside the point. Syncher was a main hub for people my age to connect and meet no matter where they were in Thalia, and screener shows were just the common conversation between anyone younger than thirty. If it weren't for the fact that I loved sleeping so much—solely to spend time with Grey—I was pretty sure I would have gone mad by now.

"I know." I sunk deeper into my chair, twirling my thumbs as my gaze met the window again. "Maybe I'll be able to find someone at Kings Court who can hack in and update my system. We might have to make friends with the nerdy types . . . only no, that wouldn't work. Our house portal would detect the upgrade the minute I used it at home, and we both know they aren't going to let me live in the dorms. Plus, if they found out, they'd suspend my portal rights completely . . . "

I trailed off, leaning forward again but still looking out the window, racking my brain for a solution almost just to spite how royally unfair my real life felt sometimes. The contrast of night and day when it came to being Carson Wallace was the epitome of poetic injustice.

"I just don't get it. How do they expect you to meet anyone new or make any memories when they won't let you sync up with classmates online or live on campus? It's not like you'd be alone. You'd have me." Mina's hands made a grand gesture toward herself as if she were the next-best thing to a mama bear.

We both knew that, of the two of us, I was without a doubt the more responsible one. Living on campus with Mina would likely result in me taking care of her all the time, not the other way around.

I shook the image of Mina and I bunking as roommates, drinking coffees before class, and attending dormitory events together from my mind before the blow horns and streamers of my pity party could shoot back up again.

I was shrugging her off, not really wanting to dwell on the topic, when her fingers tapped her Syncher Screen back to life.

"Well, I just don't agree with them. So for that reason, my dearest best friend, I am making you a Syncher account. Happy birthday biatch, you are welcome."

I jumped from my chair, landing swiftly beside Mina as I took in the words on the screen.

"Mina, you can't!" I squealed. My palms instantly became slick, but my body was torn, positioning itself in a state of both protest and excitement. I saw Mina's hand flick to her side, clicking the "create profile" button with an evil smile on her face.

I stared at it in disbelief.

"Mina, my parents are going to kill me," I gawked.

"Not if they don't find out," she responded.

I turned my body, glaring at her.

"What! You'll only ever be able to use it when you're with me, so it's not like your home portal will tell on you. You can log on and off anytime we hang out. And it's not like your parents use Syncher. How would they ever find out?"

Placing her hands on both of my shoulders, Mina gave me a solid, loving shake.

"Come on Carson, you need to live a little. Make a little noise, shake your tail feathers, stretch your limbs—rebel for heaven's sake! You're officially eighteen! Break free and spread your wings, girl."

By the end of her spiel, Mina's voice had changed to a thick accent, and as she snapped her fingers with a glorified attitude, I burst into laughter.

This was why I loved Mina. The girl could make you laugh no matter how weird you felt.

I motioned my own fingers to the right, signalling her to open her screen back up, and she followed suit. My Syncher file finished blinking into existence, and I stared at my name stretched across the top right-hand side of it in bold letters. I expected some euphoric moment, but the cold simplicity of it made my high expectations sag, along with my shoulders.

"Maybe you should delete it. It's not like I have anything to post about," I mumbled. Filing back to my seat, I collected my empty mug and threw my bag over my shoulder, completely forgetting, in all the hype of the Syncher profile, that it carried an earlier source of rebellion.

"No way!" Mina rebutted, quickly jumping up with her own mug and planting herself in the seat beside me before I could get up. Lifting her arm to reveal her wrist port, she used her other hand to hold her mug up to her face, leaving only her kind eyes staring at mine from the other side. She waited for me to do the same, refusing to let me fall back into my usual pool of self-pity.

Puffing out a defeated breath, I lifted my mug to my face, rolling my eyes at her as she squealed in excitement.

Turning so our shoulders met, she lifted her arm, stretching her wrist port out in front of us. "Say 'happy birthday to me!'" she sang before snapping a photo of our four blue eyes peering over two large, coffee-stained Cove mugs.

And, without leaving a moment for me to protest, Mina dropped the photo into my profile as my very first post.

Though I wanted to object, I couldn't deny that the sight of Mina and me at our favourite spot sent a warm wave through me, especially as I thought about what the next year might do to our friendship. And she was right: it would be nearly impossible for my parents to find out about this, if my profile only ever lived on her port.

"You liiiiiiike it," Mina teased, dragging out the "i" in a victoriously high-pitched voice. "Carson Wallace, you are officially just like the rest of us!" she grinned.

"Now, pick a photo layer . . ."

CHAPTER 2
notion – tash sultana

AFTER EXPLAINING the filtering qualities of a photo layer, complete with skin-smoothing and eye-brightening features, Mina helped me add in a short bio and adjusted my file to include my latest portal playlist.

"You're always listening to such droopy bop music. Maybe you'll find your future droopy bop babe on Syncher and live happily ever after, thanks to me and this moment," she declared.

Within minutes, someone had already arrowed-up our photo, and Mina squealed again in joy.

Who it was, I had no idea, but it didn't matter. I suddenly felt a little less like Carson, the disconnected girl who knew no one, and more like Carson, the girl who had Syncher like every other eighteen-year-old in Thalia.

Walking home, I realized that I'd forgotten to tell Mina about the matches.

I would tell her about the matches on sixth day, I decided. That way we might actually be able to sneak out somewhere and flick them to life. For tonight, I just wanted to linger in what it felt like to be normal—try to pack it up and bring it home with me, into the final hours of my birthday.

I spent the remainder of my birthday reading a new book Uncle Char had sent me from his latest air-train run to Keith's Quarters, a city in the northern hills of Thalia. It had been waiting for me on the kitchen counter when I got home, wrapped in a bow with a birthday card written in coding we'd made from the cyphering book he'd given me two years ago. With most things being loaded into portals, reading physical books had become a favourite pastime of mine over the years. It started when Uncle Char slipped me my very first poem book when I was eight. Every year after that, he gifted me another book, and I spent the long, winding second-state days leading back into social schooling lingering over their pages during the sunlit hours. This time, I would be poring over words that would fill the time between now and going to specialty school, and I was glad for the newest distraction from my anxiety.

After decoding the birthday card message along with a hack to new music that hadn't hit portals yet, I flicked on the latest Trampled by Turtles tune and sank away into the egg-shaped chair in our family lounge. My parents sat on either end of the adjacent couch, their portal screens synced to some doc-series show about the newest form of life found in a solar system encompassed by the Andromeda Galaxy.

We had settled on pasta for dinner, since our neighbourhood wasn't due for gateway deliveries until tomorrow. Following dinner, my parents brought out a solo peanut-butter-and-chocolate cupcake, with a holographic flame standing tall on top.

They awkwardly sang the birthday song despite my protest.

"Make a wish," my dad said, holding the cupcake out in front of him, toward me.

I rolled my eyes as I secretly racked through a list of wishes I could pull forth. Mom tapped her portal screen back to life, leaving it on private so no one would notice. But I could always tell.

Looking back and forth from my parents to the flame, I landed on two wishes. One was the same wish I had every year, and the second was a new wish—one that I'd tucked away. Leaning forward, I blew out the flame.

I couldn't help but feel a little ridiculous for putting that much weight into the chance that an energized candle stick on top of a chocolate cupcake could change the fate of my future, but what did I have to lose?

I planted my cards face down, pushing both wishes out into the ethers and leaving it up to the birthday gods to decide which they could work with.

Yorker, or Grey.

☾

By the time I made my way up to my room to get ready for bed, my leg muscles had stiffened from my morning run along with walking to and from the Cove. I moved to the side of my dresser, peeling off my usual full-length pant suit and collecting it with my dirty tracksuit from earlier. I opened the door to my closet portal and dumped the clothes in, then turned and caught sight of my knapsack on the floor.

The matches.

I had almost forgotten about them since coming home from the Cove. Picking up the bag, I pulled them from its front pocket and flipped them between my fingers again. I walked back to my closet and punched in for a large T-shirt and shorts as I stared at the plain white packaging.

Taking them to my bed, I set them down for a moment while I slipped into my pyjamas and pulled the covers back, climbing into the welcoming puddle of blankets and pillows. Then, tapping my temple, I flipped through my music to my usual pre-bed playlist before bringing the matches back into my hands.

As the soft beat of BØRNS filled my ears, I took in the new edges and shapes of the thrilling object I was holding. The lingering smell of wicker made my fingers flip back the cover to reveal the black-dotted sticks inside. Without thinking, I pulled one free and caught it against the ragged stripe on the back of the pack.

A sparking burst of pungent oranges and violent yellows burned into the air, and I felt the warmth of the flame spiral its way around my thumb and finger. Shocked, I blew it out instantly, my heart pounding in my chest.

I froze, waiting for alarms to sound or the house portal to light up in threat.

Nothing.

I leaned over my bed, letting my shaking fingers drop the matches into my bedside table before slamming the drawer shut. I made a mental note to leave them there until sixth day, when I would show Mina.

I tapped my bedside portal, adjusting the light settings to dim and wishing I could do the same to my heartbeat. As I leaned back, tucking the duvet up around my chest, the portal rang out, making me jump even though I should have been expecting it.

"Goodnight Miss Wallace," the flat voice said before the last flicker of light left my bedroom.

I rested my head against the mountain of fluffy pillows piled onto my bed. The thought of sneaking off somewhere desolate and seeing bonfires of flames in the flesh flashed in my mind. I imagined what the flame from my match might look like dancing in a slow motion layer on Syncher. I wondered if anyone else on Syncher had ever posted real fire.

We could do it. If Mina wanted me to rebel, then what was stopping me? We could sneak away, somehow, and play with fire. Uncle Char's book would still be waiting for me, my parents wouldn't have a clue, and I might finally enjoy a moment of magic in the real world.

The thought both excited and comforted me as my mind drifted away into a blank canvas of black, imagining places just outside of Vancity we could go to execute my ever-so-rebellious teen act, before finally giving in to the heavy weight of a long day's sleep.

CHAPTER 3
fight the fire — layla

BEFORE MY EYES had the chance to flutter open, I became aware of a thick, black stench burning in my nose, making my eyes water.

I jolted up, and my muscles protested at my sudden alertness, aching from the movement.

Weird. Why was I still so sore?

Looking around, my eyes adjusted to take in the dimly lit details of the pale white bedroom I rested in; an atmosphere that, I was acutely aware, didn't belong to me. Walls that didn't look like mine, shapes in corners that weren't my things, unfamiliar blankets that wrapped around my tense body.

I shot a hand to my throat, as if to convince it to take a breath, as I turned my head from side to side, desperately searching the room for something familiar. My eyes dashed to the flashing blue light of a portal that rested on the bedside table, where 0445 shone above the port's night-mode screen. I had seen other numbers tell other times across that same bed portal, I realized, the familiarity finally catching up with me.

I was in my cousin's room.

My hands felt around beside me, my skin brushing against the scratchy charcoal fabric that cocooned my limbs. Images flooded through my mind, memories from a time just after Axel had died. I'd slept here, in my cousin Sasher's room, for a month back then, after my family had moved into my Uncle Char's house short-term. In Thalia, it was common practice for families to gather in mourning for weeks at a time following the death of any loved one. Accidents happened rarely here, and untimely death—especially that of a child—was so rare that it was never taken lightly.

I lifted the covers from the bed and planted my feet on the cool floor. After feeling my way to the bedroom door, I clicked open the handle and made my way out into the hallway. I passed the doorway that led to Uncle Char's room, remembering what it looked like when we came and spent another three weeks in this house after my Aunt Zandra had passed. Hers had been another fatal accident as she left for work one late afternoon. On her way down the elevator shaft, its suspensions broke. She was estimated to have fallen nearly ninety-two floors.

My Uncle Char handled her death a lot better than my parents had handled Axel's, still managing to raise Sasher on his own and, with time, find joy in the simpler things of life again.

As my feet carried me down the hallway, I heard a stream of whispers flooding the entrance to the lounge, and slowed my pace.

"Well, she started the fire for Christ's sake." My mother's voice was sharp even when it whispered.

"Now, we don't know that for sure. It's not unheard of for Catcher marshals to set a fire to make a death seem like an accident," my Uncle Char responded, his calm voice hushed as well.

My jaw dropped. Had I heard that correctly?

"You think this was Donte?" My dad's voice, this time.

I narrowed my eyes, struggling to figure out whether I should be scandalized or if I was just delusional.

Donte Kingsley was Lead Catcher of Thalia, the second ever to rule since his father had grown it back into the civilization it was today.

I didn't know much about the politics of Thalia, aside from its laws and rules. I knew Donte to be the face of the Catchers, but had never perceived him to have any say or control over them. Rather,

39

I thought of him the face they presented to the people to make the whole system seem a little more . . . human.

The way my uncle and dad had always spoken of it, most things were run by machine nowadays, keeping mouths fed, lives happy, and the country running smoothly. Catchers were around to keep the peace, if they were needed for anything at all.

The voices in the lounge must have heard my muffled gasp, because the conversation stopped suddenly, and the entire house fell silent, leaving nothing but the dim kitchen lights and the hum of the food portal between them and me.

I hesitated a moment, my stomach turning at the sudden realization that I wasn't going to like whatever I was about to walk into. Then I took a deep breath, and stepped away from the shadows of the hallway, into the lounge.

The faces of both my parents and Uncle Char stared at me from where they sat in the centre of the room, their eyes following me as I made my way down the two-step entranceway into the lounge, where I stood wringing my hands. Uncle Char scratched his balding head, his discomfort getting in the way of his normally witty greeting. I did my best to assess the looks on their faces for an answer as to what was going on. A pained smile crossed my Uncle's cheeks as he glanced toward my father in desperation. My parents looked to each other and then me, neither rushing to speak.

"What's going on?" I heard my own voice croak, making me suddenly aware of how dry and scratchy my throat felt. I looked behind me toward the kitchen, a sudden desperation for water consuming me all at once.

"You're up!" my dad said, his voice laced with forced enthusiasm. From the way everyone looked at me, I knew that whatever was going on had something to do with me.

I wanted to know what was happening, but the chalky thirst that clung to my throat screamed for higher priority. So I crossed the bar-style dining table of Uncle Char's sky-rise loft and tapped the kitchen's portal screen to life, its more advanced options leaving me puzzled for a moment before I found my way to the largest ice water the thing could make. The air in the room behind me felt eerily uncomfortable as everyone waited for me to chug down most of the contents of my glass.

Finally, I walked back over to where they sat, deciding to play ignorant to any of the information I had already overheard—not least of all because it didn't make any sense in the first place.

"What's going on?" I asked again, taking another sip from my near-empty glass. My eyes flashed from face to face, curious to know who would be the first to let me in on the secret and lift the current confusion.

"Honey . . . " my father trailed off.

"There was a fire last night. Catcher marshals are saying it may have been some sort of bad circuit in the energy panel," my mother cut in, stating it matter-of-factly.

"Right. You know how that damned power circuit would always glitch," my father added, jumping on the bandwagon.

My stomach fell. That explained the smell of smoke coating my clothes and hair as if every molecule of my existence had absorbed it.

Then, in an instant, my mind lit up with the memory of the snap of the match against its lighter strip, last night.

There was a fire?

"What? Wait, why don't I remember this? How did we get here?" I lowered my arm, setting the glass on the kitchen counter just behind me. I paced toward the high-rise windows, looking out over the lights of Vancity. Scratching my forehead, my brain began racking through questions. "Is the house okay?" came out first. My mind jumped to the sealer box beneath my bed. Sealer plastic was said to be fireproof, but the stuff was old. And the rest of my journals, in the closet . . . My heart leapt into my throat. Were they okay?

"Well, most of the house is still intact . . . but it's uninhabitable for the time being. We already sent out a claim for Catcher approval, to get some builders working on it as fast as possible," my dad responded, a sense of hope hanging questionably from his words. I couldn't tell who he was trying to convince: me, or himself.

My stomach sank again, and my thoughts rose and fell in tidal waves of worry and questions, struggling to process the information I was receiving. If Catcher marshals did a claim and found the matches, not only would I be in deep trouble, but my parents would lose our house. There was no way claims would cover the illegal acts of a delinquent. I shuddered.

"We couldn't get you out right away," my mother resumed, picking up where Dad had left off. "Your door was locked, so by the time we broke it down, you had inhaled quite a bit of smoke. The medical team finger-pricked you after your father carried you out to the front, and your test came back fine, except that your lungs needed O2 puffs. They put you on a quick ventilator and fed you sleeping gas so your body could recoup faster. That's probably why you don't remember any of it. You were still completely asleep when your father put you in Sasher's bed." Her explanation bounced into my ear, drawing an image in my mind of everything I had missed.

Uncle Char shot me a half-convincing smile at the end of my mother's explanation, his obvious pity emanating from his awkwardly pained face.

I could tell by his shifty eyes and sky-high shoulders that he wanted nothing more than to lighten up the situation with a joke or jabber. He always made an effort to keep the energy light, especially after Axel died—pretending to steal my nose, pulling pranks on me, sending riddles in secret codes and letting me have all of Sasher's cool hand-me-downs even when my parents said no. I remembered wishing sometimes that he was my father instead of the one I had, and the sudden guilt and shame that always followed at such a dismissal of my own father always hit me in the gut.

In contrast, his daughter Sasher wasn't always the nicest cousin to be around, so I was in no way missing out on having her as a sister.

Her cold shoulder and mean pranks of stealing my toys and leaving bugs in my bedsheets made it very apparent every time we visited that my presence was invading hers. She tolerated me better after we got a little older. When she turned sixteen and I was eleven, her cruel jokes settled into an acceptance of my presence anytime we came over.

And yet, even though she was horrible to me, in a weird way Sasher had become my go-to role model for most of my childhood. Anytime she left the house to hang out with her fellow elevenths from social school, I would snoop through her bedside and closet portal systems, dreaming of what my life would be like five years from now, when I could grow into all these system upgrades.

It had been over two years since I had last seen her. After she graduated from twelfth year, she took off for Terigon to attend Yorker Specialty School. I faked sick the night of her family farewell dinner. Having spent the majority of my childhood after Axel's death watching her gain more freedom while I only gained more restrictions, I decided to give myself a break from sitting through another dinner full of praise and excitement for a dream she would get to live out and I wouldn't. The image of her making her way down Terigon's busy streets full of city lights in a sea of thousands of Yorker students, or stuffing her face with takeout portal food or delicious café coffees . . . it all filled me with so much envy that it made my heart constrict in pain and longing. Longing for a life that, deep down, I already knew that I could never have, and that she had no reason to apologize for. The last I had heard, she had been offered a job in Elcer City right after graduation and was now an anchor for their daily portal news show.

Shaking Sasher and Yorker from my thoughts, I looked down, staring at the floor in an attempt to regain any sort of memory from the fire. *I must have been dreaming of Grey*, I tried to reassure myself, fearing any alternative reasons. *That would explain why I didn't instantly wake up from the smoke.* If I was in a deep dream, my brain might not have responded to my body's signals from that state of sleep paralysis. It wasn't the first time it had happened to me. It was only the first time it had happened during something serious.

Judging by the thickness in my throat and the smell of my clothes alone, their story made sense . . . but my mind kept flashing back to the matches in my hands, and the whispered words I had heard spilling into the air before I entered the room.

What had actually started the fire?

Could I have been the reason our house went up in flames?

Would Catcher marshals actually start a fire on purpose? And even if they would, why would they have set our home ablaze?

I dropped my heavy head into my confused hands, my thoughts coming up like thick tar rather than light conclusions. Everything seemed mired in such thick clouds of uncertainty that my brain felt as though it were stalled in a long portal upgrade.

My mother stood and made her way to me, placing a hand on my slender shoulder. Her faded blue eyes searched my face with a focus I wasn't used to. The act made me raise my own eyes to hers, and I watched her face fall into a softness she saved only for very special occasions. Pulling me into a hug, she took a deep breath.

"We are so happy you are okay," she mumbled into my smoky hair, her hand patting my head.

I let the weight fall from my mind for a moment, accepting the hug in a way that felt oddly suppressed between us. As if we both longed for the embrace, but couldn't communicate it properly. All our love and vulnerability made their way through that hug in the brokenhearted language our family spoke.

As she released me, my mother gestured back toward the hallway, and I followed her down it, catching the worried glance between Uncle Char and my father from the edge of my peripheral vision as I went.

"It's going to be a long night, Car, and we've got a lot to figure out here. Try and head back to bed for a few more hours. We will wake you up if we hear back from the Catcher marshals on next steps."

Her voice faded back into its normal matter-of-fact tone again as she guided me back toward Sasher's room.

Though I wanted to believe that my mother's lone intention was to comfort her only daughter, the secrets I heard beneath her words mixed the sweetness of her gesture with a sour flavor—one that suggested that there was more they weren't telling me . . . and, somehow, I knew I had to find out what it was. I felt as though I had woken up in some sort of parallel universe where everyone was saying one thing, but their faces and body language were singing a song that was slightly out of tune to a beat I wasn't hearing yet.

As we walked down the hall, I felt my weak and heavy muscles longing for rest. I blinked my dry and heavy eyes, which were now pulsing with the pain of a forming headache. However many questions I wanted answers to, the one and only thing I could be sure of in that moment was that my body still needed sleep—or, better, my mind needed Grey.

I let my mom navigate me back into Sasher's bedroom and watch me climb into the now-cool blankets again. She waited in the doorway while I punched a request for ocean sounds into the bed portal before ordering the lights out.

"Get some sleep, honey. We're going to figure all this out." Her reassuring words slipped through the crack of space between the wall and the door as it shut, leaving me in the darkness I had originally woken up in.

Lying back, I promised myself that I would discover the truth behind the fire in the morning. For now, I needed sleep. Sleep would be good. Grey would be good.

Yes. Grey would know exactly what to say to help me make sense of what had happened.

CHAPTER 4
this must be my dream – the 1975

I LOOKED DOWN *at my hands, the white pack of matches contrasting against the darkened shadows of my skin. They called to me, beckoning me to scratch their itchy ends across that dark line of friction, making me feel desperate to ignite another flame without thinking about the consequences. I ignored the thought of my parents down the hall. I ignored the idea of never seeing Grey again. I forgot about myself.*

All I wanted was fire.

I wanted it to consume me, to set light to the floor beneath me and burn around me in wild, reckless abandon. I wanted to be swept away in its heat, to burn bright with its power and to melt away in beautiful destruction. My bones yearned to become kindling, my skin felt desperate to be touched by the flames, my soul hungered for heat to rid it of its cold, dark hollows.

But with each flick of a stick across the rough strip, the matches only sizzled. They popped with promise, but left me pale-faced and powerless as I struggled to free the next one. I tore out the next match, and then the next, running them over the strip at different speeds and pressures, but none would light. None would give me the burning power I was longing for—the heat I needed to fill the space around me so that there would no longer be any differentiation between me and it. I wanted to burn down, bold and bright . . . but I was met with no flame.

46

Force built its way into each stroke I made, until there were no matches left.

"It's your fault," came those same words, spoken by my own tongue.

A few soft knocks at the door snapped me to attention, and I bolted upright in the same, stiff bed I had gone to sleep in.

How long had I been asleep?

Blearily, I glanced at the bed portal, which read 1014. Later than I usually woke up, but then again, I hadn't really been setting alarms these past two weeks. I tapped the port and ordered the blinds to be raised just as the door began to creak open.

As the sun punctured the room, two figures made their way to the edge of the bed while my eyes were still adjusting. Rubbing them, I let the daylight slowly flood into my pupils, giving new life to the room.

My mother and father stood at the end of the bed waiting for me to become fully conscious and greet them.

I yawned, my hand rubbing at my sore neck as I tried to let the ghostly words from the nightmare that had haunted me every night for the last two weeks float away from me.

"Is everything okay?" I asked, another half-yawn kicking in at the end of my question, making my words sound more whale than human.

"Actually . . . " my mom said, a grin stretched across her face as she flashed her eyes toward my dad before returning them to me.

" . . . we have a surprise for you," my father finished.

Sitting up, I gave a final shake of my head to rid it of the last remnants of the nightmare so I could focus on my parents. Which was when I noticed my father's hands tucked behind his back. Warily, I sat up a little straighter.

I wasn't sure how much more weird I could handle after the last two weeks of dead-end answers and cut-short conversations between everyone in the loft except me. Mina had come to visit twice now, and even she agreed that there was weird "juju" in the air—a term that she had heard Zara, her latest Syncher super-obsession, using in her daily snaps called "Morning Moments with Zara." Zara lived in Elcer City and had a nearly unheard of 88 percent Syncher status, making her one of Thalia's elite and therefore famous for nothing other than the high-level profile she held with the public. Girls all around Thalia copied everything she said and did like dolls, or at least that was what Mina had told me. It was because of things like this that I sometimes appreciated my portal walls.

Returning to the moment, I tipped my head toward my dad, publicly noting the hands behind his back.

"What is it?" I asked.

My mom glanced at my father, nodding once before he brought his hands forward and unrolled a thickly knit, navy sweater. Its long sleeves fell loose, leaving the snow-white letters of a specialty school staring back at me. I did a double take, not sure I was reading the large block letters right.

Did that say . . . Yorker?

"What is going on?" I almost choked on the words. Was I still dreaming? If so, this was so cruel.

"Uncle Char got in touch with some of Sasher's old teachers at Yorker over this week to see if it was too late to get you into some of their classes," my father explained before tossing the sweater on top of my blanketed legs.

I stared at the sweater, then looked back at them in disbelief. This had to be a dream.

"The house is going to take longer than we thought, since the marshals still haven't been able to determine the cause of the fire. We'll be staying here at Uncle Char's for the time being, but we need to get you into specialty school. We know this has been your dream for a long time, so we've decided to use the funds that the Catchers gave us to cover housing expenses during the investigation to pay for your air-train ticket, and for stocking the portals to Sasher's old apartment over there. Oh, and to upgrade your systems so you can keep up with the curriculum . . . ." my mother listed, her voice giving away that all this would soon be followed by a "but."

Before I could say a word, a hand shot out with its index finger held up to stop me. *Here it comes*, I thought.

"You'll have to be a part-time student, because they only had space for you in some of the classes. You'll have to live in Sasher's apartment, which both me and your father will have full portal access to, and Uncle Char will be there with a watchful eye every third week during his air-train runs to Terigon. And you will call every fourth-day night at a curfew that we can work out once you are there."

After she finished, I waited one last moment for their heads to spin straight around and Grey to walk in the room laughing. But when my father leaned in, awaiting my reaction, I realized this wasn't a dream.

In awe, I reached down for the sweater on my lap, pulling its rich texture toward me before staring back up at my parents. The faces of the two individuals who had locked me away my entire life looked back at me as if full-heartedly expecting me to believe that they were suddenly going to let me up and move across the state.

I couldn't believe this was actually happening. Images of colour-coated streets and fast-paced strangers danced in my eyes like unexpected fireworks.

"What . . . actually? You mean Yorker Specialty, right? Yorker being in Terigon. Terigon being halfway across Thalia . . . "

The words tumbled from my mouth as my eyes snapped back and forth between them, half sarcastic, half pleading with them to confirm the reality of what they were telling me. I thought about leaving behind the sea beaches and tall mountains of Vancity. About replacing them with city buildings three times the height of my Uncle Char's building where we were right now.

I thought of the loud sounds, busy streets, and vibrant energy of life in Terigon—and of myself, standing in the middle of all of it.

My father placed a hand on the bed and sat with half his body on the edge of the mattress. "Yes!" he said. "Your uncle made the call after insisting that we just stay here until the house is redone. It's closer to your mother's work, and realistically . . . " he paused and glanced down at the blanket for a moment, then back up at me. "We know we haven't been able to provide all the things you've wanted, all these years. So we've decided we're going to at least give you this. And a portal update. It's not much," he added quickly, seeing my eyes light up. "Your portal will still block you from things like Syncher and screener shows. But it should be enough of an update to keep you on top of your classes over there."

He smiled, trying to mask the anxiety I could see hiding in the crease between his eyebrows.

"When do I go?" I asked, reaching a hand out to settle the whisper of nerves that shook his fingers ever so slightly.

"Uncle Char is doing an air-train run to Terigon tomorrow night. He said he can get us a ticket if you would like to run with him. Otherwise, we can get you a ticket for later in the week, only Uncle Char won't be on the ride. We'd feel much more comfortable if you went with Uncle Char . . . " my mom began to argue her case, but I cut her off before she could finish.

"I'll go tomorrow!"

Uncle Char was a train runner in Thalia. Though we could drive street lifts within city bounds, trains were the only means of transportation from city to city across the state. I had never been on one before, but the sound of them always fascinated me. My whole life, I could hear the quiet *whoosh* of air pulsing from the air-train tracks near our house as trains came and went in the night, filtering their sounds through my bedroom window to soothe me when I couldn't sleep.

My mother paused a moment. Then that same smile that had greeted me this morning crossed her face.

"We will tell him to get you a ticket," she said before motioning to the sweater. "Guess you should try that on. Come on, Kyan." She tapped my father's shoulder, and the two of them headed for the door.

"We're heading downstairs if you need us," my dad called out before leaving the room, closing the door behind him.

Bolting out of the bed, I tapped my temple, clicking play on my recent favourite song, "Problems," before reaching back for the sweater. I tore off the old social-school T-shirt of Sasher's I had been sleeping in and pushed my arms through the sleeves of the sweater as the beat began to pulse its way through my body.

I tugged it down over my head, then stopped to look in the mirrored surface of Sasher's closet portal, taking in the name of my dream specialty school across my chest just as the song boomed into a faster rhythm.

A smile slashed across my face as my eyes filled with tears.

"I'm going to Yorker," I laughed, octaves higher than usual, my voice catching in my throat. I spun, hands flying up in the air before I began dancing my way across the room. Ripping open the door, I made my way down the hallway to the lounge where my parents were sitting. In a gesture that was totally out of character, I draped my arms around my mother and spun her around in circles, then repeated the dance with my dad.

"Thank you, thank you, thank you!" It was all I could manage to say, about a thousand times over. Standing back, I stared at them in a state of bliss. We weren't always the most functional family, but it didn't mean they didn't love me. This made me sure of it.

Then, out of the blue, as I looked at my dad's proud face, the source of what had caused my dream to become reality hit me with sudden force. And I remembered.

This was happening because of the fire. A fire I still wasn't sure if I had started.

"Are you sure you guys will be okay? I mean, I'm still not entirely sure what's going on and I feel bad leaving you with the state of our house . . . " I started, trying to imagine my parents' interactions without me around to witness them. Would my mother notice my dad's stress as he tried to fill out Catcher claims paperwork? Would my father notice when Mother skipped another breakfast, too tied up in whatever she was working on next in her specialty field to eat? Guilt bubbled up inside of me, contrasting with my excitement like oil in water.

"Yes honey, absolutely. We've got to go through a fire site investigation with the marshals this week. Once they approve of the accident and the rebuilding begins, we're going to be so wrapped up in the process we won't even notice you're gone. Don't you worry about us."

My dad's words, meant to be reassuring, instead stirred up the question of whether they would truly miss me. Suddenly, it was almost as if . . . as if they wanted to get rid of me.

I took a step back, no longer sure how to share this life-changing moment with the two people who were meant to be closest to me. I could tell they felt it, too. We were lost in translation, none of us really knowing what to say next, before my mother stepped in.

"Now is as good a time for you to go away to specialty school as any," she said. It was one of her talents—closing down conversations with statements that left no need for replies.

I nodded my head, exchanging one last smile and thank you with them before trotting back into Sasher's room and tapping my temple to dial in Mina. She was the second person I couldn't wait to tell about my new life, the first being a boy who had been replaced in my recent dreams by packs of matches and the haunting hunger for burning flames.

CHAPTER 5
goodmorning, goodbye – FRENSHIP

WARM CANDLELIGHT *flashed and danced across the sharper angles of Grey's face as the smell of warm teakwood filled the air. It seeped from the walls of the treehouse we were tucked away in, towering high above the ground in the canopy of a thick forest. My ears filled with the sound of midnight crickets and soft music that trailed from the record player sitting in the far corner, beating out echoes of the song "Beige" as it painted the walls of the room in sound. "Beige" had been my latest favourite tune, and I played it repeatedly during my waking hours. It made comforting sense that it had leaked its way into my dreams, too.*

We had wrapped ourselves up the massive blankets that dripped and fell from the corners of the floor cushions beneath us. Leaving our arms free to roam out of the tangled mess, we held warm mugs of caramel apple cider so sweet and rich that the tiniest sip sent my taste buds into a frenzy. I let my eyes wander over the tiny flickers of flame that danced from the many lit candles around the treehouse, the fire swaying back and forth from the wicks in synchronized fashion, captivating me with their light and the tingling feeling of heat they seemed to leave on my skin.

"Want to play a card game?" Grey asked, sitting up to pull a deck from a wooden shelf that lined the back wall we were leaning against.

I nodded, my attention still lingering on the mesmerizing feeling of real flame.

He dealt the cards one at a time, pausing once to sip from his mug. Finally, I sat up too, adjusting the pillows so that we were sitting at a square angle to one another, but still close enough to touch. I watched him carefully, my eyes pausing on his lean arms, moving smoothly as they passed card for card into two messy haystacks. Feeling heat rise into my cheeks—and not from the candles, this time—I directed my attention to collecting my side of the deck, genuinely curious to know which game we would play this time.

The moment was unfolding perfectly. But I knew that, with one added touch, I could hit ultimate dreaming bliss point.

"You know, there's only one thing I love more than card games in a treehouse," I teased, hoping Grey would catch on.

"Me schooling your ass in a card game in a treehouse?" He gave me some side eye to indicate that he was sizing me up.

I snorted. "Let me remind you that the last two times we played one of your games, I won. Which reminds me, you owe me one well-planned dream date some night this week. I haven't forgotten."

I pointed my free finger at him in accusation as I brought my eyes down to my cards, taking a look at my hand. But then the sudden patter of raindrops on the roof of the tiny cabin filled the air, and I dropped the cards from my face, matching his smile with mine.

There was only one thing I loved more than Grey and a tree-house, and that was Grey in a treehouse to the soft soundtrack of a thunderstorm.

His eyes held mine, the playful grin on his face growing as he, too, took stock of his cards.

"The game is called Fates," he began. "We each place a card face down and guess the fate of our cards. There are six fates: Rich and poor are the fates of numbers. Evil, pure, lucky, and corrupt are the determining fates of the suits. Spades are evil, hearts are pure, clubs are lucky, and diamonds are corrupt.

"I am to guess your fate and you are to guess mine before flipping the cards over. If you guess rich and evil, then you are assuming my card

is a spade of seven or higher. If you guess that my fate is to be poor but pure, then you are guessing that my card is a heart of six or lower. You must guess the fate of the number and suit. Get it?"

"So what if we both guess wrong?" I asked, trying to follow the information.

"The person who predicts the correct fate gets the cards, and if we both predict wrong, then we flip our next cards until one of us lands a heart. A heart card is an automatic fate-war win."

"Good thing I'm psychic," I joked, tapping my temple. It felt weird to do so without my portal screen blinking awake and asking me to give it a command. There were never any portals in my dreams.

"Good thing I've got a big heart," Grey quipped back, smirking as he patted his chest. I rolled my eyes despite the smile that cracked over my face.

Even though I didn't fully understand the rules, I picked the game up quickly after a few rounds and finally began predicting fates as if my psychic declaration hadn't actually been far off the mark.

"It looks like fate is on your side," Grey smiled, a hint of tease in his voice.

"You're making me win, aren't you?" I accused, leaning forward to knock the cards out of his hands. As I did, they fell empty-faced, indicating that either thanks to my mind or Grey's, his cards had been changing to the ones I was predicting. Grey always took credit for these things, saying he was the one constantly manipulating our dreams. But when I woke up in the morning and reflected on our adventures, I could always tie symbols from my life to whatever solutions we'd come up with in my dreams the night before.

Pushing the cards aside, I leaned forward, landing softly on his chest. Ducking low, he kissed me, and my lips tingled in that ghostly way at the touch.

"Carson Wallace, I can confidently confirm that fate is definitely on your side," he reiterated before lacing his fingers through my hair and leaning in to kiss me again. Anticipating every second, my heartbeat *rose and my lips softened into a numbness from the pins and needles.*

Eventually, I nestled into his chest, tucking my head under his chin as we laid back into the wall facing the large opening to the treehouse, all cuddled up in the blankets from before. Just past the terrace that led to the ladder stretching to the ground far below, I could just make out the thick forest of trees dancing together in the dark storm outside.

"Have you ever kissed anyone before?" Grey's voice was soft, as if he wasn't sure he wanted to hear the answer.

My face flushed red, caught off guard by the suddenly invasive question. We talked about my real life often—the weird dynamic of my family and the latest things Mina was up to—but we rarely broached the subject of other guys, outside of the one who lived in my mind.

"Uhhh . . . " I stalled, trying to decide if I wanted to answer the question. His laugh rumbled through his chest, echoing in my ear.

"Don't get all weird on me. I'm only curious," he reassured me, fingers running through my hair as he started to brush it back affectionately. I closed my eyes, trying to hear his heart beating; it always sounded more like an echo than like a steady beat. Even so, it had become one of my favourite sounds. I decided to answer.

"No," I said casually, my fingers twirling with the hem of the blanket around us. I looked down at it, and admitted, "I've been a little preoccupied."

I could tell by the sound of his voice that he was smiling.

"Oh yeah? With what, exactly?" he asked.

Sitting up, I turned, laying a tingling hand on his chest as I faced him.

"Sleeping," I replied, confirming the smile I had predicted with my own two eyes. Maybe I really was becoming psychic.

"Good," he stated, trying to suppress the smile, but it kept creeping back onto his face.

I leaned forward and kissed his cheek before returning my head to his chest. He adjusted the blanket, pulling it over my shoulders, and we both settled back into each other.

Lying against the back wall, we fell silent, staring out into the sea of green trees for what felt like a lifetime. Our ears followed the soft, booming thunder and the peaceful patter of the rain as it seeped into the quiet, plucking strum of my favourite Filos song. I breathed deeply, trying to burn the soft edges of the dream into my mind so I could put every detail into proper words, come morning.

My daze broke what felt like an eternity later at the sound of his voice.

"One day, you'll know what it's like to really kiss someone . . . " he said. "It just won't be me."

We both sat there, his thick words hanging in the air, heavy with reality. Grey wasn't real. This was only a dream, and any moment I would wake up and he would be gone. We both knew it, though we rarely talked about it.

"I know," I answered softly. And that was the last thing I heard before I woke up.

I shut my newest notebook, a gift from Uncle Char after I mentioned the journals I needed him to check on for me at home, once the marshals finally let my parents back in to collect whatever was salvageable. I trusted my uncle not to tell my parents about my hidden sealer bag. I only hoped it had made it through the fire.

Until he had a chance to check, however, I was on an air train, putting old-school pen to paper, recalling as many of my old dreams as I could and writing them into this newest journal in case my old ones were unsalvageable. I started with the most significant dreams, pulling forward as many vivid details as I could from our night in the treehouse dream, which I'd had just two months ago. It had been one of the very few times Grey had ever asked me about my romantic interests outside of him, and for some reason the smile on his face that night was the one I went to whenever I found myself searching for comfort on a bad day.

Flashes of green flickered from the other side of the air-train glass. I was about halfway to Terigon, my hands clenching and unclenching with excitement as I ran them down my bouncing legs, between writing down dreams. Finally, I let my mind take a break from my dream journal for a while, so I could take in the view outside. Thick sheets of streets gave way to reveal rolling hills of green, alive and reborn. Here and there, I caught the scars left on the land from the early cities. Mountains coated in tombstones of broken trees told a story of the life that had once dwelled on their slopes. Pockets of dry land with smooth edges marked the ghostly rivers and ponds that might have once sat in their shadows.

When we first left Vancity, my eyes counted trees, imagining that each one represented another mile toward freedom. I had to keep reminding myself to let out the air that I caught myself unknowingly holding anytime the anxiety of what was actually happening bubbled up. I was on my way to Terigon, a full day's air-train journey from my parents, Mina, and the only city I had ever known.

I was going to Yorker.

I was free.

My stomach flipped each time my mind narrated the circumstances of my present moment. I longed more than anything to have the chance to talk to Grey about it all, knowing he would know exactly what to say to feed my excitement and starve away my fears . . . But it had been more than two weeks since I had last dreamt of him. Instead, my nights were filled with the repeating nightmare of unlit matches or, if I was lucky, nothing at all.

The minute Uncle Char navigated me to my sitting pod on the air train and shut the door on his way out, after making sure for the millionth time that I had everything I needed, I had grabbed the new notebook he'd left me and started regurgitating old dreams, hoping that they might trigger a new one that night.

They didn't. But, after falling into a doze and waking up again, I figured I still had a few hours of train ride left and not much else to do to distract myself from my nerves besides recollecting more dreams, anyway.

This wasn't the first time Grey had disappeared from my dreams, but it hadn't happened in a while. I usually attributed his disappearance to sudden changes or stress; like the time I was fifteen and my parents suddenly decided we would take a weekend trip alongside Uncle Char to his cabin in the woods. I was relieved to learn that Sasher wasn't coming, only to find out later that she'd be coming in a few days after all, with all of her snobby teenage friends in tow. The anxiety of the trip made Grey go missing from my dreams each wretched night I was there, tossing to the sounds of forest frogs outside and the whispers of Sasher's clique mocking my baggy, old clothes and how I carried around old-fashioned books.

When Aunt Zandra died, Grey disappeared again . . . for the entire time our family stayed with Uncle Char to console him on his loss, in the usual Thalia fashion. It was then, one late night when I couldn't sleep—unable to subject myself to another Grey-less disappointment—that I went to the kitchen portal for a glass of water. There, I found Uncle Char reading books with words written in messy ink, rather than typed lines. When he spotted me, his smiled, telling me they were my aunt's journals.

He gestured toward them, allowing me to take a look, and my eyes ran over the long swirls of her imperfect yet all the same beautiful handwriting.

"Wow," I gasped. My eyes seemed to breathe in the words on the paper that shared everything from the early days of Sasher's life to poems that I had never read before.

"She had extras, you know. Ones she never got the chance to fill. I let Sasher take the ones she wanted, but there are still a few left. Would you like one?"

I nodded, taking in my uncle's saddened yet kind face. He leaned down and pulled up a white notebook from the box beneath the table. Handing it to me, he smiled, giving me a moment to look it over. I traced my fingers over the stitched embroidery that lined the thick front cover. The billowing shapes there, dotted by stitched lining, reminded me of clouds.

"She loved to write. She learned from a book I found in an air-train run to Pocasso, and then she taught it to Sasher when she grew up." My uncle smiled at the memory. "Nowadays, you can learn that kind of thing just as simply from portals."

It was that week I learned to write, that white journal marking the first wobbly letters that recorded as many dreams as I could remember, until Grey finally returned the following week.

I prayed again that the sealer bag had kept at least my most recent journal safe. Leaning my head against the train pod pillow, I stretched out my legs in front of me, barely brushing the empty seat pod that sat across from me. These pods could hold up to four people, but Uncle Char had hooked me up with an empty one, leaving the vacant seat across from me to become a resting spot for my small duffle bag of belongings, and the seat beside me to serve as a potential headrest for the nap I felt coming on.

Another two hours and I would be in Terigon.

I reclined to my left, collapsing my head onto my crossed arms as I kicked my feet up, bending my legs so that I lay sideways across the two seats.

A loud bell rang, waking me from a blank sleep, and I sat up, stretching my arms above my head. Tapping my temple, the time lit up at 1500—and "ARRIVED" sprawled across my screened vision. *Arrived.*

Nerves tingling, I tapped again, collapsing the screen. Then I stood and gathered my journal into my bag. Opening the pod door, I made my way through the hallway of pods and down the steps to the air-train platform, only to become instantly lost in a sea of other humans doing the same thing.

Clusters of people of all different heights, weights, and ethnicities darted left and right, roping me into a tornado of diversity. At first, my chest tightened, feeling a little overwhelmed by the sheer vastness of humanity.

But then I let out a breath, allowing myself a moment to relax into it. And as soon as I did, I started to find the hints of beauty in all the lives racing past me, running parallel to my own.

Uncle Char was running the front end of the air train and warned me that it might take a while before he was able to leave, so I followed his instructions to part with the crowd. I went left and down the escalators to a café in the train hub called The Grounds, where I ordered myself an iced latte before sitting at one of the tables and chairs and pulling my journal back out.

Before I began tracing the words of another dream, I took a second moment to absorb the commotion going on around me. I had never seen this many people in one place before, and the energy left me bubbling with excitement.

I inhaled a deep breath, and began writing out last month's dream of racing power bikes with Grey through desert streets on a cool, dusty night. Then, too, I had felt this bubbling excitement in the pit of my stomach.

Only this time, it was real.

Two more dreams made their way into the early pages of my journal before I heard Uncle Char calling my name.

I looked up and spotted his balding head bouncing its way around travellers as he worked his way over to me. His goofy smile and peppy step were so similar to my father's that, for a split second, I almost mistook him for my dad in the bustle of my new surroundings.

"How was the ride?" he asked when he reached me, taking the duffle bag I had hauled up onto my shoulder as I gathered my things. I tossed my empty cup into the recycle portal and followed his lead as he directed us away from the café toward the exit doorway that ended the huge hallway of the train hub.

I spoke loudly, trying to keep up with him as we wove our way through the people around us. It helped that I could feel the caffeine seeping into my veins as I walked, kicking up my pace.

"Not bad, got some reading done," I shouted, doing my best to follow his stride while craning my neck in all directions to take in even more of my surroundings. Screens lined the walls of the hub, flashing vibrant images of the latest screener show or the newest sweater now available for portal purchase. I gawked as an advertisement promising 2-HOUR DELIVERY in bold letters burst across the closest screen. In Vancity, we had to wait a week for any portal purchases, since the mail truck only made its sweep through our neighbourhood on third days.

I thought of our house again. The last I was told, Catcher marshals still hadn't figured out what had caused the fire. Instantly, I felt my usual caffeine high deteriorate into what felt more like anxious jitters.

I still couldn't remember if I had been the one who started the fire, nor had I forgotten the words I had heard Uncle Char say, that night.

"It's not unheard of for Catcher marshals to set a fire to make a death seem like an accident."

I shivered, hoping that once we made it to Sasher's apartment, I would be able to find the right way to broach the subject with him. I needed him to clue me in to what he had meant.

Uncle Char had insisted that I take over Sasher's old apartment, which had lain vacant ever since she got her job in Elcer City. It was covered in most of my Uncle Char's things now, being the place he stayed whenever he did his air-train runs to Terigon. Per my parents' many conditions, living here meant that Uncle Char would be crashing on the couch for a few nights every time he had a train run that passed through.

When we arrived, taking the elevator up to the fourth floor, my uncle walked down the darkly painted hallway punctured by yellow doors to the third entrance on the right, tapping his temple to demand an unlock. He pushed open the heavy metal door, and the motion lights inside brought to life a small, high-ceilinged loft overlooking the busy street below.

Walking past him toward the far window-lined wall, I took in the motion of life unfolding below, colours brushing past each other in a hurry. Turning, my gaze fixed upon the abstract wire shapes pinned to adjacent wall as art, then moved on to the steel appliances that matched the sleek grey cabinets of the white-walled kitchen. Sasher's shadow lingered on the perfectly matching furniture, including the yellow couch that sat in front of the central window, which was the same shade as the apartment door.

I took in the portal projection screen that sat on the wall across from the couch. My heart lifted to find bookshelves lining the far wall leading to the kitchen, stocked with old-age books of all sizes and shapes that instantly sparked my imagination.

"Between the two of us, we keep quite a collection stocked. You're welcome to read any of them," my uncle chuckled, noting my wide-eyed intake of breath as I stared at the shelves.

"This place is . . . amazing," I managed. I spun around, taking it all in again. Side tables were scattered around each side of the couch as well as beside the front door. Off to the left, I walked through a doorway that opened onto a queen-sized bed perched in front of another large window, which faced the street that crossed the one in front of the lounge. Between being the corner unit and having such high ceilings, the entire place felt bigger than it actually was, yet cozy at the same time.

Falling onto my back on the bed, I let out a loud squeal that set my uncle to chuckling again in the next room over.

I still couldn't believe this was happening.

A few hours later, the sunlight from the lounge window began to fade as the sky outside changed from blood orange, to rich purple, and finally into a royal blue as the bright lights of the city began their nightly reign.

I spent the last hour of dusk lying in my new bed, watching the windows of strangers and nearby work offices light up in golden squares. Eventually, Uncle Char called me into the kitchen, motioning me toward the small portal screen attached to the food-simulation door. He punched in a portal order for two bean burgers from Billiards, the restaurant a block over, showing me exactly how to use the new system. In Terigon, portal food wasn't solely reliant on your kitchen stock. The portals here ran through systems that connected back to a main hub beneath the city, making it easy to port meals through underground tubes that filtered through buildings, placing orders right inside the doorway of your kitchen portal. The same was true for ordering groceries, apartment supplies, or even closet clothing. My mind flashed back to the two-hour delivery ad at the air-train hub.

"That's how manual orders work," Uncle Char was saying. "I should be able to sync your system to the apartment portal so that you can even make orders from your temple port."

I looked at him, wide-eyed. My parents never allowed me to sync to our homes portal system's, saying the easy access to everything in the house made for lazy habits.

"I get to sync to the home portal?" I asked in disbelief.

"Not only that," Uncle Char grinned, pacing back to the small dinner table in the centre of the kitchen. Picking up the portal plate, he motioned for me to hand my wrist port over so he could initiate my system upgrade.

As I did so, a soft ding from the kitchen alerted us that our food had arrived. Uncle Char ignored it. He touched the thick grey strap of my wrist port to the portal plate, and a blue light began to flash as my system began its upgrade. The blue download bar filled in a matter of seconds, and a second ding sounded through the apartment.

My uncle handed my wrist hub back to me, indicating a quick tap to my temple.

"*System upgrade.*" The words sounded in my head, and my portal screen came to life with the same blue loading bar. I blinked through the subtle difference between this and my usual system setup. Sifting through the newest additions to my port, I heard Uncle Char list off a few of my new features.

"You now have full access to portal commands around the apartment, camera access on your wrist hub and, finally, I took down the Syncher firewall."

I looked at my uncle in shock. Did he say Syncher? I opened my home apps and, sure enough, there sat the soft-circled "S" indicating that the feature was officially available on my port. Blinking it open, a sign in-screen lit to life. I blinked my portal screen closed again before turning back to my uncle, still frozen in shock.

"You're officially an adult, Car. You should be able to live your life like one. Just don't let your parents know it was me if they ever find out," Uncle Char winked.

"I won't. Thank you!" I threw my arms around him, fighting to hold back an excited squeal.

"You're welcome, kiddo!"

After the update was complete, we munched down our bean burgers, trading half and half of our curly versus yam fries and talking about all there was to do and know about Terigon. Shortly after, I packed up the recycled papers from our meals, dropped them into the waste port, and tapped my temple for a recycling removal.

When I turned around, I noticed my uncle collecting his things from the living room.

"Are you sure you've got everything you need? Just want to double-check we've gone over everything before I head out." His words followed him as he made his way to the bookcase, dropping a book he must have just finished reading before picking out a new one and placing it on top of his things. Then he shrugged into his jacket before pulling his bag up and over his shoulder.

"You're leaving? I thought you normally stayed a few nights before heading home," I said, trying not to sound as scared as I suddenly felt. The minute Uncle Char left, this became real. Believe me, I was excited, but I was also comforted by the thought that he'd be here for a little while as I adjusted to the new city.

"I've got an air-train ride heading east tonight. It's been a while since I visited Sasher in Elcer City, and the station had a train runner call in sick . . . " Seeing the look on my face, Uncle Char trailed off, and lowered the bag from his shoulder. "But I don't *need* to go. I can stay if you'd like . . " he started.

"No. No. Go; I'm fine, really. Excited if anything!" I tried to sound more confident than I felt, not wanting to be of any more inconvenience to him. If it weren't for Uncle Char, my parents wouldn't have a place to stay, and I wouldn't be going to Yorker. I didn't want him to have to do one more thing for me.

"Are you sure?" he asked, scratching at his shiny head, clearly torn about what he should do.

"Seriously. We've gone over city shuttles, portal systems, and how to look up the route to Yorker. There's only a few days left until school starts, and I should settle in on my own before then. Go. And let Sasher know I say thank you to her for the apartment, too!"

I smiled my biggest smile, and Uncle Char let out the breath he had been holding. Walking over to me, he pulled me into one last bear hug.

"It's only for a little bit. I'll be back in five days, 112 at 0100, so I'll be here to see you off before you start your first day at school." His eyes crinkled at the corners as he smiled. "You're going to do great, kiddo!"

Suddenly, it all felt too real. The thought of him actually leaving me all alone in this big new city started to sink in, and for a moment I found myself wanting to beg him to stay just a while longer—to maybe steal my nose, or pull some ridiculous prank on me. But I fought down the urge to tell him I'd changed my mind.

"Thank you so much for everything," I said, my voice muffled against his shoulder, feeling my last fleeting moments of being a kid slipping away from me.

He pulled back, keeping his arms on my shoulders and bending at the knees to make his eyes level with mine.

"I'm going to be in town for the next hour or so," he said. "If you need anything at all, you give me a call. Which reminds me, don't forget to call your parents tonight. They'll want to know you made it safe."

Nodding, I kept my eyes on his, summoning my courage. There was still one last thing I had to ask him, before he went.

"Uncle Char . . . what really started the fire?"

My question caught him off guard, and his eyebrows furrowed in confusion. "You mean back at home? Don't worry about that now, kid. I'm sure it was just a bad energy circuit," he said, fidgeting with the strap of his bag.

But I couldn't let it drop that easily. "Could Catcher marshals have started it? Would . . . would they actually do that?"

I searched his face for a reaction as I spoke. Eyebrows still furrowed, he looked back to me, and managed to send a laugh puffing into the air between us.

"What on earth would make you think that?" he asked.

You would, I thought, remembering what I had overheard. But outwardly, I shrugged, and waited for him to continue.

"Bad circuits are usually what cause these types of accidents. It's just taking them a while to find where the circuit caught. Don't stress about it, Car, you've got Yorker and Terigon to discover. Your parents will get it figured out."

He hugged me one last time, ending the conversation. I bit my tongue, knowing that he wouldn't say any more about it. His answer didn't convince me that he was telling the truth. But I trusted Uncle Char more than anyone. If there were something I needed to know, he would tell me.

Right?

I shook off my feeling of uneasiness as he shouldered his bag again and left, closing the large yellow door to the now empty apartment behind him.

As I turned back to the space, I took it in again. The couch I would now lounge on, the kitchen I would eat in, the table I'd do portal work at, the white duvet on the bed I would spend my nights sleeping in until further notice. I wasn't sure I was ready for all of it. But there was no going back now.

As the sounds of horns seeped through the far windows, I let out a breath. This was all I had ever wanted, and for whatever reason—be it my own doing, a mistake by the hands of fate, or the questionable hands of someone else—I was here. I would figure out which of the three it was soon enough. And, in the meantime, it couldn't hurt to try living out a dream, for once.

Once Uncle Char left, I dug into exploring the apartment in earnest, pulling open drawers and cupboards and tracing my fingers over the spines of the old, antique books stacked on the shelves. When I was sure I had seen everything there was to discover, I keyed in a closet-portal order for a new set of pyjamas, remembering that my parents had mentioned stocking the portal systems, before sauntering into the bathroom. Tapping the washroom screen to life, I punched out the request for a long, hot shower set at 60°C before peeling off my clothes from the train.

Stepping into the glass-panelled washer, I let the warm water beat down on and loosen the tightness that had bunched up in my shoulders, which felt as though their muscles had been pulled together in tight leather bands. I released a long sigh and turned, closing my eyes as the water hit my face. When I opened them again, I felt a rush of exhilaration sweep through me, suddenly acutely aware that I was taking my first shower in my brand new home.

The thought instantly had me bouncing with excitement, and as I took shampoo from the dispenser and began washing away who I was before, my mind raced with the idea of waking up and exploring my new city in the morning. Despite my euphoria, my eyes felt heavy, and my limbs were sore. For now, I wanted nothing more than to crawl into my new bed and get a full night's sleep—one where I could tell Grey all about my new home . . . and ask him to help me formulate a plan to get to the bottom of what really happened to my old one.

But I knew I couldn't sleep yet.

Coming out of the shower, I punched in an order for peppermint tea and made my way over to the couch. Sitting down, I tapped my temple, and my portal screen blinked to life.

I dialled a call back home, sipping away at the warm tea as I relayed the details of the train ride and the new apartment to my parents, and they shared their minimal updates on the fire with me. Before long, I was wishing them sweet dreams and hanging up.

My parents were unaware of my new camera and Syncher upgrades, so I held off on actually showing the apartment until I made my next call to Mina. Who screamed and squealed over it with me, like I knew she would.

Finally, once the calls were made and my mug was empty, I took a deep breath, resisted the urge to crawl straight into bed, and toggled open the web port.

I typed in a request for house fire statistics over the last year in Thalia. A total of sixty-three house fires came up on the screen, each originating from a faulty circuit in the energy panels. The numbers and explanations made sense, yet my heart ached as I totalled up the deaths from each fire, one of which had taken out an entire family.

Wait.

I narrowed my eyes, and counted back through the death tolls of each fire. As I did, an obvious fact suddenly hit me.

Every single one of those sixty-three house fires had resulted in at least one loss. My family's fire had been the first in the last year to not end in some kind of fatality.

Was that normal?

I tried to work through it, but the thoughts crossed and blurred together in my brain. It had finally reached its limit, and it was going on strike.

Shutting down my portal screen, I stumbled into the kitchen, where I set my mug in the cleaning port and ordered a cleanse and store for it before making my way to the bedroom.

Climbing under the rich white blankets that draped across the bed, I tried to shake the images of burned-away homes and the lives that went with them. I slid the rest of my body into the cool sheets, planting my head onto the pillow before rolling back toward the window so I could gaze out at the life still jostling around outside.

My exhausted mind raced with tangled questions about how the fire had started, if we had just been lucky to survive, and what was taking the marshals so long to formulate a report and clear my parents for a rebuild. Questions that I knew I needed one person in particular to help me answer.

Grey. His name was the last thing I thought before I drifted into oblivion.

CHAPTER 6
grey – EXES

I WATCHED THE SUN rise from behind the buildings that stood tall just outside of my new bedroom window. The entire wall that faced the street was lined with long panels of glass that kissed both the ceiling and the floor. Small specks of dirt and dust glistened from the rays burning through them like the flakes of ash that had visited me in my sleep last night.

This time in my nightmare, when I had stroked the match, it lit, catching my bedding on fire before lighting up my house in flames. When I woke up, a wicked smile was still stretched across my face—which only horrified me more.

I had been awake ever since, counting the hours one breath at a time, until the lives of Terigon began to thicken the streets outside again.

I'd spent the sleepless hours before dawn scrolling through maps of the surrounding area, taking note of cafés and the route to Yorker. I decided that, once the sun had risen to an acceptable height, I would throw on my trackers and grab a much-needed coffee before walking the new route I would be taking to specialty school.

I had been hoping the nightmare of the fire wouldn't find its way into my duffle, seeping its presence into my new Terigon routine just as my morning coffee or evening jog would. But I still couldn't shake the feeling that there was something bigger going on, with our house burning down. My nightmares, I knew, must be from my building fear that I had possibly started the fire myself. A guilty smile crawled onto my face every time I looked out the window, and I wanted more than anything to immerse myself in my new life. But, for some reason, Uncle Char's cryptic words remained glued to my waking worries.

I took a breath, and squared my shoulders. This morning, I figured that navigating my way to a new coffee spot along with finding the route to Yorker only made sense, having just moved to the city. But I left my afternoon open to start digging further into anything I could find about accidents tied to Catcher marshals.

I stood up from the bed and walked over to the closet portal tucked into the wall panel between me and the living room. There, I threw on a pair of black joggers, topping off the look with a grey T-shirt that scooped low in the back. The mixed shades of charcoal and smoke reminded me of Grey's eyes; a quick glance down today, and I'd find a quick sense of comfort from the colour of the eyes I had been missing. Finally, I snatched my black cap to conceal my wavy blond curls springing out in all directions and slipped my feet into my white sneakers, making a note to map out a new running route as another item on my portal to-do list.

Heading out, I locked up my loft behind me, struggling to remember the security code Uncle Char had told me time and again, insisting that I'd better not forget it. I could already feel the sense of protection I had over my new oasis. The thought of returning back to it filled me with a sense of comforting excitement. I had to resist the urge to lean against the large, heavy yellow door and whisper, *I'll be back soon.* A neighbour could greet me at any moment, and that was not going to be the first impression I made as the new girl in the building.

Making my way down and out onto the street, I felt instantly alive. A mess of people walked in all different directions around me, the colours of their jackets and sweaters melting into each other like an abstract painting. Lifts honked and whisked by with riders sitting in the back seats, their faces trained on their portal screens, most of which were set to private, making them look like they were staring into nothing like zombies, to the outside eye.

Following the route around the block and down a street, I took in the world around me. The smell of rich pastries and bold coffees hung in different pockets along the sidewalk, inviting people into their respective shops with scented swirls of cinnamon and brown sugar. People of all sizes and shapes hopped on and off the city air train, issuing commands to their temple ports as they dodged one another.

"Location reached," my own port announced to me, so that only my ears could hear it. Looking ahead, my eyes fixed on a black-and-white sign sticking out from a store in a matte black building that towered high into the sky.

The word "KOZE" was slashed in white cursive writing across the neon sign, a distinct round coffee stain sitting in the spot where the "o" should be.

The familiarity of Koze to Cove struck a chord with me—as if I were somehow channeling Mina here as I stepped toward what would become my new morning special. As I thought of her, my stomach pinched. Missing Mina had been something I hadn't had time to process. I wondered if she had already rooted out her Kings Court coffee spot, too.

Making my way over to the shop, my eyes peeked inside to see large black bucket chairs contrasting against sandalwood floors, bar tables, stools, and side tables. Large-bulbed string lights twinkled from the perimeters of the windows and blanketed the ceilings of the café in small waves as customers made their way in and out of the main entrance, which was surrounded by leafy green plants.

I pulled open the heavy door, the soft *ding* signalling my arrival going unnoticed by the busy crowd. My nose instantly filled with the warm, comforting smell of roasted coffee beans and sweet, buttery baked goods, both so enticing that my mouth watered. I made my way up to the counter, scanning the old-style black menu with its interchangeable white lettering before training my eyes on a portal screen below it and tapping in my order.

Walking off to the side, I waited for my name to ring in on the order screens, announcing that my large, vanilla iced coffee was ready.

"CARSON WALLACE," the portal voice rang out. I caught a glimpse of the barista as she leaned over the counter and handed my drink to me, her strawberry-blond hair dripping with streaks of pearly whites and sorbet pinks—a hairstyle I had never seen in Vancity.

Before heading out again, I scanned the seating area scattered with customers, a majority of their faces fixed on portal screens. Everything in the café was a golden colour from the crystal-strung bulbs above, warming the air around me with invitation. Making my way back to the street, I turned left, continuing on my route to Yorker . . . already promising myself that I would return here on the way home.

I knew I had found my new coffee spot.

My feet ached, having walked double the distance I would now be travelling on a daily basis.

On the plus side, I had figured out that it should take me roughly fifteen minutes to make it to campus, minus the ten-minute detour I had taken today, having gotten lost twice. Once I was finally there, I took my time walking around Yorker campus, relishing each slow step as I explored its benches and small alcoves with excited eyes.

Eyes that were now trained on the same order portal they had discovered this morning, only this time they were settling on a warm latte to soothe the aches of my tired legs from the inside of a deep mug.

When the latte arrived, I sipped from the coffee cup, shocked by the rich, smooth taste embracing my existence with the promise of a soon-to-be caffeine kick. There was no coffee like this in Vancity. Mina would lose her mind if she tried this stuff.

I nestled into one of the vacant bucket chairs that looked out onto the street, taking in the movement rushing by. The café was much less busy at this hour, presumably due to the fact that morning rush hour had ended some time ago. Around me, the sound of soft acoustic music was muffled by the overlapping conversations of customers muttering to each other and into portals, along with the buzzing of the espresso machine.

I sank deeper into the pleather cushions, taking another large sip of the warm coffee before settling in to look up the first thing I wanted to investigate.

Tapping my temple port, I joined the sea of screen zombies that filled the space around me.

"Thalia Lift Accidents," I recited, my words filling the search-engine bar as I, too, dropped my voice to mutter quietly into the microphone of my wrist port. I had privatized my screen, leaving me staring into oblivion in the direction of the strangers outside, as accident reports began to fill my field of vision.

I scrolled through the most recent accidents in Thalia: the lift that veered to escape an oncoming pedestrian and ran off a mountain in Watersedge; the lift that had run down three individuals after a mechanical malfunction in Calcove. With each accident, I totalled together more deaths, waiting for a report that hadn't resulted in any casualties. A sinking feeling grew in my stomach as more and more lift-related lives lost filled my screen.

Forty-two names listed themselves in a gruesome line inside my mind of people who were no longer here, just in the last year, because of these accidents. I thought back to the day our lift crashed into the river. There was a casualty that day, too. A casualty that changed my life forever. A casualty that led to me never knowing the only other sibling I ever had.

How could it be that *none* of these accidents allowed all of the people involved to walk away with their lives? Could this be a coincidence? If what Uncle Char said was true, could some of these deaths have been at the hands of the people who were supposed to be protecting us—the Catchers?

I shivered. Pulling up an empty search bar, I began looking through more accidents, tracing them back year by year, determined to find the last time everyone involved had escaped one of these tragedies.

I had only combed through two years of listings when a voice cracked my concentration, sending chills down my skin in waves.

"Charli, you look absolutely dashing this afternoon. Could you possibly add a shot of cinnamon to my Americano order today? I forgot to punch it into the portal. Must have been thinking about those crystal eyes of yours."

My hands turned to ice, and the hairs on the back of my neck stood up as my breath caught like a hard ball in my throat. I blinked my screen away, taking a second to register what I was hearing before turning to crane my neck over the back of the chair, straining to locate the source. My heart raced with each second that ticked by, and my hands turned clammy.

Standing at the front counter of the café, I caught the back of chestnut-coloured hair tossed perfectly on top of broad shoulders and a lean build, outlined by a black tracksuit in material that screamed "rich" even from a distance. My heart pounded in my chest, the seconds stretching into what felt like hours as I waited for the man to turn around. Inch by inch, I slowly leaned forward in my chair.

Taking the mug from the same barista who had served me, her face flushing from the contact, he turned around—and my body froze.

As the slap of shock hit, I gasped, losing my balance. Catching myself on the table in front of me, I knocked my coffee to the floor— shattering the mug into sharp, tiny pieces. The piercing sound caught the attention of the room, all the zombie eyes brought suddenly to life as they turned toward me—including his.

The moment stood still, my eyes transfixed by the sheets of granite in his, even from across the room. I struggled to take him in, unable to materialize a thought or cultivate any movement. My breath caught in my throat as I finally croaked out a single word.

"Grey?"

CHAPTER 7
only you – yoke lore

THE EYES OF STRANGERS bore holes through me as I waited for him to respond. My brain locked into place, the gears grinding slowly together, trying to process the details of the face that was staring back at mine. It was the same face I had seen thousands of times, only now it was somehow crisper. The sharp grey eyes, the chiseled jawline shadowed with scruff, the angular cheeks . . . it was Grey.

I watched as his eyebrows knitted together, a flash of confusion crossing his face before he turned to look behind him. Facing forward again, he motioned a thumb toward his chest as if to say, "*Me?*"

Blinking hard, I tried to regain a sense of reality. I felt as if I were frantically searching for the ground beneath my feet. I had to do something, yet all I *could* do was stare at him in disbelief. My mind and body felt as though they were made of cement, leaving me unable to move or speak. My eyes scanned the room from side to side as I slowly realized that the only barrier between myself and everything around me was the soft acoustic music that filled the silence. Not a single eye was trained on a screen as onlookers waited in awkward anticipation of what I might do next, obviously amused by the new source of entertainment.

But more dominant than anything else was the confused face staring back at me as if I were a complete stranger touched by a hint of crazy.

The barista, whom I now knew as Charli, broke the moment as she turned to grab a broom and made her way swiftly over to me from around the coffee bar. Bending down, she began sweeping the shattered glass off the floor as a few eyes that were too impatient to wait for the conclusion of this drama started peeling away from me.

"Watch your feet there," she said to me softly as I forced my gaze away from Grey's familiar face and down to her. I stepped quickly out of the way, and she continued to sweep with a sympathetic look on her face.

Looking back up, I made eye contact with the same grey eyes that had made my stomach tie itself into knots countless times, this one being no exception. They were still looking at me, waiting for an explanation.

"S-sorry, I thought you were . . . somebody else," I stammered, fighting the faint feeling that swept across my mind, leaving me dizzy. Giving my head a shake, I apologized to Charli as well before stepping around my mess.

Snickers rose from a group of peers sitting at a long table just feet away from the guy with grey eyes. As I made my quick escape, I looked back once, only to find that he, too, was biting his lip to keep from laughing as he looked back at his friends.

"Okay then . . . " he smirked, setting his Americano on the table as he sat down to join them. Readjusting his jacket, he leaned forward and muttered something quietly to the group. Bursts of laughter erupted into the room. Satisfied, he leaned back, taking a long sip from his mug and looking back at me just as I turned to close the door. The side of his mouth perked up in a cocky grin I had seen on Grey's face a million times, only this time it didn't stem from playful banter.

As the fresh air caught my skin, I stumbled over my feet, my face burning with embarrassment. Standing up straight, I was hit by a new wave of nausea. I had forgotten to grab my bag and belongings.

I wanted nothing more than to be anywhere but here. A bed, a black hole—I'd even consider going back to Vancity if it meant escaping this moment.

Charli was just gathering my stuff as I made my way back into Koze and over to her, head ducked. My throat tightened as I struggled to hold back the tears digging their way through the backs of my eyes.

"Here you go," she said, handing my black bag over, her voice low but kind. By now, all the eyes in the room had turned back to screens or to each other, probably sharing a quick moment of "glad it wasn't me."

I smiled at her and turned quick to leave again, but she grabbed my arm. Glancing around, she smiled, leaning in close so no one could hear.

"Don't you know who that is?" she asked, darting a glance at the guy with the grey eyes.

I slowed my frantic attempt to escape this hell just long enough to send a quizzical look back to her.

I don't know . . . do I? I thought to myself. I shook my head, deciding to play it safe, curious to know who she might say it was. The moment seemed to stretch on and on as I waited for the name "Grey" to fall from her mouth.

"That's Hale Kingsley. Son of Donte Kingsley . . . "

Donte Kingsley, as in, Lead Catcher of Thalia?

I had heard that name just last week, on the night of the fire. My dad had asked my uncle if he thought Donte had been the reason it all happened.

This guy who looked exactly like Grey, my Grey . . . was Donte's son?

"Right. Thanks." I ducked my head again and ran quickly from the café, trying to ignore the whispers from the table he was sitting at. This time, I didn't look back.

I barely noticed my feet as they made their way back toward my loft, questions spilling over me in waves.

Was Grey really Donte's son? And if he was, what did that mean, then? Why had I spent my entire life dreaming of Hale Kingsley? Did it have anything to do with the fire, or his dad?

My chest tightened, my stomach rolling and flipping with each new question as I finally made my way inside of my building. I kept my head down, focusing on putting one foot in front of the next until I made it home. Fussing with the lock code at the door with shaky fingers and blurred vision, I finally got it open, spilling into the loft before slamming the door behind me. My chest rose and fell rapidly; I couldn't get air into my lungs quick enough. I leaned and then slouched against the wall, head lowered between my knees, before sliding all the way down to the floor.

That face.

Hale Kingsley.

My heart raced, pounding like a jackhammer in my ears as the room spun in every direction. I pushed down on the sides of my head with the tips of my fingers, curling my knees up to my ears before tucking my head between them. It was a calming mechanism I had learned in the days after the accident, when panic attacks crept their way into my body at night. A doctor told me to drop my head low and count my breaths like the cascading waves of an ocean until the spots in my vision went away and my heartbeat slowed.

It took some time, but eventually it always worked. I stopped getting panic attacks a few years after the accident, but every now and then one would hit me out of the blue, and when they did, they hit hard. I could feel the pricks of pins and needles pinching their way across the skin of my hands and feet like fire ants as I tightened my grip underneath my folded knees. Tears stained my cheeks, their salty smell helping to aid the vision of white-caped waves in my mind.

. . . five . . . six . . . seven . . . eight . . . breathe. Just breathe . . .

My mind fought against me, a strong force insisting on racing my thoughts a mile a minute, but I kept fighting back with the vision of a wavy blue sea that promised safety, pulling it slowly into the forefront of my thoughts.

Hale Kingsley.

Donte Kingsley.

The fire.

I stomped on all of the questions and confusion that stormed my mind, desperate to centre my thoughts and my breathing. If I continued to run all the hamster wheels that were screaming for attention, I would completely unravel, and I wasn't sure I could handle that. Not right now. I needed to get a hold of myself so I could get to the bottom of this.

After a few minutes, my breathing finally slowed, leaving me lying in a puddle on my side. I set my cheek against the cool floor, staring at the walls, counting each gush of air before finally returning back to a quiet state of breath.

Hale Kingsley.

My entire life, I have been dreaming of Hale Kingsley.

I rested my hand on my chest, letting it rise and fall with my breathing, my brain reaching desperately for some sort of explanation as to what the hell it all meant.

That was Grey. There was no denying it. I knew it the second I heard his voice. Everything from the smirk on his face to his saunter as he made his way to the table played out again in my head, like all the Grey shades of a black and white film. This was no close call. Every detail was exactly the same.

"*That's Hale Kingsley . . .* " I heard the barista's words again. Which meant only one thing.

I needed to know more about Hale Kingsley.

I thought back to the things I was taught during my homeschooling about the Catcher government. Donte's name came up multiple times, but it never stuck as something I deemed important to really care about or remember. It wasn't like he was going anywhere. No one who wasn't blood of the royal family had any chance of working their way up into any sort of government position. You had to have the blood of the founding families of Thalia in your veins to be able to be a Catcher. The public had very little say in the way the country was run, and for that reason, I didn't care to ever try and involve myself with any of it. I knew it was the founding family of Kingsley that brought Thalia together after the nearly unfixable destruction the old world brought on human existence. But that was about it.

I tapped my temple, blinking my portal screen to life before I opened the search bar. I typed in his name.

Hale Kingsley, son of Donte Kingsley and grandson to Catcher Kingsley, filled my eyes, and the recognition hit me like a wave as more lessons from early homeschooling popped into my mind, connecting some of the dots.

Catcher was the man who brought Thalia to life. He was a young scientist at the time, having just married his wife Laina Kinson—a rumoured gypsy—at the age of eighteen. When the hostilities hit, he and Laina had survived the war of the world in one of the many bunkers filled with leading scientists, physicists, politicians, and doctors, along with many other officials and highly trained professionals deemed necessary to salvage human existence. He was said to have been the smartest man of the old world, and he used this to his advantage in order to demand space for Laina in the bunker. After living underground amongst fifty-six people for ten years, they were two of the forty-nine to walk out alive, and they set to work turning Thalia into what it was today, along with the remaining survivors.

I blinked open the link leading to the Kingsley family tree, reading the paragraph at the top that described how Kingsley blood had grown Thalia into the country I knew. Easy-read pictures showed Thalia's first people working in labs and establishing laws as more of the world's survivors joined the new nation, livable land having become scarce.

Word of Thalia got out, and as new settlers arrived, telling stories of nuclear forests and acid seas, it became one of the three remaining sanctuaries of community left in the world.

I scrolled past explanations of how food-runners turned into food portals, how old scrap metal was melted and reworked into the first-ever lifts, and how old building foundations were reworked to house the population of survivors still left in the world.

Then, my eyes caught on the headline "Future Ruler, Hale Kingsley."

"Using new laws and regulations established by first Catcher and now Donte, Thalia has grown into the thriving source of life it is today. It is said that Donte's son, Hale Kingsley, will take future reign of the country, ensuring that the fate of our lives never mimics that of the ones who came before us."

The information confirmed what I had already assumed. Hale was to be the future Lead Catcher. With most of the country being run by machine now, weapons banned, and crime rates barely having a pulse, Catchers were merely supposed to keep things running smoothly. Guns and bombs were something of the old world and were never recreated with new civilization. They would probably even have been thought of as myths, if it weren't for the photographed proof they had on screeners and in old history books to prove not only that they had really once existed, but that they were the final kiss of fate the old world used to nearly demolish all life on earth. All the leaders did these days were sign laws and host lavish dinners in a massive mansion here in Terigon, Thalia's capitol. All of the richest families and royalty from the two other remaining countries that survived the rubble of war from the old world were invited to attend the events, at which thousands of photos were taken, and some sort of speech was always made about making Thalia, and the world, a happier and safer place.

I could recall Mina telling me about the videos and pictures of those state dinners that she'd steal peeks at on live screeners, before she herself was allowed to use Syncher. She was always wrapped up in this world, but it never enticed me. Anything about Thalia, from its government to all the royal families of the other visiting nations, was as dry to me as cardboard in terms of knowledge and information. It held no real interest for me.

Little had I known that I was more wrapped in it when I was completely asleep than I ever had been, awake.

I needed to know why I had been dreaming of Hale's face for what was almost my entire life. To know if, or how, it tied into the fire. To find answers.

Standing, I trudged over to the yellow couch, planting myself on it before taking a deep breath. Now wasn't the time to freak. I had to focus.

I tapped my portal screen back open, bringing the Syncher app to life. I hadn't signed in, having been so wrapped up in the move.

I blinked through my login credentials, and my home screen came to life with the image of Mina and me on my birthday. My stomach turned again.

Focus.

In the search engine, I blinked, mentally gathering the name in my mind before it typed into my screen.

H-a-l-

His name was the first to pop up, three letters in. I blinked it open, his profile unfolding across my eyes.

His Syncher status was 92 percent. A small star sitting beside the scale indicated that his profile was authentic. A quick glance at all the fan accounts listed underneath Hale's profile made it instantly obvious that the leading family made more of an impact of the vast majority of Thalia than they had on me.

I scrolled through his profile, staring dumbfounded at the feed of photos that flashed back at me. There were photos of him at group gatherings and events he had attended with thousands if not millions of hearts and comments coming in from people all over Thalia. It was like he had fans.

The weirdest part of it all was seeing the same face I had been calling home masked on a complete stranger in circumstances I could never have pictured Grey in or enjoying. A grid of photos and short videos showed Hale dressed in tailored, expensive suits and driving futuristic lifts. These sat alongside photos of what looked to be insane parties, his arms draped over his friends' shoulders, and high-profile events where he stood tall beside his father.

My heart sank when my eyes fell on a photo of his arm around a tall, lean girl in a gorgeous floor-length, glittery silver gown. Her black hair was slicked back into a high ponytail, sharpening her staggering features while her lips split into a stunning smile. His face, on the other hand, was perfectly proportioned, his dark, smoky eyes striking against the backdrop of the black suit.

I felt my body tense, rejecting the sight of the boy I loved with a girl who clearly wasn't me. My mind flashed to my wild hair and chicken legs, wondering what I would look like standing next to Grey in a photo like that.

Only this wasn't Grey. It was Hale Kingsley. Someone I'd had no earthy idea existed a matter of hours ago.

But just seeing that face—the side grin and strong arms I knew so well—wrapped around someone else sent a sharp pang so deep into my chest that I thought I might throw up.

I collapsed the screen in a blink, suddenly unable to take it. It didn't help that I was still drowning in questions, struggling to play out their possible answers, each one coming up blank.

Who was this boy, really?

Why had I been dreaming of his face ever since the accident?

Suddenly, a new realization dawned on me with such force, my hands reached for solid earth to steady themselves.

Donte. The Catchers. The fire. The accidents.

What if all of this had something to do with Axel's death?

I shook my head to clear it. No. The coincidences just didn't line up. The map they created was peppered with holes of uncertainty, leaving too many pockets of black confusion that clouded my mind.

With the discovery of Hale, everything seemed to weigh on me ten thousand times more than it had before. I felt the walls closing in around me, caving in and crumbling as flecks of grey filled the air, leaving me aching for my version of a boy who had somehow escaped my dreams and now entered my world.

CHAPTER 8
six feet under – billie eilish

MY FACE FLOODED WITH HEAT *and licks of hungry flames snapped like whips in my ears, making my eyes shoot open. I was standing in the main loft of my house in Vancity, only the walls were torched in amber flames that engulfed the furniture and floor.*

My house was on fire. I had to get out.

Only, wait . . . where were my parents?

I turned down the hallway, making my way up the staircase two steps at a time. With each step, I prayed the tail of my pyjama shirt wouldn't kiss the flames. The minute I reached the top floor, my legs turned to sludge, a sudden thickness weighing down any move I tried to make.

Down the hall, I heard my mother scream, and my heart lurched into my throat.

I tried with all of my might to push my legs down the hall, but it was like moving through liquid cement, quickly drying as I tried to force my way through.

I needed to get to them. I needed to save them from the fire.

I opened my mouth, about to scream their names, when I felt a sudden crack under my feet.

My eyes darted to the floor, and to my horror, it crumbled as I watched, the groans and booms of the thick panelling thundering in my ears. As the floor broke apart, it gave way to a sea full of blackness that swallowed me whole.

My body plummeted through the pitch dark, leaving me no way to tell how far I had to go or when I'd hit the bottom. The air raced into my throat, choking me with its sweet invisibility the whole way down.

A scream bubbled up my throat, my arms flailing in desperation to grasp anything I might find. No use. With another awful crack, my body hit a sheet of ice-cold water, its freezing temperature cutting across my skin like razor blades. My muscles froze instantly, and my body began to sink into deep oblivion.

As my eyes adjusted to the darkness of the water, edges began to blur into focus, my surroundings becoming more and more visible with every passing second.

Then I saw it.

Off in the distance, an old lift rested at the bottom of the river.

Instinct took over as I started to wave my arms through the cutting water, each movement pulsing a brain-freeze sensation throughout my entire body. As I neared the lift, I poked my head into the back window to see the tousled head of blond hair drifting in the water. Attached to it was the body of a small girl.

I struggled with the door, frantically fighting to pull it open and save her. Just then, her hair swished away from her face, and I choked on a scream.

She was me, only younger.

I swam toward the front of the lift to see my parents floating in the front seat, drifting unconsciously in the water like seaweed. But that meant . . .

Axel.

I thrashed my way over to the opposite side of the lift, dropping my body low enough to look inside the window. An empty car seat sat next to my small, lifeless body in the back. I pushed off and away from the lift, my head turning rapidly in all directions, looking for where he could be. My lungs were starting to burn. Where was the surface?

I dropped down to the sandy floor of the river and then pushed off hard, swimming toward the black, seamless surface. After a few moments, I broke through to air, my body instantly relieved by the taste of oxygen.

I gasped for air, its sharp sting clinging to my wet face, colder than the water below.

"Axel!" I screamed, my breath puffing out of my lungs in clouds like warm smoke as my voice echoed over the now moonlit water. I spun around in every direction, treading water as best as I could despite my aching muscles.

It wasn't long before I spotted the body of a baby boy lying along the dark, muddy bank of the river.

I swam as fast as my muscles would allow, desperation burning inside of me, turning my adrenaline into fuel that pushed my body to move faster. When I felt my feet touch down on solid ground beneath me, I stood, kicking and thrashing out of the water toward Axel's body. As soon as I was near, I collapsed to my knees beside his limp, lifeless body and reached down, placing my hands on his small, cold shoulders before turning his body over.

Once I did, I jumped back in shock.

His eyes were staring right back at me, his face in a state of frozen shock.

"Axel, you're okay! Oh my god, you're okay!" I screamed, leaning in to hug him. When I pulled back, his face hadn't changed . . . but his lips parted.

A deep, dark voice husked out of his mouth, and I was sure the devil himself was speaking to me.

"It was supposed to be you."

☾

I gasped, sitting up fast in my bed. Sweat clung to my chest and body, making my hair stick against my forehead and down my neck. My chest rose and fell as I desperately drank in air and my surroundings.

It was just another nightmare. It wasn't real.

Kicking the comforter off, I swung my legs over the side of the bed to rest my feet on the cool, solid floor below. As I pulled myself to the edge of the mattress, I dropped my head into my hands for just a moment, taking long, deep breaths to steady the lingering jitters from the nightmare. Then I rose to my feet and pulled open the glass window, letting fresh air infused with the sounds of horns and engines fill the room while I made my way out into the lounge and kitchen.

The dimly lit walls indicated that it was still early morning, as did the pale blue dripping like paint from the buildings outside, moments away from being kissed by the sun.

It must be anywhere between 0500 and 0600, but I knew going back to bed wasn't an option. I had hit my limit with fire-related nightmares, even though I knew the fear of them was probably working its way into my psyche even more because of my insomniac habits.

Walking to the food portal, I punched in my coffee order, catching a glimpse of myself in the reflection of its door while the machine inside came to life as it brewed.

It looked like I had barely slept a wink, the heavy circles surrounding my eyes impossible to miss even in the dark glass of the portal. I shook my head, tapping a shot of almond milk into the order and waiting for the ding. A minute later, settling into the couch with coffee cup in hand, I draped a blanket over my bare knees before taking the first sip.

I allowed the early hours of the morning sit with me in silence, letting my mind catch up with my body. Each sip from the mug eased my burning thoughts into smouldering ash.

Getting up briefly to grab my new dream journal, I returned to my spot on the couch and peeled it open to the next blank page. I etched down the details of the nightmare, my intention not so much to document it as to just get it out of my head and onto paper; to release the knots that had formed in my brain. I felt the unraveling release of those knots with each word I wrote. If they were just words, they could no longer haunt me. They were just thoughts in a book, nightmares on paper. Not some hidden truth from my subconscious.

Once finished, I closed the journal and placed it on the coffee table in front of me, then took the last swig from my mug. Sinking deeper into the couch, I stared out onto the street below, watching the scarce amount of pedestrians make their way back and forth on the walkways below. Some walked holding hands. Others jogged, a steady beat in their ears.

I tried to imagine what each of these strangers' lives might be like. What the pepper-haired man and woman holding hands would be having for dinner, or if they had a grown child living somewhere whom they missed and spoke to everyday. If the woman who jogged, looking to be in her thirties, had a man waiting for her at home still curled up in a bed she would climb back into just after her jog for a few moments, before they both began getting ready for work. What the boyish-looking man walking his dog could possibly be thinking about, so deep in thought he didn't notice that every third step or so, his golden-haired dog looked up at him with so much love and admiration in his eyes that even I could feel the bond from four floors up.

I wondered if they had ever lost anyone. If they were tied to lives that had been taken too soon. To mistakes that maybe weren't such accidents after all.

I let my mind play out these questions in my head, drawing up the lives of new faces I would probably never meet until all the details of my own life vanished amongst the sea of others out there, if only for a moment.

Everyone had nightmares. Everyone woke up. Everyone moved on with their lives.

I should, too.

It had been a while since nightmares took me as their midnight prisoner so frequently. Night terrors came to me in strong waves after Axel died, but once my mind latched on to the idea of Grey, they slowly disappeared, replaced by skydiving into cotton-candy clouds and flying dragons to castles built high on cliffs, overlooking fields of green.

Lifting a hand to my neck, I worked out the tight rubber bands that seemed to have permanently tensed there from the haystack of anxieties pulling at me. My fear that I might have started the fire, the possibility that Catchers might be capable of terrible things, the question of whether there could be a connection between all of it and Axel's death . . . it all played wicked games with my mind anytime I tried to rest.

Most of all, I knew now more than ever before that, despite his doppelgänger, Grey wasn't real. All the years I had secretly hoped he somehow could be had crashed down around me in the form of a stranger who went by Hale.

Even so—even knowing all of this—all I wished for every time I closed my eyes was to be with Grey again.

I got up, placing my cup into the dish port before making my way back into my bedroom. The white walls had brightened, painted warm by the rising light of a new day's sun.

I pulled up the corners of my comforter and tucked them under the fluffed pillows. Then I plopped down onto my freshly made bed, rolling onto my back before tapping my temple.

The screen lit to life in front of my eyes, causing the ceiling above me to blur. Blinking open Syncher, my mind worked faster than my thoughts as I typed in his name.

H-a-l-e K-i-n-g-s-l...

I needed to know more about him. I knew I was digging for answers I didn't quite have the questions to, but it was all I could do to keep myself from unraveling.

His profile filled the screen, but my hopes were instantly dashed by the sight of no new posts since I had checked last night. I returned to the Syncher home page, where my eyes fell on a string of faces that topped the Syncher feed.

Do You Know . . . ?
   Kycer Snare

A picture of a light-haired boy with dark eyes stared back at me. I knew that face. He had been at Koze yesterday with the group at the table. I'd caught a glimpse of him as I was running out. He had been sitting in the seat beside Hale Kingsley.

I clicked his profile, making sure not to sync my profile with his while I blinked delicately through status updates and mutual photos, many of which overlapped with the group shots on Hale's profile. A post marked the top of his page, showing his live location.

He was just outside of Yorker.

I looked at the description beside his location.

"Kycer is attending Yorker orientation as a tour guide starting at 0700."

It was a long shot, but it was all I had. Based on the amount of mutual photos, events, and friends Kycer and Hale had in common, it was safe to assume they were friends.

If Kycer was attending Yorker orientation, maybe Hale would be there, too.

My eyes collapsed the screen with a swift blink, and my feet carried me toward the washroom. Punching in a shower, I untangled myself as best I could, hoping that somehow, all at once, everything around me would come back together.

My brother's death, my family's divide, my dreams of Hale Kingsley, the fire . . . I knew more by instinct than anything else that there was an answer to all of it. Some kind of foul play was at work here, and I just couldn't blanket myself in the ignorance of possible coincidence. Something wasn't right. Someone was a fault.

An increasingly familiar fear flashed through my mind as I wiped away the steam of the bathroom mirror, catching in my throat as the reflection of my fresh skin dripped back at me.

Maybe the person at fault was me.

CHAPTER 9
something real – breakup

I WALKED DOWN the same slick, paved path I had stumbled along just yesterday morning. Young trees just beginning to burn with the colours of second state lined my progress on either side. I took in the campus in its entirety for the second time, a pocket of planted greenery in the middle of the sea of tall buildings that was Terigon. The slate path that led the way to the front doors of the specialty school matched the walls that lined the main building on campus. Yorker was tucked into the city the way a heart is tucked into a body cavity, its presence obviously a main hub of life in Terigon.

As I dodged fellow students, climbing the large set of stairs to the doors, it suddenly dawned on me that I had no idea what I would say to Hale if he was actually inside.

"Hi, so, I've been dreaming of you since the day my brother died and now my house has burned down and I think your dad might have something to do with all of it. Thoughts?"

Oh boy.

Despite knowing there was no way this could go well, I was unable to stop the inner urge that kept my feet moving forward, one in front of the other. Knowingly walking toward another potentially humiliating doom, I pulled open the doors and made my way into Yorker headquarters.

My first thought was that I had never been around so many

people my own age. Around me, faces chatted and eyes blinked at live screens as people weaved through one another.

In the distance, I spotted a long table of portal screens and a sign flashing above them that read, "Orientation Sign-Ups."

I made my way toward it, my eyes subtly panning the crowd for a certain familiar face.

When I approached the table, I typed my name into one of the tablet sign-up sheets, not caring to look at which orientation leader I was falling under.

Hale Kingsley was nowhere in sight, but my eyes caught the contrasting eyes and hair I now knew to be Kycer in the far corner of the room. He laughed, punching another familiar face from Koze in the arm as they waited by a coffee order port.

To their left, silky black hair stood out against a fitted white pantsuit, making the girl from Hale's Syncher photo unmistakable.

I turned my thumbs around each other as if to spin a web of invisibility around myself in fear that anyone might recognize me from yesterday. Quietly, I walked to the far wall, leaning back against it as I took in the crowds of commotion around me, my eyes peeking over at Hale's friends periodically.

Fifteen minutes passed, and the crowds fell silent as orientation leaders began calling out groups. I kept my eyes peeled on the sea of faces, searching for features I knew as well as my own.

"Carson Wallace," a high-pitched voice pierced my consciousness. I turned toward the sign-up portals, my eyes instantly falling upon the pretty girl I had seen on Hale's arm. Her eyes scanned the crowd, impatiently waiting for her newest group member to step forward.

God, no.

I pulled away from the wall, walking toward her with an awkward smile on my face. As I neared, I got a clear look at her sharp features, softened by symmetry and coated with just enough makeup to enhance her high cheekbones and doll-like eyes. She was beautiful, no doubt, but the expression she wore on her face was less so. Vanity dripped from her shoulders with cutting precision, accented by the hands on her hips.

She lifted an impatient arm, waving me along faster before calling another name off the list.

Nope. I definitely did not like this girl.

After the last name was called and the clusters of students had been broken into pockets, our guide turned to face us all, her eyes still trained on a live portal screen. She stared into it as she spoke to us, her voice matter-of-fact.

"I'm Temperance, your orientation leader for the next hour. Follow me and don't get lost. Save all your questions until the end of the tour."

With that, she blinked closed her screen, scanned the crowd for a brief moment, flicked her hair across her shoulder, and led the way forward.

As we filed out of the grand hall, we turned left, our group hustling to keep up with Temperance's long strides. Passing a windowed hallway, our portals rang in our ears, notifying us that we had entered Section A of the campus. Suddenly, everyone's eyes blinked open live screens, and a map of Yorker was laid out for all of us with a star indicating where we were on the map.

Surrounding this main hub were the classrooms of all sciences, maths, and engineering.

"Section A is the largest part of the Yorker Campus," the monotone voice filled our ears again, playing from the multiple individual portals keeping our group in tune with each other.

From the corner of my eye, I caught the blurred edges of Temperance as she leaned against the nearby wall, arms crossed.

I blinked my screen closed, taking in the architecture of the building with my real eyes instead. The stone walls rose high until they met the crisp edge of the ceiling, boxing us into a perfect square. On the middle panel of the far wall, a portal screen was mounted among a thick curtain of ivy, water dripping down its leaves and into a soft fountain build into the floor. The portal screen was displaying the same map that had been inputted into our temple ports, its screen following along with the parts of the orientation I was missing. I blinked my screen back open, rejoining the other students around me in an attempt not to steal another peek at Temperance.

I had bigger things to stress about than why I had been born with a messy mop of blond hair while she was graced with a silky sea of thick black locks.

At the end of the Section A screenplay, our group went left, filing down a hall of classroom doors as we followed the clicking heels of our tour guide.

When we neared Section H, I realized our tour was walking around the school backwards in what I assumed was an attempt to keep the different tour groups separated.

We lined up in front of a wall filled with windows as we faced Temperance, her back to another row of doors.

Once she had counted everyone in the room, she tapped her temple, and our next virtual tour flickered to life.

Section H was for urban agriculture. Research done in the adjacent small lecture rooms had helped to push forward the invention of things like portal food and Thalia's ability to produce simulated foods grown in indoor solar rooms—sustenance that kept its population not only alive, but thriving from the improved food's modified nutrient density.

Temperance opened one of the lecture-room doors, and our group filed along behind her into a clean room whose four walls were covered in greenery. The room breathed with life, motion-activated lights blinking and giving shape to metal desks that stood on its waxy white floors.

A massive screen attached to the far wall of the classroom mimicked the smaller ones placed at each desk, wristlet ports ready for students to sign in with their individual portals. I looked up, catching the cameras planted in the far corners of the room, sticking out among the green leaves.

The room had life, yet as I stood in the middle of it, it left me feeling lifeless in a way I couldn't quite explain.

After making our way through Sections G, F, and E, we ended up back outside, following the back pathways in the direction of Section C of the campus. We turned at the second pathway toward another building lined with windows, getting closer to our destination with every step.

The doors opened automatically as approached and we made our way inside, where we found more plants, this time twining up pillars as well as walls as they climbed all the way up to a sky roof. Rows of tables lined with screens took up the majority of the room, a handful of students scattered among them. To the far left, I caught a small section tucked away from the light of the sunroof. Walls of shelves lined with the spines of what I instantly knew to be antique books made my heart jump. My eyes pored over the room, finishing on the right, where I spotted an empty coffee bar fitted with a portal order screen.

In a matter of seconds, the space had become my favourite part of Yorker.

"This is the library. There are a few late years and summer students who are currently in a program using it right now, so keep quiet and don't take too long looking around. You've got 0010 time."

Temperance shuffled off, joining two girls at one of the empty benches in the centre of the room.

The walls of plant-lined windows grew high and tall here, like the Vancity mountains. Without wasting time, I found my way to the shelves of old books that no one else seemed to show much interest in.

I walked up and down the aisles of books, my fingers tracing the bindings and textures of each one. It was easy to spot the really ancient ones by their obvious scars and bold colouring, in contrast to the sterile feel and block lettering on the slightly newer volumes. Portal screens lined each shelf, making it easy to navigate the large collection and find exactly the book you needed. I couldn't wait to get my hands on all their pretty words, titles already jumping out at me from each of the shelves.

At the end of the third row, I weaved back out of the books, taking a short set of stairs into the pit of benched screeners. A half-wall divided students from whoever was sitting on the other side of them, giving the space a sense of united focus. A few students were sprinkled into the seats, heads down and wrist ports plugged in as they concentrated on their private screens.

I wondered if this time next year I would be one of the long-haired heads bent low as I cultivated the newest sleep simulation, maybe a walk in the wilds of the mountains, or a surfing experience in an ocean of clouds.

A cough sounded from a chair at the end of the table, pulling me from my daydream. The arm of the culprit rose to scratch his head, and his profile came into view. My heart leaped at the lines of his face even before my brain registered exactly who I was seeing.

Hale Kingsley sat low in the farthest study cubby, his eyes trained on his own invisible screen, head ducked, as if he were trying to stay out of view.

Panicking, I skipped back into the row of cubbies behind him, sinking low into the nearest seat as well to block my face from his field of vision if he were to turn around.

A bitchy demand to keep up sounded from behind me, and I saw my group shuffling out of the back end of the library to move on to the next section of the tour. I waited until they were gone before peeking my head back up over the half-wall, catching a glimpse of the back of his head again.

I sat back down, taking a deep breath before channeling my focus. No matter what, I needed answers. I couldn't let this opportunity pass.

Standing up, I lifted my chin in an attempt to project confidence as I made me way toward him. Reaching his cubby, I stopped short of his chair, lingering a moment as I waited for him to look up.

When he didn't, I cleared my throat.

Still nothing.

"Um, hi. Sorry to bother you, I'm new here. Do you happen to know if this library holds any antique books written by a guy named Sholstire?"

Grey and I quoted Sholstire all the time. He had become one of my favourite writers after Uncle Char gave me one of his books for my fourteenth birthday. After a few romantic words about the beauty within despair, I was instantly hooked, sharing lines of his golden, wisdom-soaked words—always cast with just a shade of realism—with Grey so often that, after a while, he had no choice but to join the game.

I hoped to see a flash of recognition in his eyes, some kind of response that would let me deem him Grey-worthy. But I regretted the entire idea when he didn't even so much as glance at me as he spat out a quick response.

"Not a clue."

I blinked, hoping he might say more. He remained turned forward, his focus trained on things I couldn't see.

"Well, I'm not sure where my group went off too. Any chance you know your way around here?" I cringed at my own words, knowing I was reaching desperately for any sort of interaction. Anything that would leave me better off than I was this morning. "You see, I'm not from here . . . "

An abrupt laugh barked from his throat. Finally turning, he had obviously closed his portal screen as his eyes took me in with utter annoyance. Dropping one arm across the back of his chair, he leaned back, his arrogance holding him in place like gravity.

"Do you have any idea who I am?" he asked.

That's what I'm trying to find out . . .

"Um . . . Hale Kingsley?" I replied, fighting off the urge to say "Grey" pulling at my tongue.

"So you're not completely incompetent then," he leaned forward again, positioning himself to spin back away at any moment. "Would have guessed otherwise from your spill at Koze. Listen, I'm a little too preoccupied at the moment to feed into this pathetic crush you seem to have on me. Drop me a follow on Syncher, sweet cheeks. I'm busy here."

Turning away, his eyes lost focus again, returning to a screen I still couldn't see.

I blinked, frozen by the shock of his conceit. Boredom settled over his shoulders again in seconds, like he'd already forgotten I was there. He seemed utterly unfazed by the interaction. As if he dealt with this kind of attention every day.

When I continued to stand there frozen, he puffed out a breath in annoyance, and pulled his wrist port from the cubby, attaching it swiftly back onto his arm.

"I was just leaving anyway," he muttered under his breath, rolling his eyes as he made his way around me and up the stairs of the pit.

As he walked away, I stared at the back of his head, still unable to process the sting.

He looked like Grey. They even walked with the same confidence in every step. But Hale Kingsley was without a doubt not Grey.

CHAPTER 10
in the end – vancouver sleep clinic

LIKE WAKING FROM A DREAM, the shock slowly faded as Hale exited the library, leaving me standing in the middle of it and wondering, dumbfounded, what to do next. I had been right. Grey was never real, only a figment of my imagination, tied to the face of the future asshole leader of our state.

I didn't know why I had tried to talk to him. What insanity had taken over my brain to present myself to someone who seemed to be lacking one? I shook my head, breaking through the tornado of thoughts so I could take action.

I sat in the chair Hale had left empty, pushing my wrist hub from my arm and placing it into the table socket before tapping my temple, bringing to life my portal screen. The flat screen attached to the table below synced to my port, coming to life with a touch-screen keyboard that made it easier to type and navigate through my personal screen at a faster pace. Opening the Webber app, I settled in to do more research.

I typed in "Hale Kingsley" again, only this time information filled my screen at length, rather than just giving me the soundbites from before. Connecting to the library's system had granted me access to all the stored books and articles of the Yorker database—a wealth of information that the lingering firewalls in my portal still kept me away from, even after my latest upgrade.

A grim smile cracked across my face. Suddenly, the day no longer felt like a total loss.

Everything about the history of the Kingsley family, from its very first origins to articles like "Hale Kingsley Graduates Social School with Honours," were listed like countless potential hints and clues to my mystery. A vast, tangled web of new information at the tips of my fingers.

As I combed through the results, images cropped up of Hale finishing first in the hundred-meter dash, along with a list of the awards he had obtained during social school for his work with the sick and elderly. There was even a photo of him at one of Yorker's early admittance events . . . with Temperance standing behind his right shoulder, a painfully perfect smile on her lips.

It all seemed a little over-the-top to me. As if every article and image had been strategically calculated for the public eye. There was not one bad photo of him, each picture somehow highlighting his pearly white teeth and those icy grey eyes that dazzled even on a portal screen.

Not knowing where to start, I blinked open the first link that topped the list, which seemed to be a complete bio of not only Hale, but his entire family.

> *Hale Kingsley*
> *Future Lead Catcher of Thalia, currently attending Yorker*
> *Specialty*
> *Related: Donte Kingsley and Portia Kingsley (deceased)*
> *Age: 21*
> *Birthday: 481st*
> *Syncher Status: 92%*

"Lead Catcher of Thalia" was hyperlinked, its graphics flashing in my eyes before I blinked it open.

"Catcher History" titled the screen.

My eyes rolled over the words as I tried my best to retain as much information as I could, eating it all up to feed my ravenously curious mind. I trailed through sentences laced together with proud, patriotic rhetoric about how Catcher marshals lay at the core of safety in Thalia. Between advanced technology and a promise for a better fate by our leader, Donte Kingsley, no harm would ever come to the people of Thalia.

I felt my blood boil, my stomach turning at the thin veil of deception that came from those words. The thought of people buying this stuff when, in all likelihood, Donte and the Catchers could very well be the ones committing the only untimely deaths that ever found their way into our unsuspecting lives—and passing them off as "accidents"—made me want to throw up.

Backing up to Hale's bio again, I blinked open the hyper-link of Donte Kingsley's name. My screen flashed as a new wave of words—"Our Hero Donte, Lead Catcher of Thalia"—topped the screen. The motion picture to the left of Donte's biography and basic information bore the look of an aged man giving a forced smile to the camera. His sleek grey hair was slicked back and smoothed, his collared shirt trimmed with metals that granted him a sophisticated look; not a piece of his appearance was out line. But his eyes held a darkness I couldn't quite place, especially in combination with his attempt at a warm expression. Those unsettling jet-black eyes seemed to stare through me from my screen, bringing back my urge to vomit.

I had seen flashes of Donte before, when my parents share-screened as they watched the Thalia news. But with the monsters that I now suspected might be hiding in his closet, it was impossible to not see shadows dancing across his face like the ghosts that might very well be haunting him.

I scrolled away from the disturbing smile of his photo, my eyes desperate for a break from this face. As I did, I crossed a motion photo that stood in such contrast to his that I instantly felt the warmth and peace of it radiating toward me. I blinked open the link below it, titled "Portia Kingsley," and her bio flipped onto my screen.

Portia Kingsley
Spouse: Donte Kingsley
Children: Hale Kingsley
Age: 27 (deceased)
Birthday: 251st
May the queen of fates rest in peace.

The photo to the left showed a woman with soft, angelic grey eyes and smooth, wavy brown hair that poured past the borders of the photo. As she smiled warmly at the camera—with her pinched-pink cheeks and eyelashes so long I could only assume they weren't real—a gentle laugh tumbled from her mouth . . . and then the entire moving image played over again.

Looking at her, all of the chills I had gotten from Donte vanished. She seemed to beam with rays of light like an angel. I scrolled down to find any information on her death, a new curiosity suddenly taking me over. I landed on a paragraph titled "Final Moments."

Portia Kingsley had passed away tragically on the day following the birth of her first and only child, Hale Kingsley. It was said to have been known by the Kingsleys that Portia had a condition that put her at risk of death during childbirth. While she made it through the birth of her son, she nonetheless passed during a dark hour of the morning the following day. Prior to her death, she had summoned the energy to leave a statement of comfort to the public.

I blinked the video to life and her face filled my screen, still looking peaceful despite her exhaustion, only this time I caught a touch of sadness in her expression, dimming some of her light.

"Do not cry for me, for I know my fate has been fulfilled. To pass only moments after fulfilling my destiny, to bring something so beautiful into this world . . . I cannot think of anything more I would need to accomplish to have known I lived a full life. I ask of you all that you do not mourn my passing, for in him, I will continue to live on.

"People of Thalia, know that I truly love you. Your fate rests in his hands. May you teach him to share great love and to create a destiny of dreams, so he may one day repay the kindness by leading you to do the same."

My heart sank as the playback ended, erasing her face from the screen. It was weird to feel the loss of someone I had never known existed until a few short moments ago . . . but something inside told me she was one of the good ones.

Though I wasn't very fond of Hale, to say the least, after hearing his mother's words, I couldn't help but feel more of an understanding for his putrid, childlike behaviour. Maybe if he had been given the chance to be loved by a mother like that, he would have been different.

Instead, she died in order to give him life. He probably blamed himself.

"What are you doing?"

My mind snapped back into focus, blinking closed the screen I only now realized I hadn't privatized. Temperance stood a few feet from my right shoulder, one hand on her hip as her eyes tore into me with accusation and annoyance.

"Sorry, I lost you guys," I responded, standing quickly.

"You weren't supposed to trail off on your own. You may be a student here in a few weeks, but as of now you're still a nobody. Got it?"

I nodded, deciding it was best to brush off her comments. She stepped closer, and my eyes were suddenly able to take in details about her appearance that I hadn't noticed from afar. Like the freckles she had clearly erased in photos, and a small scar under her right eye.

I waited for her to turn and walk away, but she continued to glower at me. I fought the impulse to roll my eyes. How long was this power trip going to take? I had bigger problems to deal with than a few snide remarks from Thalia's most edited Syncher model.

"By the way, I saw your pathetic attempt to talk to Hale. It was cute. Pathetic, but cute." She flicked her hair over her shoulder, and I caught a waft of cherry scent in the air as she slithered away like a snake, her nose lifted high from the awareness that all eyes were on her.

Glaring, I trailed after her, back toward the group.

I really, really did not like this girl.

⸱

Silken ribbons of purple, green, and indigo stroked across the midnight sky, bleeding into each other like blending paints. Heavy waves crashed like thunder against the ship we stood on, the salt from the sea filling the air and my nose.

"Ahoy there, matey."

Grey was standing on the highest deck of a wooden ship that he claimed came from the old world. A patch covered his left eye, shielded by the oversized black hat of an old-time pirate, which sat atop his usual perfectly tousled hair.

"So we're pirates again?"

My hand moved quickly over the paper, trying to jot down as many details of the old dream as I could pull out of my mind.

After the orientation, I had returned home to try to jog my memory for any dreams that might help me discover more about the connection I was sure I had to Hale and the Catchers. The memory of a night we'd spent on the pirate ship hit me first, so I sat back on the lounge-room couch just as I had that morning, only this time I wasn't writing about nightmares. The contrast of old-world ink on paper brought a comfort to my eyes that portal screens never seemed to. I sighed, and tuned back into the blurred images of that dream from years ago.

"I thought you were enjoying the pirate theme lately?" Grey

said, walking to the side staircase before leaping over all its stairs, landing swiftly on the deck I was standing on below. As he made his way toward me, his arms spun out toward the open sea with a little too much enthusiasm.

"Arrrrrrr, we've got the world at our fingertips. Where would you like to go, me lady?"

Facing me, he wrapped his arms around my torso as my face broke into a laugh.

"Shall we fight the great creature of the sea with tentacles as long as city streets, or shall we take to the land, seeking an island to overthrow?"

His thick eyebrows pondered the question as he continued to stare out at the sea ahead, one hand making a dramatic motion to block the soft moonlight from his vision. I chuckled again, breaking from his grasp so I could walk to the edge of the ship.

I looked up at the massive black flag that whipped billowed in the sea-filled air above us, a massive skull and bones spread across its surface. Just behind it, I could see the ebb and flow of what looked like the northern lights, twisting and fading in and out of their cool-toned colours like melted sorbet leaking into the sky above. I let my eyes get lost in them for a moment, realizing I wanted nothing more than to swim in their sweetness.

"I want to go up there, in the sky," I said, not knowing how long I had been lost in the beauty of the lights.

"As you wish, me lady . . . though I will miss the eye patch," Grey replied, coming up behind me. He flicked the eye patch overboard and took my hand. Leaping from the edge of the ship, we flew into the waves of colour, stopping to land softly on a pillowy cloud of green that whisked back and forth through technicolour shades even as we sat on it. All the clouds around us alternated colours in unison, as well, leaving us lost in a wonderland of lights.

The cool air lapped and tingled at my skin, but I wasn't cold. Everywhere, stars twisted and fell, and snowflakes began to drift down around us, melting on my skin in seconds. My mouth widened in a smile as I tilted my head up to the sky. The white, shining flakes fell all around me like confetti, lit by the endless stream of starlight.

This was more like it.

I stuck my arms out, falling back into the multicoloured night cloud of the aurora.

Grey lay down beside me, one perfectly sculpted arm resting across his torso as the other stretched up and relaxed above his head. He turned his head to face me, an amused grin crossing his face, and I followed suit.

"I think you're the only person I know who gets this excited about snow," he said, his hand leaving its place on his chest to find mine.

I nestled my head against his chest as he pulled me in. He smelled like a heavenly mixture of lemon, honey, and teakwood that made my stomach lurch and turn. I breathed in hard, trying to burn the scent into my memory. If I could bottle it up, I'd keep it on me at all times. I'd burn it in every corner of my room and coat my life in its essence, marking everything with a touch of something I loved.

"I'm the only person you know, dummy," I joked, the side of my head tingling as it rested against him.

We lingered in the moment for a while, neither of us feeling the need to fill the air with more words.

"Are you thinking about Axel?" His question yanked me back into my living reality.

Today, in the real world, it would have been Axel's birthday. The day he was supposed to turn twelve.

"A little bit," I admitted slowly, not sure if I really wanted to talk about it this year.

I felt his body tense, waiting for the words he was holding back to make their way out.

"Have you ever thought about looking into his death?" he said finally.

His question puzzled me. The thought had never crossed my mind.

"No," I responded. I knew how Axel died. I was there. Reliving it *didn't top my list of things I felt like putting myself through. Plus, I didn't want to dwell on it tonight. I just wanted to be.*

"Car—" Grey began.

"Shhhh," I cut him off, placing my hand on his chest and feeling the tickle of contact that danced on my skin. "Right now, this is all I need," I said.

A moment passed. Then I felt Grey's hand on my hair, brushing it back softly. When I titled my head back, I could see the dancing colours of the sky behind his head, outlining his face in hues of purple and blue. In the moment his eyes caught mine, I felt like I was truly home. We smiled, and a gust of wind brushed my skin . . . before taking the dream with it.

I shut my dream journal, the regurgitated dream still weighing on my mind. I remembered wondering, the next day, why Grey had asked if I researched Axel's death. The idea had lingered in my thoughts for a brief moment, a tiny nibble of curiosity making me wonder how far I could get with the firewalls of my portal . . . but in the end, I had dismissed it. What more was there to know? It was best to leave the entire horrible event at rest.

We had never spoken of it again.

🌙

After dinner, I decided to throw on my running shoes, hitting the pavement with all the frustration I felt fizzing in my bones. Once again, to make sure it was deeply ingrained, I ran the route to Yorker and back, and the entire run only lasted fifteen minutes.

After washing up, I tapped an order for sleepy-time vanilla tea into the food port before making my way back to the lounge-room couch, my mind feeling much clearer and ready for the emotional upheaval I was about to subject myself to.

Pulling up my temple port screen, I clicked open the search engine and typed in "Axel Wallace."

No results.

Curious, I tried again, only this time following it with *lift accident.* This time, a lone link popped up, matching the keywords of "Wallace" and "lift accident."

The screen came to life, listing our lift accident to be the third of that year. There was no mention of Axel in the entire article. In fact, the only listed passengers in the lift were myself, my mom, and my dad.

I scrolled past the photo of our wrecked family lift after it had been retrieved from the water, continuing down until I landed on the Catchers' write-up of the accident. It listed the date and time of the event, along with the one individual who had become deceased.

I blinked, and my eyes did a double-take, yanking themselves back to the name that followed the word "deceased" in the report. No, I wasn't reading it wrong. I stared at the screen, trying to process what I was seeing.

Deceased: Carson Wallace.

CHAPTER 11
kill our way to heaven — michl

MY EYES FLUTTERED OPEN *and I took in the dark shadows of the unfamiliar room surrounding me. Groggily, I scanned the far wall until I found my own reflection shining back at me from a mirror, planted dead centre. I looked down, and gasped. My arms were tied to the arms of a chair.*

But, in front of me, my reflection showed no binds.

I stared into the mirror, taking in the image there. My body rested in a white armchair with my hair in front of my shoulder, a few inches shorter than I expected it to be. I concentrated on looking myself in the eyes, but the eyes of my reflection didn't follow, looking me up and down instead.

The reflection wasn't actually me.

My face, a little paler than usual, caught me staring at it and looked back at me with a wide, wicked smile that made my heart skip. I tried to pull my arms free, fighting against the thick wire rope that was keeping me locked in place. My reflection began to laugh, a sound so sinister it sent chills down my spine.

A doorway flew open, and the sounds of voices rushed into the room. Their chatter and laughter was familiar. Mom, Dad, Uncle Char! Even Mina's ditzy giggle was recognizable in the mix. For reasons I couldn't quite place, I knew I needed to save them. I knew something bad was about to happen.

My heart sped up, each beat skipping faster as my breath began to come in quick, panicked gasps. I fought harder against the chair, but I could feel it cementing me into place, steel thread making its way into the fibres of my skin.

I looked back at my reflection. An amused expression was dancing on her face now, her cheeks turning pink as she smiled at me, lovingly this time. The look in her eyes was soft, melting my anxiety away with the reassuring sign of her love and acceptance.

"You want to sit there." My own words filled my mind from a place I didn't have control over. "Relax. Sit. Watch me," she said.

Another roar of laughter from the people I loved came pouring into the room, and I looked toward it, again feeling a sudden desire to run to them. Didn't they know I was in here? Why couldn't I scream for them?

I bit my lips together, trying to form Mina's name, but my jaw locked tight.

"Don't," my reflection hissed. The heavy feeling in my bones deepened.

"Watch me," she demanded, and I turned my head back to face her. All of the colour drained from her cheeks as they hollowed out, her eyes darkening with shadows at the creases. Her dry, cracked lips were still smiling at me.

"The only way you survive, is if you smile," she said tilting her head. Her eyes twitched, suggesting fissures of insanity, and her teeth began rotting as they fell from her mouth. She lifted her hands, their skin aging with scales.

"Smile," she said again, her hands rising to her throat. Without my permission, my hands did the same, suddenly free from their wire bindings. My fingers laced tight around my neck, squeezing so hard they began to drain of blood. My lungs buckled, begging desperately for air, but I didn't ease up. Instead, I stared at my reflection in the mirror— only this time, it really was me.

And I was smiling.

⏾

I shot up, gasping for air. Sweat slicked my skin, and strands of hair stuck to my hot face and neck in a way that was becoming unsettlingly familiar. I wiped my forehead, my hand slipping across my forehead. It was burning.

"Breathe," I gasped to myself, trying to force my lungs to ease into a slower rhythm. Sitting up, I took in the yellow cushions beneath me.

I hadn't been able to make my way to bed after discovering my own apparently documented death. I must have fallen asleep on the couch while trying to process everything.

The sudden confusion from last night hit me all over again. I was, apparently, dead.

What did this mean?

I needed to talk to someone about it all. My parents flashed across my mind, and I realized that, despite my mother's rule about checking in on fourth-days at curfew, I had missed calling in last night. How had that happened . . . and how I had I gotten away with it? I hadn't even noticed the days passing, being so heavily immersed in my discovery of Hale that I hadn't checked in on things with the house. Would they even tell me what was going on, if I asked?

My mind shifted to another comforting voice, realizing it had also been days since I last spoke to Mina. I opened my portal screen, blinking in her name so I could call her up. I wanted to tell her everything. How I found the matches and could have set the fire. The words I'd overheard about the Catchers, and all the new information they were leading me to. My dream about Axel, and my discovery that the death documented from our accident was mine, with Axel's existence nowhere to be found.

But as I looked at my screen, one glance at the calendar stopped me in my tracks.

It was day 112. Uncle Char would be coming back from Port

Edward today, arriving at 1000. I tapped my temple, and the screen shifting to the current time: 0800.

He'd be here in two hours. And he couldn't shut me down this time. This time, I had proof.

Time passed slowly, but finally, a knock at the door announced Uncle Char's arrival.

Opening the latch, I let him in, his familiar face granting me more comfort than I realized I needed. Having punched orders for two stacks of pancakes into the food port, I listened as he updated me on Sasher, anticipating the moment I would be able slip a word in edgewise and redirect the conversation into uncharted territory.

"Oh, and I got you a new book. It's called *Midnight Mind*. It's about old tales of time gypsies and fortune-tellers," Uncle Char said, his eyes filling with excitement as he took another bite of his pancakes.

His energy was at a height I hadn't seen from my uncle in some time. Presumably, seeing Sasher had left him in good spirits.

"Thanks, Uncle Char. Can't wait to read it. Actually . . . I've been doing some portal reading lately, and I stumbled across something I wanted to ask you about." I twirled a piece of pancake in a pool of maple syrup, unsure of how to tackle the topic.

"Sure! What'd you find, kid?" My uncle forked another fluffy bite into his mouth, chewing in bliss.

"I found the Catcher statement from the day of the crash," I said, figuring there was no other way to break the ice.

He stopped mid-chew, staring at me.

"Axel's name wasn't anywhere on it," I continued. "In fact, it actually had me stated as the deceased." I popped the piece of pancake in my mouth, signalling that my turn to talk had finished, and I expected him to pick up the topic from here.

Swallowing, Uncle Char took a drink from the soy milk I had ordered on the side, gulping down a big chug of it before setting his glass back on the table.

"You saw that, huh?" He wiped his mouth with a napkin before resting it back on the table, letting out a breath.

"There was a mix-up on the documents on the day of the crash. Your parents were so torn up about Ax that they didn't notice it in the marshals' write-up of the accident. Your dad signed the thing off in a state of tears. By the time the documents were filed, your parents had gone into the mourning ceremonies. I'm not even sure they ever noticed the files were wrong."

I nodded slowly, feeling instantly relieved that I hadn't called them this morning. If what he was saying was true, they had no idea those documents existed. But he did.

"Shouldn't we tell them?" I asked, hoping that by "we" my uncle would know I meant "him."

"I'm not sure it would do any good, kid. That paperwork is numbered, filed, and stored away without any value. It's not like it makes much of a difference now." His hands seemed to shake a bit as he picked his fork back up. Cutting another piece of pancake, he popped it into his mouth and smiled at me. I looked back at him thoughtfully.

How much of what he was saying was true?

It felt weird to question Uncle Char. He had always been nothing but a rock for me. Someone I felt I could trust even more than my own parents.

So why did I feel like he was lying to me now?

"You excited for your first day tomorrow?" he changed the topic. I kept my eyes on him, hesitating as to whether I was going to let him shift the conversation away from the accident.

"Very," I replied finally, cutting into my own stack for a second bite. I decided that at least our talk had made one thing clear.

If I wanted to know the truth, I was going to have to seek it out for myself.

A buzzing from my wrist hub brought my arm to life before the rest of my body.

My eyes, peeling open, caught the graphic screen of the silent alarm I'd set before going to bed last night—the first time it had actually had the chance to wake me up, instead of one of my nightmares.

I let the dark room seep into my consciousness, slipping out of a deep sleep and into the real world again. Then I sat up quietly, lifting the blankets from my legs as my feet found the floor.

Standing, I tiptoed out into the main area of the loft.

More and more of the apartment's edges came to life with each second as my eyes continued to adjust. Uncle Char's snores sounded from the couch in the lounge, the soft lighting from the city pouring into the room and over his sleeping face. Pushing down my guilt, I looked around for his things, spotting his duffle bag in the kitchen corner where his wrist hub lay charging. Walking over to it, I pulled the wrist strap free before creeping back to my room.

Shutting the door with a soft whisper, I climbed back into bed, freeing my own hub to secure his onto my arm instead. Putting my wrist to temple, I watched my uncle's portal screen blink to life, a passcode resting in wait.

Six characters.

S-A-S-H-E-R I typed, the screen giving a jarring wiggle to let me know that the password was wrong. What else could it be?

Z-A-N-D-R-A, I tried again, and this time the screen blinked to life.

I was in.

His screen layout was so different from my own that it left my brain momentarily puzzled. I scanned his apps, a little in awe. His software was clearly many levels above the capabilities of my own.

"Would you like to say a command?" a calm, female voice spoke into my temple. I double-checked the sound options, ensuring the setting was on private.

Tapping my temple, I spoke as quietly as I could.

"Search Axel Wallace," I directed, the screen flashing quickly into action. I figured voice commanded would crunch down on the time it would take to navigate through his system.

Instantly, photos of a baby-faced kid with eyes that matched mine filled the screen. My stomach knotted. Axel's face having faded in my memory, over the years. My parents kept no photos of him around after he died, so the face staring back at mine shocked my system with a sense of déjà vu. Like I had known it before, yet was still somehow only seeing it for the first time.

I sifted through the files, seeing no official Catcher documents with Axel's name. Tapping my temple portal, I tried something else.

"Search Carson Wallace."

This time my face lit up the screen with all the photos and videos that had been taken of me over the years: me blowing out artificial flames on my tenth birthday; a photo of Sasher and me sitting on opposite sides of a dinner table, my eyes drifting off into a daydream.

Then a folder labeled "Official Catcher Records" filed into view. I blinked it open.

All files containing my name were highlighted at the top of the folder's listed documents, which held everything from Catcher population records to simulation- and portal-system updates.

Three folders topped the screen under my name.

Carson Wallace Birth—Catcher Certification.
Carson Wallace Death—Catcher Certification.
Carson Wallace—Kill List *LOCATION UPDATED TODAY*

My heart lodged itself into my throat as I stared at the labels. I blinked open the third file, afraid of what I was about to find. A list of names flooded the screen, mine highlighted at the top under a chilling heading:

"Catcher-Certified Kill List"

My name flashed, and I blinked it open, feeling my hands beginning to shake in my lap.

"Carson Wallace. Fate previously recorded as sealed by lift accident on day 218 of year 102. Syncher file created on day 218, year 116 indicating that her fate was still alive and unfulfilled. High-priority kill. Location last updated at 1000 day 224."

My stomach fell.

Blinking closed the screen, I pulled my uncle's hub from my wrist, too shaken to search for anything else.

I was on some sort of kill list. A Catcher-certified kill list.

This could explain the fire. It certainly explained the day of the accident.

It really was meant to have been me who died that day.

Only, I saw Hale's face and chose to live. Axel died instead. The Catchers had believed me to be dead this entire time, because I was so off the grid. They had no way of knowing otherwise . . . until Mina made me my Syncher account.

I followed the timeline in my mind, piecing together the night of the fire with sudden conviction. It must have been caused by the Catcher marshals. The Catchers wanted me dead; why, I had no idea. A bigger question hung over me instead . . .

Why did my uncle have this list?

CHAPTER 12
back in the water – HAEVN

I MADE MY WAY out into the kitchen, punching the largest order of coffee into the food portal before making my way to the bathroom to quickly wash up. I didn't try to hide my alertness, not caring if the sounds of my early morning routine woke Uncle Char, who was still sleeping on the couch.

As I brushed my teeth, I caught sight of my reflection in the mirror. The bags under my eyes wore on my face, telling anyone who looked at me how little I had slept. I was torn between confronting my uncle again, or allowing him to leave today while I pretended to remain unaware of the things I had found on his portal screen last night.

If my location had been updated yesterday at 1000, that meant something had been able to report where I was at that time. And the only overlapping detail I could see was that 1000 was when my uncle had arrived back at the loft.

At this point, I wasn't sure if the files he had on his port were a means of protecting me, or if he was somehow complicit in creating them.

The possibility of the latter shuddered across my skin.

I made my way back to the kitchen port, pulling the door open to retrieve the mug I had ordered earlier, to go. My first class at Yorker was in an hour—a concept I hadn't even begun to process, amongst all the chaos going on. Still, I got ready for it all the same, unsure of what else I could do at this point.

My uncle sat up on the couch, scratching his shiny head before turning to look at me, one eye still glued shut.

He tapped his temple, and a screen activated in the air. To my horror, the kill list created a holographic wall between the two of us, making me choke on my sip of coffee.

"Carson . . . " Uncle Char croaked. "Did you tap into my portal last night?" He collapsed the screen in a quick blink, and his eyes searched mine, suddenly more alert than they had been moments before.

There was no way out of it. I was caught red-handed. I decided to charge right into it, answering his question with one of my own.

"Why is my name on a kill list?" I demanded, standing straight and lifting my chin, unsure if I would even be willing to accept whatever answer left his mouth this time.

"Carson, you can't begin to understand what you've gotten yourself into," he said flatly. Pushing tiredly off the couch, he crossed to the kitchen and secured his wrist hub to his arm.

"Someone needs to tell me what's going on," I insisted, frustrated at how childish I sounded as my fear cracked through the words.

Uncle Char punched in an order for a coffee, his back turned to me and his head hung low. Turning, his face held a defeated look as he gestured for me to take a seat. I lowered myself into the dining-table chair, waiting to hear what he had to say.

"The day Axel died, he was only two, still months away from having his blood tested for disease and entered into the Catcher database," Uncle Char began. That much lined up. It wasn't until your third birthday that you were required to be admitted into the database and have a portal surgically fused to your temple. The surgery itself was short and decently noninvasive. Even so, it kept most parents from entering their children into the Catcher database until the last possible moments before they turned three.

I leaned forward in my chair, waiting to hear more.

"When your lift ran off the bridge, it was meant to take your life with it. The kill list carries the names of unrelated strangers—people I can't begin to understand why the Catchers would want dead. But all the same, it exists, and yes kiddo, your name is on it." His face softened as he tried to cushion the confirmation.

"Your parents had no idea that you had been confirmed dead. It was me who helped the Catcher marshals wrap up the details of the accident," he continued. I looked at him, puzzled. He had kept this from my parents this entire time? The prospect seemed unlikely.

"Why would you have anything to do with the Catcher write-up?" I asked. There was no way a marshal would just take his word that the deed was done, for a life that was ordered for murder.

Uncle Char hesitated, the truth sitting on his tongue.

"Just tell me, please. I can't handle any more secrets." I knotted my fingers in my hair, the truth of my words pinching at my brain.

"Well . . . technically, I myself am a Catcher marshal," my uncle admitted.

My head shot up, shock snapping me back into focus.

"You're a what?"

"I'm one of the undercovers," he admitted quietly. "I play the role of a train runner, but ultimately I work for the Catchers as a system hacker. I mainly work on system upgrades for temple portals. I . . . leave back doors open into the minds of Thalia's people, to make it easier for Catchers to gain access to information that would otherwise go untapped. Most of the time it's useless. Unless they gain access to someone on the kill list through an upgrade."

My arms braced against the table, my body rigid as I struggled to take in this information. Uncle Char was a Catcher marshal. My mind flew back over all the constant portal hacks and updates that the Catchers had sold to us as "the new dawn of connection," tying them to the words he was saying.

"That's why you found those documents. They aren't available to the public eye," Uncle Char confessed.

"So is that what you did to my temple port?" I accused, suddenly pushing myself up from the table. "When you upgraded my system, did you leave a 'back door' open for them? Are they coming for me?" Tears welled up in my eyes, my chest starting to rise and fall with heavy breaths.

My uncle was quickly on his feet, crossing to me and putting his hands on my shoulders in an attempt to calm me down.

"No, absolutely not. I've been updating your system to keep you safe. Even the Syncher app. I deactivated its ability to track your location, since that was how they found you in the first place. Now that they know you're alive, I've had to go into hiding. They realized that I lied to them about your death, all those years ago. That's why I took that train up to Port Edward for a while; I wanted them to follow me away from you instead of to you. Did you check the place listed for your current location?"

He tapped open his screen, the kill list flashing to life again as my name painted itself in the air backwards, from my side of it. As he blinked open the location, "Port Edward" filled the screen, recognizable even with its letters flipped backward.

"But . . . how?" I asked.

"I attached your name to the Sasher's location. While they go looking for you, they'll have no idea they're really following her. She agreed to it no problem," he hurried on, seeing the look on my face. "Once they discover it's really her, she knows they won't touch her. It's not her fate they're concerned with."

I thought of Sasher, instantly grateful for her help despite the years of rivalry and all the time it had been since we had last seen each other. Clearly, she deserved more credit in our later years than she had in our earlier ones, I thought. I felt all the grudges I'd held against her falling by the wayside.

"So why are they so concerned with mine?" My eyebrows knitted in confusion as Uncle Char sat me back in the chair.

"That I haven't quite figured out. I have to head back to Vancity tonight, start a new trail for them to follow in search of you. If I stay in Terigon any longer, they might find you here," he said, crossing over to the lounge and beginning to pack up his belongings even as he spoke.

"Am I even safe here?" I asked, suddenly feeling as though the walls were watching me.

"You're safe. The apartment actually belongs to a good friend of mine, and I've put a firewall around it, blocking any potential hacks into any of the portals inside. The guy who owns the place is in with the Catchers too, but I can assure you he's on our side," he said, catching my eye to emphasize the last of his words.

I stared at him, blank-faced. Was I supposed to just take his word for it?

"So what do I do now?" I asked, the idea of heading to class suddenly feeling meaningless in light of the new stakes at play. The Catcher government wanted me dead. How was I supposed to leave the house?

"You need to carry on as if you know none of this," my uncle told me firmly. "It wasn't until you created your Syncher profile and took that photo with Mina that the Catchers got wind you were even alive. Luckily, thanks to those mugs you covered your faces with, they can't pull together a full physical profile for your search. For all they know, you could have been Mina in the photo."

I thought of Mina's face, our features different but similar enough to be labeled based on the same criteria.

Light eyes, blond hair, fair skin.

"Any and all photos of you taken by your parents or myself, I firewalled, so they are nearly impossible to hack. Same with your enrollment at Yorker; you can even use your temple port there, and no one will know it's you. And I made sure your air-train ticket into the city was untraceable. Not only do they have no idea you're in Terigon, they aren't even 100 percent sure what you look like. You have nothing to worry about," he insisted again. Then, stopping to place his belongings on the table, he rounded the corner of it and pulled out the chair beside me. Sitting in it, he levelled his eyes with mine.

"Carson, I need you to promise me you'll carry on as if you don't know any of this. We need you to look as normal as possible. You can't tell anyone, not even Mina. I've been blanketing any call and port signals that leave the apartment, so no one can pick up on your temple port, but even particular words picked up by portals can trigger alarms back to the Catchers, flagging and notifying them of potentially harmful calls and messages. Do you understand?"

I nodded, grateful again for not having called Mina or my parents yesterday morning.

"What happens next?" I looked up at my uncle, feeling the fear that had settled into my eyes.

"Next, I need to find out why you're one of the top priorities on their list. My friend, he's deeper into the Catcher government. He says the kill list is made up of lives whose blood tested not for diseased bodies, but for diseased fates. Their bloodlines foreshadow violence or mass murder. My friend thinks this is the reason the Catchers take out their lives and cover them up as accidents."

A new shock punched through me, making my eyes go wide. I hunched forward in the chair, trying to process what this meant about me.

Uncle Char was one step ahead of me. "Before you freak out, we don't think that's why they want you gone, specifically," he said. "We think it's got to do with something else, but we need some more time to find out. First things first, I need to create a new decoy trail leading as far away from you as possible, which I'm heading back to Vancity to do. From there, I'll get some information back to you on your next steps. Until then, I need you to go on as if everything is fine and dandy. Can you do that Carson?"

Uncle Char placed his knuckle under my chin, bringing my eyes up to meet his again.

"We're in this together. I won't let anything happen to you," he promised.

I nodded and took a shaky breath, reaching forward for my mug. Unsteadily, I took a long gulp of the warm liquid, feeling it slide down my tight throat.

I was going to need a few more cups to make it through today.

CHAPTER 13
can't wait – filous

I HUGGED UNCLE CHAR goodbye, promising I'd do my best to go about my days without causing a scene until I heard from him again. He took some of the weight off my shoulders by reassuring me that he'd have an update for me in a few days. If I could just make it through my first week of school, I'd be told what steps I might need to take next.

I decided that, in that time, I would try and find out some information about why the Catchers wanted me dead so badly myself. It helped to know that my loft was firewalled, leaving me protected so that I could hunt for a few more answers on my own. I could even use the library's system, if I was careful to limit my searches there to some of the more generic questions I had, like why someone might dream of certain people or things for long periods of time.

When I finally arrived at Yorker, I stumbled through the hallways, distracted. Having missed half of the orientation tour, I got lost finding two of my classes. Each classroom was lined with pristine seats, our temple portals syncing with the day's lesson at the teacher's command. We all sat staring blankly into our screens, scribbling down information from the first day that mainly covered class curriculum, Yorker rules, and which classes actually required regular in-person attendance—most having the ability to load the class from anywhere on the Yorker campus so long as you were signed in during class hours.

By the end of the first day, I felt like I had merely drifted through the entire routine, my mind perpetually checking the time and jumping at every Yorker automated message that flashed to life on my portal screen. They mostly consisted of information about the first day of school, and each time they popped up, I blinked them closed again within seconds. The only school information I could retain that day was the basic map of campus and the nearest coffee ports.

By the third day, I moved more slowly through the halls, my mind fogged by restless hours of barely there sleep. Each night, if I wasn't thrashing awake from another nightmare about fires, kill lists, or created accidents, I was scrolling through my portal screen, desperate to find out all I could about Catchers and the Kingsleys.

I hadn't caught even a single glimpse of Hale Kingsley since the week had started. I tried to fool myself into thinking I wasn't looking, but anytime I entered the wide hallways of campus filled with roaming students, my eyes scanned the faces around me, searching for the familiarity of one particular face I missed desperately from my dreams, despite the real person now attached to it. During the hours I wasn't at Yorker or at home, I found my way back to Koze. Despite my lingering embarrassment over what had happened there, I decided that I couldn't allow my ego to get in the way of good coffee and a break from the quiet echoes of my lonely loft.

I hadn't realized how comforting having parents in the next room was until moving out on my own. Despite loving my freedom—however complicated it had become—my heart still sank a little when my dad's feet didn't saunter into the kitchen at breakfast, or when my mother's hands weren't tapping away at a screener pad in the next room.

We had been sending messages back and forth, updates on how my first week at Yorker was going, as well as my mother's news that the Catchers had deemed the fire an accident and that our house was under reconstruction. For all that, I kept dodging their calls, leaving them unanswered anytime they tried to reach out. I wasn't sure how to talk to them, given everything I now knew. There was no way I could tell them most of what was going on, but there was also no way I could play pretend.

I was dodging Mina's calls, too. Her Syncher profile had been exploding with pictures and playback videos of all the new friends she was making at Kings Court. I missed her more than anything, but I didn't have the time or the heart to stay up and listen to her banter on about boys and how totally awesome her new best friends were.

It was a bitter thought, but with everything weighing on my mind while hers seemed to be on cloud nine, I couldn't take the potential hit to the friendship bubble we had been leaving untouched.

So I kept finding myself back in the worn black bucket chairs of Koze, sipping from a large mug and jotting down more memorized dreams in hopes that more bygone conversations with Grey might help to serve me in my quest for answers. And, as much as I liked to think it was the soothing smell of coffee beans and the dim lighting that made the corner café the only bit of comfort I seemed to be able to find, a part of me was also silently hoping the door would ding and Hale would walk in to order another Americano.

I spent each night before bed cruising his Syncher account. I tracked him across Yorker, including the few times he went to Koze café and once even to a simulation bar, the first night of classes. Hale didn't usually post about these things himself; rather, Kycer's profile left a trail of live locations he was tagged in. When I wasn't doing that, I dove into articles on Thalia's government, gathering together more details about Donte Kingsley, the process of temple-portal fusions, and what exactly the Catcher database granted them access too.

Now that I was almost certain that it had been the Catchers who caused the fire, I was curious to know how they did it. The nightmares of my hands on the matches kept dancing in my mind, leaving me to wonder if they could have somehow hacked into my portal, feeding me commands to light our house on fire.

It was a far-fetched assumption, but I couldn't keep my mind from running wild as the days ticked by slowly. At this point, I wasn't crossing any possibilities off the list.

By the time the week came to a close, my brain needed a break. I decided to head back to Koze, desperate to dive into a book instead of into my own mind or the Kingsleys and Catchers again. I wanted a time out, a place to sit and wait for the call from my Uncle Char without feeling so alone.

Settling into my usual bucket chair and placing the new book he had brought me at the beginning of the week on my lap, I took in the front cover.

Midnight Mind: Tales of Gypsies and Fortunes, it read.

I smiled. Uncle Char always picked out the best books. If only someone could tell me my fortune now, or a gypsy could grant me a wish or two.

I thought back to my birthday wish, realizing that both of them had come true, in a way, despite the questionable circumstances surrounding them. Grey was technically alive, although not at all like himself or in the way I had hoped. And I was at Yorker . . . thanks to the fact that I was on some sort of kill list. I puffed out a somewhat bitter, ironic laugh.

Guess it really was true: be careful what you wish for.

It turned out that *Midnight Mind* had been written just before the end of the old world by a man who suffered from chronic depression. Seeking out time gypsies and fortune-tellers, he had learned to cure his mental illness by translating the magic of the mysteries and dreams within him.

I gently opened the worn cover, careful not to add to the damage a war had left on it. Its weathered pages and torn back end gave the impression that its homes had been dirty and its travels long before finding its way into my hands.

Flipping to the first pages, I drank in the words, the pressure in my brain releasing like a valve as it absorbed new ideas and fresh thoughts to ponder. Section one started with the author's quest to find a time gypsy—one of a bloodline of women who could apparently read fates. Again, I smiled wryly at the irony of how much I could use someone like a time gypsy to tell me my fate right now.

I lost track of time passing and had become completely absorbed in the book's world of fantasy and imagination when the words of someone standing just a couple feet away ruptured my concentration.

"Going with the silent treatment, are we? Well, I guess it's deserved. Last I saw you, I believe I was a bit of a dick."

My eyes shot up from the book, goosebumps rising across my skin at the sound of his voice. He sounded so much like Grey that, for split second, I almost forgot he wasn't.

On the other side of my table I saw Hale Kingsley, one of his extended arms leaning his weight onto the back of the empty chair across from me. His other hand was tucked into his pocket, and a piece of his perfectly tousled hair curled in front of one of his ocean-grey eyes as he stared down at me.

"S-sorry. I didn't know you were standing there." I sat up a bit, fixing my posture. Part of me wanted to tell him to screw off and give him a taste of his own medicine. But the minute my eyes met his, all I saw was Grey.

He moved, pulling out the chair before spinning it around with ease and straddling it. He did it fluidly, like he knew all eyes were on him, yet seeming to be unfazed nonetheless. He rested his elbows on the top of the chair's back as he leaned forward, the side of his mouth pinched like he was trying to hide a cocky smile. He looked straight at me again, leaving me struggling in the attempt to pull my eyes away from him and back to my book, and to keep my mouth from gaping open.

Being identical to Grey, he was desperately handsome, his edges crisper and more defined than Grey had ever looked in my dreams.

It was like seeing him again for the first time, but with sharper vision and surrounded by strangers—including the one who had taken possession of his eyes. I trained my gaze harder on the blur of words in my lap, doing my best to find the spot on the page I had been at before.

After a few moments, I raised my eyes back up to his, curious as to why he hadn't said anything yet. He was studying my face, his mouth finally having broken into the grin it had been hiding. He jutted his scruff-speckled chin toward my book.

"What's so interesting about . . . " Leaning over the table, he used his fingers to tilt up my book so he could get a better look at the cover before dropping back into his original position. " . . . *Midnight Mind: Tales of Gypsies and Fortunes*?" His head tilted from side to side, as if easing himself into the idea of reading such a thing. "What, are you afraid your future might be filled with more shattered mugs?" He smiled, sending my stomach into a flip. Then he raked his fingers through his chestnut-brown hair and shot me a satisfied smile, awaiting my response.

He was trying to be playful, I realized. Some nerve.

My blood boiled, but I wasn't quite sure if it was for the right reasons.

"What I am reading is none of your business," I said, returning my eyes to the page. I did my best to channel my mother with her matter-of-fact tone, daring anyone to even attempt to challenge her. This wasn't a game anymore.

I had to remember what he could be tied to.

My heartbeat fluttered, clearly indicating that my head and my heart were not on the same page with this decision. But I propped the book up in front of my face, creating a pathetic barrier between the two of us. His feet shuffled. Then came the scrape of the chair pushing back, from the other side of the book.

Did he leave?

I waited a few minutes, not daring to check.

"Let me know if it says anything good about the gypsies. God knows I could use a few wishes."

I dropped the book on the table and found that his face was still on the other side of it. The chair had been flipped back to its original direction, and he leaned back in it like we were two old friends enjoying each other's quiet company.

Everything about him was a concoction of confidence and cockiness, and I was unsure of which of those to label him in my books right now. Grey had always been confident. But Hale Kingsley, I decided, was definitely just cocky.

"Can I help you with something?" I snapped, trying not to look too long into his eyes for fear I'd see him for who he wasn't. He sat up, the smile fading into a look of penance. Damn, he was good.

He leaned forward, taking in a breath before opening his mouth to speak again.

"I'm sorry I was so rude to you the other day. I was having a bad day and you were . . . close by. I swear I'm normally much more pleasant." He smiled, extending an arm in my direction to top off his apology. "Let's start over. Hey, what's up, I'm Hale. What's your name?"

If this was an act, it was impressive. I looked at the extended arm, my eyes falling on hands that looked strong and sincere. I wondered if I would feel the sensation of Grey if I took his hand. Would the sleepy pins and needles tickle the tips of my fingers, or would he actually feel firm and real? I blinked back up to his face, snapping myself back into focus. *Remember who he really is.*

"Not interested," I said.

"Well your body language is telling me differently," he replied quickly, smirking again as he kept his arm extended. I leaned back, only now realizing that I had moved in my seat, leaning in toward him like I was sure all the other girls did.

God, I was pathetic. This wasn't Grey. I had to stop feeding his ego before it required liposuction—an old-world surgery I'd read about in a book Uncle Char had given me when I was eleven. The image of it had stuck with me; how people used to pay to have the fat sucked out of them, due to their addictions to things like grease and sugar. Back then, portal foods were called "fast food," and companies could pack them full of all the sugar and fat they wanted, breeding a high in human brains that kept them coming back for more. With Thalia's improved food systems and portion controls, no one in the new world needed liposuction, which was fine with me. Even the idea of it grossed me out.

Right, reading. Reading until Uncle Char called. That was what I was supposed to be doing here.

I pulled my book back up, making sure to shoot an uninviting look his way before returning to the same paragraph I had been trying to read for five minutes now. He leaned back again, hands tracing along the surface of the table.

"You're feisty. I like that."

I rolled my eyes, biting tight on my lips to keep them from breaking into a betraying smile. My reactions to him were instinctual, my entire being wanting to move closer to him without my even being aware of it.

"Just so you know, I don't plan on leaving until you tell me your name. Lucky for you, this place has coffee and comfortable seating, so if I have to I can stay here all night." Over the top of my book, I caught a glimpse of his arms as they stretched up high above his head, followed by the sound of him melting more comfortably into the seat. Without looking, I could tell his gaze was still on me. Burning through the book in a way that made my chest tighten in anticipation.

He was good at this. Too good. I thought of all the girls who probably fell for his act. I thought of Temperance dripping off his arm the way I suddenly wanted to. I didn't bother to move my book, talking loud enough that he could hear me on the other side.

"I can tell you what my name is not. Temperance." Setting the book down, I looked him dead in the face, shocked by my own ability to confront him with the accusation. "How would your girlfriend feel if she knew you were out here flirting with other girls?"

His laugh cracked open his face, his teeth shining as the soft thunder of the sound melted all my muscles like butter. Finally collecting himself, he looked at me, his eyes still gleaming with amusement.

"Temperance is not my girlfriend." He leaned forward again, pressing a perfect forearm onto the table. "Sure, we're equitted to marry, so we attend most of Thalia's events together for the time being. But the equittance is only a 'just-in-case.'" He quoted bunny ears with his fingers on the last words as he leaned back, his eyes taking me in softly. "What I find more interesting is that you think I'm flirting with you."

I felt a wave of warmth flush into my cheeks, and prayed that they weren't burning through my stubbornness. My eyes met his above the worn scars of the old book that sat between us on the table, my attempt to read now fully abandoned.

"Isn't that what you're doing here?" I accused again, trying to match his confidence with a bit of my own, hoping that I could fake it till I felt it.

"Why don't you find out? Let me take you out tonight."

This time it was my turn to laugh. I reached over to take a sip from my latte, which had gone lukewarm. Damn him for making me miss the enjoyment of my perfectly brewed goodness.

"What's your name?" He was serious this time, leaning forward to place a hand on my arm before I could retract it from the latte. His hand sent lightning bolts up my skin, but not like in a dream. The friction of skin to skin hit me with a sudden shock.

After a moment's hesitation, I laughed again, trying to play the whole thing off. But he asked again, this time staring straight into my eyes.

"What is your name?"

I stopped laughing. Looking at him, I rolled my eyes, and pulled my arm away.

"Carson."

His gaze lingered on mine a moment, their pupils surrounded by wisps of grey and slate so hypnotic that, as I looked into them, the chatter of the café around us seemed to disintegrate into white noise. Then his lips broke into a smile, and he stood from the table.

"2000 tonight. I'll pick you up here." He tucked in the chair, dipping closer again as his hands rested on its back.

"See you soon, Carson," he winked before standing straight and making for the door. Looking up, he tossed a nod to the barista before pushing his way out onto the street, more than just my eyes following him the whole way.

I sat there, unable to move, my brain struggling to digest the last ten minutes. I could still feel the imprint of his hand on my skin like a tattoo. The contours of his face seemed fitted to my eyes like prescription glasses.

Hale was a jerk. Whether it was because of some deeply buried demon or truly just full of himself, the simple fact remained that he was a charming jerk.

Yet I had been dreaming of his face for the majority of my life. Since the day I was supposed to die.

Hanging out with Donte Kingsley's son—when, for all I knew, Donte himself might have put my name on that kill list—was probably crazy. But on the other hand . . .

Maybe spending some time with Hale might clue me into exactly why I had known his face for so many years. It could be a golden opportunity to search for some answers, and kill time until Uncle Char called.

That was justified. Right?

I felt my heart flip and knew instantly I was in trouble. Tapping my temple, I checked the time: 1600.

Four hours until my date with Hale Kingsley.

CHAPTER 14
better with you - michl

STROLLING DOWN THE STREET, I heard the tapping of the new booties I had ordered through the closet portal. Two-hour delivery was no joke, and now that I knew the apartment belonged to some potentially life-threatening Catcher—whom I was apparently supposed to trust in blind faith—I figured the guy owed me a cute bodysuit and new booties, at the very least.

I looked down at the lush black fabric hugging my torso. The subtle flare of my pant legs kicked out with every step I took, a flash of grey peeking up from the booties whenever the material drew back across them. The thick straps of the bodice hugged my shoulders, stretchy yet firm.

It was the nicest full-piece outfit I officially owned. Nicer than anything my parents would have ever been able to afford.

"You've got this," I thought to myself as I came to a stop in front of the now familiar coffee-shop entrance, trying to ingrain the message into my head. Taking one deep breath, I opened the door to Koze, and found him sitting in the same chair I had been planted in just hours ago.

Seeing me, he rose, my eyes eating him up in spite of myself. His hair was combed back, yet still had a familiar sense of dishevelment, his arms now tucked into a tailored jacket the same colour of his eyes. He walked toward me as I stopped dead, unsure if I should sit or if we were leaving.

"Hey, gorgeous."

The side of his mouth turned up into that pretentious smirk that insinuated there was a joke I was somehow unaware of. Did he actually think I looked gorgeous?

It doesn't matter, I tried to tell myself.

I rolled my eyes at him, then turned back toward the door of the café when his hand gestured toward it. His other hand found the small of my back as he guided me outside, and I felt my insides do somersaults.

"You look good," Hale said.

I smiled, already feeling my own personal firewalls tumbling down at the sound of his voice. I didn't turn his way before responding.

"You don't look so bad yourself," I admitted.

We walked in silence down the main street, stealing glances at each other every few seconds before looking away. Now that I was here, I didn't know what to say, finding myself wrapped up in wondering what he was thinking instead.

After a few blocks, we turned right onto a quiet back road I hadn't noticed on my earlier adventures around the area. My eyes scanned the old-style cobblestone brick that housed windows and doors, with staircases connecting the two.

I wondered who lived inside the windows. Whose feet walked this street every day, to and from the place they called home.

"This way," Hale said, just managing to brush my arm as he turned quickly and made his way down an alleyway. He sauntered over to the third door that sat at the back of a big city building. Pulling it open, a loud creak punctured the air, and I laughed nervously.

"After you." He gestured his hand toward the dimly lit staircase inside the door.

"Well, this doesn't seem like the perfect place to commit a murder or anything," I huffed. I managed to make it sound sarcastic, but inside, I was balking. I bit my lip, suddenly very unsure about how safe of an idea this was. What if Hale was part of the Catchers' plot?

Had I just walked willingly into my own death, obliviously swimming all the way here in the grey seas of his eyes?

I stood tall, unsure if I should turn around or risk it all and go inside.

"It leads to a private rooftop I like to hang out on. This . . . " he gestured around him, " . . . is to keep the emphasis on the 'private.' I promise you're safe." He extended his arm again, hand open to take mine.

Without giving myself time to second-guess, I took it, unsure if the gesture was my heart handing it to Grey or my mind handing it to fate.

We climbed the stairs since there were no elevators here; they were all at the front of the building. By the tenth floor, my legs were burning almost loudly enough to drown out my nerves, and I instantly regretted wearing a new set of booties.

"Almost there," he promised, and I smiled uncertainly back in his direction. One more flight and we had reached the rooftop terrace, marked by a rusty-looking door. Hale pushed on the handle, and the stairwell we stood in suddenly gave way to the light of the setting sun.

"Welcome to my little oasis," he said, stepping out onto it behind me as I lifted my hand to my eyes, squinting to help them adjust.

When they did, I caught my breath.

Canopies—hung high with thick white wire tangled through their beams and sprinkled with bright bulbs of light—twinkled across the patio, making it sparkle against the last rays of the sun. Tall green bushes lined the sides of a balcony that met the building, which held low-sitting patio benches and side tables in each corner. Toward the middle of the patio was a large dining set with deep-set chairs that matched the benches on the balcony, all arranged underneath another canopy hung with paper lanterns. In the farthest corner from the door was a small ladder that led to a higher platform on an upper balcony.

The entire atmosphere left me in awe, the tall buildings stretching out in all directions around us in the fading light sugaring the moment like icing to a cake. The sound of horns and life drifted up to us from below, lights flickering on and off in the windows of the adjacent buildings that were filled with lofts and office cubicles. The little bits of sky that were visible reflected back and forth between the glass panes of the forest of buildings around us, fading from bold pink to a deep-set, watercolour-like mix of blue and purple as I watched. Looking up, I could just make out the shining white pinpricks of a few stars doing their best to peek through the city lights.

"Wow," I breathed. "This is amazing."

My neck craned in every direction as I tried to take it all in, having almost completely forgotten that Hale was with me, if only for a split second. The rooftop was so simple and comforting, confiscating my breath in a way I didn't mind for the first time in weeks. I had only ever seen places like this in my dreams . . . and even a lot of those paled in comparison.

"Thanks. It's my favourite place in the city. No portal power, totally old-world," Hale replied, a hint of pride in his voice.

I walked to the edge of the nearest balcony, peeking over it at the bustle of the city far below. As I stepped out farther, leaning into the railing, the armour of the building began to fade behind me, the wind picking up my curly hair and tossing it in different directions. Life from the city hummed through the air around me as I breathed in. I stretched out the tension lingering in my arms and tilted my head back, letting the moment sweep me away for an instant as a laugh bubbled from my throat. Turning around, I looked back at Hale.

"I love it! I would never leave!" I declared.

He watched me, a smile fighting to free itself on his face. For a split second, I saw Grey looking back at me. Like a flash of déjà-vu, but for a moment that hadn't happened, with someone who wasn't really here.

"That's why I normally don't," Hale said, tilting his head toward the table. "Shall we eat?"

140

My stomach rumbled on cue, causing me to realize that I had skipped dinner. Nodding, I made my way toward the table.

I had to get my head on straight, loosen up a little so I could stop getting so lost in his eyes and take a peek inside his mind instead. My nerves jangled back to life. I was going to need a bit of help.

"Can we start with wine?" I blurted.

Hale burst out laughing.

"Love that idea," he grinned. At the table, he picked up a bell and rang it. A moment later, the door to the terrace opened, and a man dressed all in black entered the scene.

"Christoph, can you grab us two glasses of white, and bring out the first appetizers?" Hale asked, speaking in a firmer and more authoritative voice. It was the first time he didn't sound anything like Grey.

The man nodded, the dark glasses sitting on his nose keeping his expression somewhat concealed. I looked to see if the blue dot was flashing from his temple, checking as to whether he was someone I should be wary of, but caught nothing. Looking to Hale as he made his way into the seat across from me, I saw that his temple port was off, too.

I tapped my wrist hub subtly, hiding what I was trying to do, but no screen came to life. There really was no portal access here. Which meant that, if Uncle Char called, I would miss it.

I would have to call him back after. Right now, I was doing recon of my own.

"So, who exactly is Christoph?" I asked as the man in black moved off, watching Hale relax confidently into his seat.

"My assistant. Well, sort of. Half the time he's totally incompetent."

There it was again. The distinct difference between Hale and Grey. This guy was so pretentious. What on earth was I doing here again?

"Oh, nice." My eyes trailed off to the city behind him, grateful to have something other than him to look at. I felt his gaze on me as he adjusted in his seat. Clearing his throat, he spoke again.

"Sorry, that was rude. Christoph is actually a super nice guy." He studied my face, waiting for a response. I just nodded and dropped my gaze to my hands.

"I'm not who you think I am."

My head jolted up, instantly alert.

Tell me who you are. Tell me you've been having dreams of me your entire life. Tell me why your father's government wants me dead. Tell me everything. Anything.

"What do you mean?" I responded carefully.

"I know I must seem like a total jerk. From the way I treated you in the library to what I'm sure you've seen and read about me on Syncher. I can see it on your face. You think I'm just another hollow head that thrives on the eyes of pretty girls, but I promise my intentions here are good."

I looked him over, unsure of how much I was willing to buy his speech. But either way, we were going to have to pick up our pace of conversation if I was going to learn anything valuable from him.

"You're growing on me," I said back.

"Good, that's a start," he smiled, sitting a little straighter in his chair. "So Carson, enough about me. Tell me something about you."

Well, for starters, I've been dreaming of your face since I was four. Oh, and your dad wants me killed, for unknown reasons.

I decided to play it safe.

"I'm from Vancity. I'm specializing in brain simulations, and if you were to cut me open I'd probably bleed coffee."

"I'd bleed the same. I like you already." He smiled again, softly this time. I tried to suppress my own grin, but my mouth had a mind of its own, and my answering smile stretched across my face feverishly as my cheeks flushed.

"My turn to ask a question," I retorted, deciding to make it into a bit of a game—something Grey and I would have totally done.

He leaned back, draping one arm over the back of the chair. "Hit me with it," he challenged.

I weighed the options in my mind, trying to gauge whether I should start small or get right to the big questions.

"Why did you invite me here tonight?"

What?

Did I seriously just ask that? Where did it come from? I felt my heart gain speed as I waited for his response, my obvious attraction to him winning over any logical question in my mind.

"Because you're cute and I wanted to get to know you. My turn." His face was unfazed, his body language exactly the same as he pondered his own question.

"How old are you?"

"I'm eighteen. What's your favourite colour?" I asked back, knowing Grey would say blue.

"Black."

My heart sank a little.

"Only because it looks so good on you," he added, flashing a wicked smile at me as the door to the terrace opened again to admit Christoph returning with the wine.

"New rule. Anytime we don't want to answer, we have to drink." He lifted his glass just as Christoph finished pouring, and I did the same, mine having been poured first.

"Deal."

There were bigger things at play here, and guilt washed over me when it hit me that I was having fun. I hadn't realized how much I needed a bit of a fun until I felt its tingling lightness in the air. Suddenly, I was desperate to capture it and swallow it whole before returning to the nightmares that might await me tonight.

"All right, your turn," I continued, just as Christoph came back through the door again, placing warm plates of dips, breads, and bite-sized snacks on the table in front of us.

Hale stayed silent as Christoph placed the appetizers in front of us. His eyes remained fixed on mine from across the table, a playful hint of challenge mixing with the steam that rose from the luscious food beginning to fill the table. I stared back at him. *It's not Grey* repeated in my mind as I reminded myself to hold my gaze firm.

"Thanks Christoph," Hale said without breaking our gaze. Christoph nodded and headed back toward the door, exiting the patio silently.

"You said you're from Vancity. What brought you to Terigon?" he asked finally.

"Yorker. I've always wanted to go to school here." I picked up my glass of wine and took a small sip. Its buttery taste nipped at my tongue.

He nodded, leaning on the table.

"All right, we'll drink whenever we *want* to answer, then," he laughed, taking a sip from his own glass. I placed my glass back on the table, realizing I had forgotten the rules.

"My apologies, it's just so good," I said.

"Best in all of Thalia," Hale replied, winking at me again. A quick raise of his eyebrows and a nod of his head reminded me that it was my turn.

"Are you an only child?" I asked innocently. I knew that the Webber articles had said he was one, but it was worth asking. The idea of a possible long-lost twin or even a half-sibling had crossed my mind a time or two as I pondered what could have caused a link between my mind and such a familiar face.

"I am an only child, unfortunately. Always wanted a sibling growing up, though. What about you?"

I dropped my eyes to the table, Axel's name flashing in my mind.

"No, no siblings." I didn't feel like answering that question, but it was also something I wouldn't drink to.

"Hmm, interesting."

"How is that interesting?" I asked. Taking another sip of wine, I tried to refocus, the thought of Axel reminding me what I was really here for.

"I just pegged you as the older-sister type. You have an air of independence to you, which usually stems from having to care for other people or from not getting enough attention yourself. I assumed wrong. Bad guess. Your turn."

His accuracy took me aback. He could tell all that about me from the pinch of time we had spent together? I needed to catch up.

"So what exactly is the deal with you and Temperance?"

Again, I mentally punched myself for not asking a more important question. Hale's love life was not the matter at hand here.

"We're equitted, which pretty much means that we're arranged to marry if I'm not already at least engaged by the time my father passes on. It's not forced upon us. It's more of a backup plan to keep Thalia happy with the promise of a future ruled by both genders. After my mother died, the issue was never pressed, but now that the state has built itself up to what it is, the Catchers feel it's time to bring balance back to the way it's ruled. Plus, the equittance was made when we were only kids, and most people are content enough to wait a long time for the day. Temperance is more than happy to follow through with it in order to placate the state. But I haven't given up on seeking out other options."

His response drew me in. I hadn't expected him to be so forthcoming in his honesty with me.

"Temperance is a nice girl, and beautiful of course, but I'm not in love with her," he went on. "I'm not sure I ever would be. But if it came down to it, I'd do what I had to for Thalia. Not to mention her parents are the specialized Catchers who invented the temple-port fusions and blood tests. It was her father who came up with that technology. Her family has been an important asset to ours ever since."

I took in everything he was saying, wondering how much he really knew about the fusions and testing the Catcher marshals were doing. When he didn't continue, I realized that it was time for me to respond.

"I see. I would hate to be equitted. I'm sorry," I said, trying to imagine the pressure of having an arranged marriage hanging over me ever since I was young. Then again, having no choice in how I got to live my life felt all too familiar, even now.

"It's all a part of the journey," Hale shrugged, smiling at me again. "I'm sure fate has something worthwhile in store for me. We're all destined for happiness so long as we choose it."

I let his sentiment sink into me, its depth reminding me of his mother's parting words. Maybe he was more like her than I had originally noticed. I picked up a vegetable and dipped it into one of the many sauces that decorated the table, biting down as he asked the next question.

"What about you? Any boys waiting for you back in Vancity?"

Oh god, how did I answer this? My cheeks flushed with colour, giving myself away.

"There *is* a guy, isn't there?" he pressed.

"I'm going to drink on this one," I laughed, taking a big swig of the wine. It slid down my throat in a satisfying dodge to his question.

"So unfair," he laughed back, picking up a breaded snack from a platter to his left before laying it on the plate in front of him.

I took him in, letting the questions shuffle through my mind, trying to figure out how to subtly steer the conversation in a new direction.

"Are you close with your dad?" I asked, taking close note of his body language.

He sat a bit straighter, and his face looked puzzled for a moment before returning to its relaxed state.

"Depends on what you consider to be close. Aside from the weekly shadowing of his day that I have to do as part of the responsibilities of being the future heir, we don't talk much."

"Oh? What do you do when you shadow him?" I pressed lightly, seizing what sounded like a chance to find out how much he might already know.

Hale stared at me, his face not quite masking a hint of confusion that left a small crease between his eyebrows.

146

"Um, the usual I guess. Signing documents, sitting through board meetings, hearing pitches to improve our resources here in Thalia, debriefing potential threats. It's all boring, really." He waved his hand dismissively, picking up the snack from his plate and biting down on it to indicate that he didn't have much else to say on the subject.

Was I one of these "potential threats" he didn't know about? From my perspective, he wasn't showing any signs of being dangerous. If he had anything to do with the people hunting me for the kill list, he could easily have done away with me by now. Maybe he really didn't know the darker side of what the Catchers were actually up to. Had no idea what he would be one day be governing.

"I'm sorry you're not close with your dad. I'm not really close with my parents, either," I admitted, offering him a small smile and suddenly feeling guilty for making him uncomfortable.

He smiled back at me.

"Your turn."

Christoph returned about an hour later to clear the plates. After bouncing back and forth between questions about everything from favourite foods to favourite antique books we had read (his access to a much larger selection putting him at a great advantage), we stood and made our way up the small ladder in the far corner of the patio.

My cheeks were warm from the wine and I could feel the muscles in my body loosening as the alcohol pumped through my veins. I felt bubbly, the wine having instilled a greater sense of confidence and good cheer in me as the night wore on. The buzzing feeling in my head mixed with the fluttery sensation in my stomach, and my mind had long since been erased of any thought of Uncle Char's call.

We lay back in the artificial grasslands that waited above, and I drank in the starry lights bordering the edges of this upper terrace, appreciating the white cushions propping our heads and shoulders above the ground. When we got back on pace, it was my turn to ask a question. I decided it was time to go straight to the heart of something I'd wanted to know since the day I saw him.

I stared out at the buildings, working up the guts to say what I was about to say.

"You're easy to be around," Hale commented from behind me. I turned in my spot to find him leaning back on his elbows, his head craned toward the sky.

I laid back on my elbows too, craning my head in the same direction. The sky was a darkened blue now, and the tiny bits of stars struggling to shine through blanketed the sky.

"It's almost like I've known you my entire life," Hale broke the silence again.

My heart pounded. If only he knew how true that felt for me, too. He turned his head toward mine, and I did the same. For a few moments, we lingered in the closeness. My mind fizzed as I lost myself once again in the wisps of smokey grey that lined the pupils of his eyes.

Focus, I told myself, trying to pull it together despite the fire that coursed through my veins.

Just do it.

"Hale, I . . . "

Hale lifted his hand to my chin and leaned forward, stopping me in my tracks. He stopped just inches from me, and the scents of hickory and sandalwood filled my nose, making my stomach do flips.

Then he pressed his lips to mine, softly, as if he didn't want to shatter the moment with too much force.

Just like that, any lingering scrap of resolve that I had been holding on to evaporated from my being.

Before I knew it he was pulling me in deeper. I leaned into it, my hand lifting to his face on its own. The urge to stay focused, my need for self-control—all of it disappeared beneath the taste of his lips, as if it had never been. Kissing Hale was every bit like kissing Grey, only with a force and physical presence that I had never felt in my dreams. Instead of the tingling touch of phantom lips, these ones were real, and I let myself be swept away by them like ocean waves under a moonlit tide. His hand found my side, pulling me in still closer, before returning to rest softly on my chin again.

The sting of the liquor and my yearning to be near Grey took over me completely, and my hands pulled him in closer, too.

Suddenly, the sound of the terrace door opening below broke us apart.

Hale was on his feet in a heartbeat. He walked to the edge of the grassy area, looking down to the patio below.

"What is it, Christoph?" Without waiting for a response, he turned to look at me and motioned me to follow him with a finger before climbing over the side of the gardened balcony, out of sight.

I breathed heavily, trying to catch my breath. As I sat up and began combing my hair back, reality hit me like a brick wall of sobriety.

I didn't come here to get tangled up in Hale Kingsley. I came here to untangle Grey, or better yet, untangle the hidden truth that linked all of it.

"Tell them I'm out running errands," I heard Hale say from below. He tried to keep his voice low, but the obvious frustration with whatever Christoph was telling him floated up to my ears anyway.

Errands? Why would he need to lie about where he was?

"All right, fine. I'll wrap this up."

The cold indication that I was a situation that needed to be wrapped up left me feeling suddenly defensive, and I felt my shoulders crawling up my neck as he climbed the ladder back to the upper terrace. He didn't finish climb up over it, instead stopping at the top and looking me over with regret.

"Ah, I'm really sorry but I actually have to get going. Emergency Catcher meeting. My dad is ordering me to attend. Can I can get Christoph to drop you off?"

I stood, brushing non-existent dirt from my outfit as a nervous tic in order to collect myself. I didn't want him to know that the sudden wrench in the night had upset me.

I didn't even want to admit to myself how much it did.

"Sure, thanks," I said coolly, making my way to the ladder. He climbed back down, and I followed as quickly as my tipsy muscles would allow.

We made our way across the patio to where Christoph stood waiting with the door open. A thousand new thoughts clouded my mind. What was the emergency? Had the Catchers somehow discovered where I was? Was Hale about to discover that I was labeled as some sort of threat to Thalia?

Hale walked up slowly behind me, the sudden tension as huge and heavy as an elephant between us.

"Again, I'm really sorry. This normally doesn't happen. We'll do it again sometime soon, though?"

I turned back to him, a forced smile on my face.

"I'll think about it," I said, turning back toward Christoph as he led me off toward the stairs.

"Carson?"

I stopped, turning to look back.

"I had a really good night tonight." He smiled, that softness returning to his eyes, making him look more like Grey than ever before.

As I made my way down the stairwell and out the bottom of the building, I found that Christoph had a lift waiting. Its windows were tinted black, making the inside nearly impossible to see.

I wondered how many girls this lift had seen off at the end of the night.

I wondered if it would be the last lift I myself ever got into.

I kept my eyes on Christoph, sharply aware that I was completely at his disposal. I asked him to drop me off at Koze, not wanting to let him know where I was staying, just in case. When he did, I went inside, deciding to wait until he was long gone before walking home again.

The soft, comforting sounds of the café felt abnormal after such a jarring night. I walked over to the order portal, punching in a decaf cinnamon latte, thinking it might be best to skip on caffeine. I was jittery enough as it was.

Tapping my port screen to life, I took in the missed calls from a portal number I didn't recognize, its location listed as Terigon.

I knew Uncle Char was going to call, and there was a good chance the missed calls were from him. If he had gone into hiding, then calling from an unknown portal would make sense.

I decided to take my chances, calling the portal back on private so no one in Koze could hear.

A long beep pierced my ears, making me wince. Reaching for my temple, I tapped away the call, rubbing both sides of my head that now pounded from the sound.

The ding of my order sounded in my portal, making me jump. Taking a deep breath, I walked over and took the to-go cup from a barista I didn't recognize, his jet-black hair slicked back into a ponytail. I smiled faintly at him before turning, making my way back out of the café. Then I dialled up my uncle's usual portal number. He answered on the first ring.

"Hey kiddo, no updates yet! We shouldn't stay on the phone long though. Just go home," he said, hearing the noise of the city around me, "and try to get some rest. I'll call you back with updates tomorrow morning. I just need a bit more time."

The familiarity of his voice comforted me, and I slowed my breathing as I entered the building of my loft. We cut the call as I entered the elevator, tapping my temple and demanding the fourth floor.

I tried to keep my breathing steady, after his voice was gone. But the anxiety in my chest rose with each floor I passed.

CHAPTER 15
stars and moons – dizzy

I SAT ON THE YELLOW COUCH that centred the lounge area, flipping through more pages of *Midnight Mind* to try and calm my own mind down. It was a decent hour to crawl into bed, but the nerves of the night had yet to wear off, leaving me restless and hungry to gobble anything up to distract myself.

I decided the book was my best bet, having grown tired of following mostly dead-end trails on my portal. Anyway, I needed a break from everything at play . . . just like the one I had hoped to find earlier today.

Flipping through the pages, I took in the pictures of gypsies and fortune-tellers, women with wild eyes and fairy-like faces. They radiated a type of beauty I felt I had seen before, but couldn't quite place.

As my eyes traced the words, falling willingly into the tales and stories of fates and fortunes, my fingers flipped to a list of surnames known to have carried the magic in their bloodline. Wallace was nowhere to be found. Figured.

As I continued to scan down the list of names, my eyes caught on one in particular: Kei.

I knew that last name from somewhere.

Frowning and flipping back a few pages, my eyes fell upon the pictured faces I had been looking at before. On the left side of the photo, I took in features that had a hint of familiarity. A peaceful, parted smile, and eyes that radiated softly in a shade of silver.

I tapped my temple port, bringing my screen to life. Opening a search engine, I typed in Hale's name again, clicking first to his bio on Webber and then scrolling down to find his mother's name.

Clicking Portia Kingsley, her bio came to life just as it had back in the library. My eyes scanned the facts strung together into sentences about her early years, waiting to spot the name.

Portia Kingsley, daughter of Don and Perri Kei, married to Donte Kingsley at the age of eighteen.

There it was, I thought triumphantly. The surname—Kei. I knew I had seen it before.

I clicked on the Kei surname, bringing to life a Webber page full of its family history. Briefly glancing over it with tired eyes, I saw nothing mentioned of belonging to a line of gypsies or fortune-tellers.

This book probably wasn't even real. Just imaginary tales made up from the old world.

I closed my portal screen, returning back to *Midnight Mind* with yet another layer of disappointment added to the night. Flipping to the next page, I read what appeared to be an introduction to the time gypsies:

"Time gypsies were a group of women from the west world who were known to cherish and pray to the elements of earth, air, fire, and water. In harnessing the energy of all four, legend has it that they could shift through dimensions and the many realms of life they believed to exist all at one time. They were also known to be able to tell the fate of any soul merely by drinking the blood of the individual it belonged to."

My heart stopped.

Time gypsies could read fates? I thought back to Uncle Char telling me about the kill list. How anyone with a fate destined to bring harm to Thalia was placed on the list. He had said it was by testing some of the blood they took for future disease clearance that they were able to also map out the living fate of Thalia's individuals, resulting in a list of fates that needed to be stopped.

Including my own.

Could the time gypsies have been a real thing? It couldn't just be a coincidence that Hale's mother was part of a bloodline of gypsies who apparently told fates in the old world, only to now have his father ending such fates in the new one. Was it possible that the Catchers were keeping this from the common people? A secret source of psychic power, bringing a new fate of death upon unsuspecting lives?

I tapped my temple, my portal screen flashing to life again. This time, I searched time gypsies. The only credible link that came up was titled, "Portia Kingsley's Thoughts on Gypsies," an interview she had done after announcing that she was pregnant with the future heir to Thalia.

I played the video, instantly captivated once again by Portia's angelic voice that seemed to match her natural warmth.

"I have a sneaking suspicion it's a boy," she smiled, her hands cupping her round stomach.

The video cut back to the interviewer, who chuckled. "Maybe it's the gypsy blood in you, sensing the future like in the days of the old world."

As the camera moved back to Portia, she looked up in a state of peace, the beatific smile still on her face.

"Now, now, Carter," she tutted at the interviewer. She cocked her head at him and he lifted his hands in the air, as if shrugging at the possibility. They seemed to be old friends.

"We are all of this time, we are all of the elements," Portia continued. "But we are all not of such nonsense."

The video ended and I closed it out. As much as her presence enchanted me, it also felt weird to watch videos of the woman who had created the face I had loved since I was little.

One more thought crossed my mind, and I typed it in the search bar:

"Portia Kingsley and Catchers"

Multiple links flashed to life, dancing in front of me as if waiting to see which of them I would chose. Third down from the top, I saw one that piqued my interest.

"Catchers of Thalia Implement New Disease Testing after Death of Portia Kingsley."

Blinking it open, I pored over its information. The article noted how, shortly after Portia's death, Donte had insisted that blood from every citizen of Thalia be tested to seek out disease or potential life-threatening illnesses that lingered in their DNA. A test he believed that, had they used it before Portia's pregnancy, they would have been able to keep the fate of her death unsealed.

I frowned, his words striking me as being subtly resentful of the existence of his only son. What if Portia had known what would happen all along, but went through with her pregnancy anyway, in order to bring life to this earth? I read on.

Shortly following her passing, Donte had hired Thalia's best scientists to solidify the accuracy of the test he had already been researching, prior to his wife's death. The test would be taken at the same time any citizen was fused to their personal portals, making them an official member of Thalia. Anyone who tested positive for a disease would be given immediate health care in order to prevent or cure whatever illness might be at play. This also made it possible for Catcher caretakers to spot potential illnesses and diseases that might spread early and, in turn, create vaccines for them right away, ensuring that people would not have health issues later on in life. This was where Thalia's "all health, no harm" alignment principle came into play. With the banning of all potentially lethal objects, and the implementation of the new mandatory blood testing, every inhabitant of Thalia was practically guaranteed a long, healthy life.

Unless their blood betrays them somehow, I thought to myself, grimly.

I tried to think back to the day I'd had my portal fused. I didn't remember much of my test, only that my parents told me I came back completely clear, healthy as a horse. We all piled into our lift afterward and went to eat at Uncle Char's house, where I played with my new, primer portal functions, mainly programs designed to teach me things like my ABCs and 123s.

Sasher had made fun of my bandage, decorated in pink clouds, and convinced me that the portal they'd put in my mind was a robot that would take over my body when I slept. I cried my eyes out until Uncle Char pretended to fix the robot glitch in my portal and let me order another coconut ice cream sundae from the kitchen portal.

Blinking closed my screen, I puffed out a breath of air, my eyes starting to sting from dryness. I wondered if Uncle Char had succeeded in leading the Catcher marshals back toward Vancity, tricking them into skipping over the fact that I was a sitting duck right under their noses. I shivered.

Was I really capable of something horrible enough to make my fate worth terminating?

The entire thing still made no sense to me. How, at the age of three, could I be pegged as a life that needed to be taken? How could some database label my blood as that of a future killer or detriment to society, to the point that the Catchers would run a family off a road and, in turn, unknowingly take the life of an innocent baby instead?

My chest pinched at the thought, guilt creeping up my spine and seeping its dark weight into my brain. Standing, I decided to keep my hands busy until the late-night hours were ready to pull me in.

☾

Walking into my bedroom, I checked the time of my bedside portal. It read 0100, and I knew I had run out of things to do to keep myself from sleeping. My loft was sparkling, since I had just scrubbed every inch of floor or surface I could find. My clothes were washed and restocked into the closet portal. The selection of antique books lining the shelves in the main area was now sectioned and organized alphabetically. I had even scheduled a closet-portal order for my exercise gear the following day, promising myself I would get up and run. I had only blown off steam by hitting the pavement once since I made it to Terigon, and with the stress that lingered in the fibres of my bones, I knew a good sweat session would help me burn away some of the anxiety.

Pulling back the blankets, I listed off more things I planned to do with my morning as I waited for the promised call from Uncle Char. After my run, I would call Mina, finally breaking the thin ice our paused friendship had begun to skate on. I really did miss her. Maybe she'd have time to video call. I didn't have to tell her everything going on, just maybe that I was having nightmares. She'd probably tell me a good screener show to fall asleep to alongside some incense and a cup of chamomile tea.

That thought made me miss her even more. Made me wish she were here to work through it all with me, now that I no longer had Grey to do so.

Just go to bed. Answers are coming in the morning, I told myself. And, finally, I allowed the dark shadows of my loft to spill and merge into the blank canvas behind my closing eyelids.

CHAPTER 16
for you – tusks

I LOOKED DOWN *at the bodies in front of me. Lifeless on the floor lay my mother, father, and Uncle Char. They were close enough that I could see the blue edges of their cold skin.*

I knew they were dead, and somehow even more clearly, I knew I had killed them. I couldn't remember how; it was just a feeling. I stared at their bodies, and a satisfied smile crept across my face.

I was happy to have ended their lives. They needed to die.

Death was happy. Death was bliss. They could be with Axel now. All dead because of me.

I knelt down beside them, staring at their motionless bodies, curious as to what it might feel like to die myself. My mother's angular face looked so at peace as she rested on the floor.

"You're welcome," I whispered.

"Your turn," I heard her voice repeat back to me. Her body hadn't moved, but her voice rang in my ears like a portal.

"Your turn. Your turn. Your turn. Your turn. Your turn. Your turn. Your turn. Your turn. Your turn. Your turn."

I slammed my hands into my head, trying to turn it off, only there was no temple port to hit.

"Die with us," my father's voice boomed in my ears, shattering the repetitive calls of my mother.

Standing, I ran away from them, opening a yellow door that stood in front of me before leaping inside and slamming it shut.

I was in my loft now, the nighttime streets of Terigon singing their usual song outside. I walked to the window, peering below at the pedestrians—and was shocked to find them standing still, staring up at me.

With no mouth or nose to breathe out of, a sea of vicious eyes glared in my direction with venom. I backed up, away from the window, before falling onto the couch.

Just then, my name echoed, a distant trace of sound from a voice I would recognize anywhere.

Was that . . . Grey?

The sound of an air train rang out, puncturing my eardrums with so much force that I scrambled to cover them.

When the onslaught of sound ended, I stood slowly from the couch, suddenly feeling beckoned to the train. It called out for me, its promising whispers making me move, putting one foot in front of the other without my command.

Only, I could have sworn I heard Grey's voice . . .

I tried to force my thoughts back to him, the intensity of fighting to regain control like swimming through a thick quicksand of helplessness.

It didn't work.

I turned, walking out of my apartment door, suddenly knowing what I was about to do with certainty.

The lights flickered in the foyer of my loft building as I made my way out onto the now lifeless streets of Terigon. I took off sprinting, my legs carrying me in the direction of the tracks.

"It's all your fault," I heard my father say as I neared the area.

"You killed Axel." My mother's voice boomed around and within me as I stepped onto the tracks.

"Carson, don't do it." It was Grey's voice.

I blinked, the words registering with my mind but not my body. My parents were right. I killed Axel. I killed them. It was my turn now.

But Grey . . .

The image of his face struggled to paint its lines and textures into *my mind, pulling me from the moment in front of me just as the train horn sounded again.*

The horn snapped me back into focus, and I felt the certainty of my death again, ready to go willingly.

I began to see a faint source of light coming toward me on the tracks. My feet rumbled with the earth as the train came racing in my direction.

"Carson?" This voice was new, unrecognizable, pulling my attention from the train.

I looked to the side of the tracks and saw who I knew to be Axel, only much older. He looked to be about sixteen, his blond hair a curly mess of a mop atop his head. He smiled at me, and a warmth lifted my heart.

"It's not your turn," he said, walking toward me with arms outstretched. My eyes flicked back to the train headed our way.

I couldn't let him die again. I couldn't let anything happen to him.

"Axel, no!" I screamed. I had to move. I had to stop him. I urged my legs to run, but they stuck to the tracks like cement.

The train was rushing closer. It would hit in moments, and when it did, it would take Axel, too. There was nothing I could do.

We both had to go.

I closed my eyes, tilting my head upward as I thought of Grey's face again, hoping to cling to it in the painful moments about to unfold . . .

A sudden impact slammed into me from my right, cracking my body against the gravel below and leaving scrapes of dirt and blood down my left shoulder.

The train's horn sounded as it ripped over where I had just been standing. I watched as it flashed by, catching the thin, vertical slits of night flickering by between cars as it raged past, shaking my bones like an earthquake. Tears started pouring down my face as the breath I had been holding broke free, and I gasped in a huge gulp of air.

I felt arms come around me from behind, pulling me into an embrace.

"Shhh. It's okay. I'm here. It's okay." I turned, biting down at the pain it caused. When I found myself face-to-face with grey eyes, my breath caught in my throat again. Throwing my arms around him, the tears came down harder, only this time they were of disbelief.

It was Grey.

He was back.

"Grey," I sobbed into his neck. Taking in a breath, I noted his familiar scent, my brain still trying to process that he had somehow found his way back into my dreams. "I've been having so many night-mares. I can see them all happening but can't move. It's all my fault, Grey. The fire, Axel, everything." Everything real.

That was when I remembered. This wasn't real. It wasn't really even happening.

"Even you. You're not real . . . " I said, pulling away from him.

He took my shoulders, looking me squarely in the eyes so I could see his urgency. "Carson, listen to me," he began, his voice level.

Please don't let this be part of the nightmare, I prayed. I couldn't handle it. Not a nightmare with Grey.

"We have to get out of here. Now," he said.

I looked into his eyes for the slightest hint of lies or evil. Layers of grey and silver reflected into mine, the familiar warmth in them battling against their urgency.

He really was back.

Standing quickly, he reached down to help me to my feet. My body stumbled up, still shaken from the blow from the tracks. We tried to run, but the pain in my right leg left me limping slowly along.

"I can't run," I said, just as Grey scooped me up. I linked my arms around his neck, ready and willing for him to flip this nightmare into a long-awaited sea of dreams.

"Where have you been?" I asked, still working to grasp the idea that he was even here at all.

"I've been here all along," he said back, becoming more breathless with each step he took.

"Stop running. I want answers!" I wiggled in his arms, freeing myself from his grasp and landing my feet back on the ground with a wince. I used his shoulder to steady myself as a worried look invaded his face.

"Carson, we don't have time for this," he urged, trying to pick me back up. I brushed him away.

"You disappeared for weeks, Grey! I couldn't tell you about anything. You have no idea what's been going on. I moved to Terigon. I met someone who's completely identical to you, aside from the fact that he's kind of an arrogant ass. I have so many questions . . . "

My mind flickered with memories of the date Hale had taken me on, instantly hitting me with a wave of remorse. I had gone on a date with someone else. Someone who was but wasn't Grey.

What would he think when he found out?

The stress on his face cracked for a moment, a hint of a smile peeking through.

"Oh yeah? What's he like? Is he hotter than me?"

There he was.

"You guys look completely identical. But for the record, no, you are by far much hotter."

Nodding, he gestured his head in the direction we had just been running. "We really do need to go," he said. The stress was back, but his eyes were kind, and his voice lifted with a bit more energy than before. Rolling my eyes, I opened my arms, allowing him to pick me back up before taking off down the tracks.

☾

"We're here," he said finally, pulling up to what appeared to be an empty air-train cart that sat abandoned on the tracks. To my surprise, the lights were on inside, despite the fact that it wasn't attached to a string of other carts out for a train run.

Grey yanked open the door that sat at the rear end of it, climbing the steps inside before pulling me in after him. After planting my wounded body into a seat, he ran to the front of the cart and tapped the door twice before running back to me. In seconds, the air train had lifted off the ground, picking up speed as it made its way down the tracks of Terigon.

I felt the weight of my terror and emotion melt away as we sped along the outside of the city, the lights from the buildings creating a skyline blanket on the canvas of the night sky.

I had just propped myself up higher to get a better look out the windows on the other side of the cart when I felt Grey's eyes on me, checking me over to see how badly I was hurt.

I turned toward him, the bliss of having him hijack my sleep again quickly filling the void that my retreating stress had left behind. I had missed him so much. I had missed this so much.

Leaning in, I took his face in my hands and kissed him as deeply as I could. My hands trailed along the scruff of his jawline, peppered but not too scratchy. As our lips met, I waited for the tingling tattoo of feeling that his lips always made on mine . . . but it didn't appear. Instead, he pulled me closer, and I could feel the loving desperation in his body as he tangled himself deeper into me. I could *feel* him.

I pulled back, gasping.

This was real.

His eyes studied mine, considering my expression.

"I'm so glad you're okay," he exhaled finally, resting his forehead against mine.

"H-Hale?" I managed, letting the breath caught in my chest escape.

Lifting his head, a half-smile pulled at his lips.

"I'd prefer it if you called me Grey."

CHAPTER 17
cavalry – novo amor

I STARED AT THE FACE that stared back at me, its smooth skin and angular edges sharper than ever before.

Was I dreaming? I knew had been having a nightmare, and Grey saved me.

Only it was actually Hale . . . and it was real?

"You mean . . . you're real?" I breathed.

Taking my hands in his, he leaned his forehead against mine again.

"It's me," he said. "I'm here."

"How?" It was the only word I could manage to choke out, not wanting to jolt the image of him away, for fear I might actually be dreaming.

"I promise I'll explain everything when we get there," Grey said, kissing the spot where his head had just been resting against mine, firm and tingle-less.

"Where are we going?" I asked, still waiting for the moment to float into the next sequence of mirage, a flowing stream of film that tied me to a world playing inside my mind.

Only, it was as if the whole world had paused as we sped away from Terigon, the city lights now fading into the distance beyond the window.

"Back to Vancity, and then up into the mountains. I have to get

164

you somewhere safe." Grey pulled back, his charcoal eyes boring into mine. I felt tears start to well up in my own eyes, threatening to spill over.

"You know about the kill list," I stated rather than asked, my mind still struggling to process the bizarreness of my two words colliding.

"Yes, I've known all along. That's why I couldn't let you know who I actually was. It wasn't safe. But it doesn't matter now," he said, shaking his head grimly. "I had to save you."

"So I wasn't dreaming just now?" I felt the confusion bubble up between my temples again, pulling tight like a rubber band.

"No. You were under a simulation. My dad had your port hub hacked, and the Catchers were able to gain access to your mind the moment you fell asleep. They were trying to kill you." Looking off into the distance, we watched as the final shimmer of Terigon's city lights faded into the horizon, his words sinking into me slowly.

"I still don't understand," I admitted finally, despite the couple of new puzzle pieces beginning to connect to the bigger picture inside my mind. It wasn't that I didn't understand the fact that I was being hunted for my fate, or that I couldn't grasp the idea that the Catchers had found me, hacking into my mind while I was in my most vulnerable state. I could feel those pieces of the story piecing themselves together—the pulling urge to run to the train and let it take me, the fact that Hale had been Grey all along. But parts of the puzzle were still missing. Like how I had been dreaming of him my entire life to begin with.

"How . . . " I began.

"Shhh," he hushed, lifting a finger to his lips before gesturing toward the front of the train. It hadn't occurred to me that someone had to be there, driving it.

"I promise, I'll explain everything when we get there." Reaching down for my hands again, he wrapped his around mine, their warmth and solidarity easing my heart in ways I couldn't explain.

Grey was real. He was living and breathing. Someone I could feel without the depths of a fuzzy subconscious, and see without my eyes closed. A waking dream.

But if Hale was Grey, that meant I really had been dreaming of Hale my whole life. He had a world of his own that he'd been keeping from me all these years. I felt a suppressed sigh leave my lungs, the rubber band pulling tighter again at the back of my head.

Taking one hand from mine, Grey pulled me toward his shoulder, letting me fall into him as I winced. My muscles had begun to ease into the seat, but the pain from the tracks was seeping into my bones like slow venom. Slinging his arm over my shoulders, Grey's hand fell upon my arm, tracing circles into my skin and giving me something soothing to focus on, despite the hurricane that stormed through my thoughts. I leaned deeper into his shoulder, breathing in the same scent from earlier, and suddenly syncing it, mentally, to my date with Hale, reminding me of the reality of who was sitting beside me.

I felt my eyes growing heavy as I traced through possible scenarios of how this could be possible, reminiscing back on old dreams with Grey that were becoming all too clear to me now.

I remembered meeting him for the second time, when I was four, and asking him what his name was; remembered the puzzlement on his face as he told me he didn't know. I remembered naming him myself, feeling like I had a right to do so, considering that he was a figment of my imagination, after all. Back then, I was almost as tall as he was, despite the fact that he was nearly three years older. I had named him for his eyes—those silver streaks saturating the space around his pupils. His eyes were like grey clouds, comforting me and keeping me company at night as they swept me away to worlds unknown, all of them better than the one I truly belonged to.

Still remembering, I let the blurry details of that long-ago dream carry me off as I fell asleep on Grey's shoulder.

☾

I heard the clinking sounds of glasses and running water in my ears before my eyes began to blink back to life. The scents of pine and mahogany fused with the aroma of freshly brewed coffee tantalized my nose, their warmth matching that of that blankets nestled around me as I lay in what appeared to be a bed.

I sat up, brushing my messy blond curls away from my eyes and drool from my mouth, the latter of which seemed to indicate the level of dreamless deep sleep I had apparently fallen into. Tapping my temple by morning habit, I waited to see the date and time pop into my blurry vision . . . but nothing happened. Instead, "No signal" flashed across my empty screen before blinking back out of view.

I rubbed my eyes, taking in the scene around me.

Where was I?

Tall planks of wood made up three of the walls around me, connecting to a fourth one built from rust-coloured bricks behind me, instantly reminding me of homes I had seen photos of from the old world. The planks of wood were painted a clean white, their hue matching the sheets that were still tangled around my legs, housing the lower half of my sore and stiff body. Another gust of rich aroma wafted into the room and sent its delicious signal up to my brain, promising that cups of fuel awaited me on the other side of the bedroom door.

In the corner, I spotted the plump cushions of a beige chair, a thick, grey blanket dancing over the armrest where a fresh set of clothing sat.

Grey.

Dragging the blankets from my legs, I jumped up, then paused to catch my balance for a moment, having gotten up too quickly. Black spots dotted my vision before fading as I crossed the quaint room in three strides, pulling open the door.

Grey's face was the first thing I saw as he spun around, magnetizing my attention like the centrepiece of a painting. He stood by a large black oven, a flat-sided utensil resting in his hand as the sizzling sound of frying food popped and snapped from the antique pan behind him.

"You're awake!" A large smile split across his face, so warm and solid that, despite the lingering effects of my deep sleep, I knew without question that I had woken up to him, rather than the opposite.

What was happening was real. Grey was real.

I ran across the creaky floorboards of the cabin, taking a sharp left around the deep-set couch that anchored the room before jumping into his arms, knocking both of us into the back wall that housed the kitchen. His laugh rumbled into my hair as I tucked my face into his neck, my arms and legs clinging to his body like a monkey.

"I missed you so much," I breathed into his neck, hugging him tighter, suddenly aware of how much I never wanted to let go.

"I was never really gone," he said, his arms wrapping around me just as tightly as he nestled his face into my neck, too. We lingered there a long moment before I finally unhooked my legs from behind his lower back, planting my feet firmly on the ground again, with my arms still draped around his shoulders. Leaning back, I took in his face again, its contrasting lines looking deeper and realer now, in my new state of knowing.

"Hungry?" Grey asked, and my stomach suddenly rumbled at the suggestion.

"What's for breakfast?" I asked, and the simple reality of the question in the context of whom I was posing it to made my heart bloom into a euphoric state of bliss.

We sat at the small table pressed against the back window of the cabin, my left leg propped under me on my chair as I bit into the soy scramble and banana waffles he had made. The savoury flavours salted my tongue, mixing in a heavenly way with the sweet maple syrup that coated my throat and the creamy tang of homemade coffee. I had never tasted food that wasn't created from a food portal, the homemade flavours mixing in subtle ways that I knew a machine would never be able to master. The meal filled me and brought on a serene food coma, until I slowly became aware of my exhausted brain and tired limbs again.

"When did you learn to cook?" I asked Grey, purposefully keeping the questions simple until we at least had the chance to finish our meals.

"When I was young," he told me. "My aunt Ryka used to bring me to this cabin whenever my dad had official Catcher business. She taught me the ways of the old world, insisting they would be of use one day. I didn't realize how right she was," a faraway look touched his eyes for a moment. "I didn't know, then, that she could read fates."

I almost choked on my coffee, placing my mug carefully back on the table.

"You mean, your mom has a sister?" I asked, thinking back to all the research I had done on Portia Kingsley. Nothing had come up about her having siblings, not even when I had searched her maiden name.

"Yeah, she did," Grey's face fell as he corrected my statement to past tense. "My dad only let me see her whenever he needed someone to watch over me when I was little, telling me not to believe the tales she put in my head. He called her a lost cause. A rebel." Grey laughed sadly, swirling a piece of waffle back and forth on his plate.

My eyes widened. "A rebel?"

"I'm not sure they actually exist," Grey said. "He had her banned from Terigon when she refused to back the blood tests, after my mom died. She came to live here, picking me up from the air train anytime I was sent away to visit. She didn't have a mean bone in her body, but my dad always spoke of her as if she were a bad person. I'm still not sure why he let me spend time with her at all. Maybe my mother made him promise to let me know her. She was the only family we had, after all, except for each other.

"I stopped seeing her when I finally became old enough to stay home on my own, whenever he had to leave Terigon. Word came a few years later that she had died from a fatal disease. He called it a cruel irony, because she'd been so critical of the testing. But it always seemed a little *too* ironic, if you ask me." He trailed off at the end, insinuating something he clearly didn't want to dwell on too much.

It was weird to see him in such a vulnerable, human state. My heart wanted to protect him in ways I had never needed to in my dreams. The way his face twisted as he found his way through the weight of his words, the pain he had clearly been masking in the short span of days I had known him has Hale.

Placing my fork on the table, I looked him over again more closely. His tousled hair was messier than usual as his head bobbed down toward his plate. I noticed the way his tired frame rested in the kitchen chair, his skin somehow warming the bare and earthy hues that filled the room around us.

"I want to know everything," I said. It was time to end the game of dreamlike charades that masked the severity of everything going on. Who Grey really was had finally begun to settle into my waking awareness, the hows and whys of everything in between my dream state and the real world demanding to be answered.

I pulled at my pant leg, remembering the fresh clothes laid out for me in the bedroom, as Grey rose to clear away our dishes. He had the entire cabin stocked with clothing, food, and everything else we needed for survival, I realized, looking around—as if he had been anticipating this moment all along. I mentally added the question of how he'd prepared all this to the rest of my long list.

Returning from the sink, Grey sat in the chair across from me again, and nodded, smiling briefly.

"Ask away," he said.

☽

"So regulated blood tests don't just check for disease. They also read our fates, don't they?"

We were sitting on the couch now, turned toward each other with refilled mugs pressed between our hands.

"Right. How did you know?" Grey asked, seemingly impressed by the pockets of information I had already gathered on my own, as we started to unravel our mess.

"My uncle Char told me. I found the kill list on his portal and forced his hand. He also told me that the Catchers thought I had died back in the lift accident when I was four. Axel hadn't done the testing, so he wasn't officially registered in Thalia's database," I said, the realization dawning on me even as I spoke. "As far as the government knew, my parents had one child. One child's body came out of the crash. His death masked my own." I shuddered and looked down at my mug, guilt tying knots into my stomach again.

Grey rested a hand on mine.

"They're after him, too," he said quietly, bringing the conversation back to Uncle Char. I knew my uncle had been working with the Catchers before they discovered the role he'd played in helping to keep me alive. He would probably be calling me any minute now if he hadn't already, wondering why I wasn't picking up. Without service in the cabin, Grey and I were safe from locators and portal signals, but it also left our temple ports and wrist hubs useless, leaving us to rely entirely on our own senses and spoken sentences. Like in the days of the old world.

"I know. He was supposed to call me with updates this morning. I hope he's all right," I said, the fear behind the words weighing heavy on my conscience. I couldn't have another life lost because of the fate of my own, especially that of another person I loved.

"He's safe," Grey assured me, and my eyes snapped back to his.

"You know where my uncle is?" I asked, hardly daring to believe it.

"We're good friends," he smiled. "I made sure he was safe."

A pinch of the worry that had been weighing on me melted from my skin, making my heart tailspin even further in gratitude for the man sitting across from me.

"The part I still don't understand is why the Catchers want me dead to begin with. Is my fate truly that hazardous?" I wondered aloud. "What is the accuracy of these tests, anyway? How are they even sure these fates are sealed enough to kill innocent strangers?"

Grey took a deep breath, settling himself before diving into his explanation.

"Back in the day, it was said that time gypsies could taste the fate of any blood that touched their lips, and one bloodline in particular excelled at it. My grandmother, Laina, was a gypsy. My grandfather fell in love with her the day she said his fate could not be told."

Grey smiled briefly, then continued. "He thought she was being cheeky, playing hard to get, maybe. Only she wasn't lying. Before the war, my grandfather grew up very sick, with a disease they couldn't pinpoint using old-age technology. That was why he became so invested in the sciences, when he grew up. He was determined to find a way to heal anyone touched by disease."

I nodded, weaving this new information into what I already knew about the history of the Catchers about and his grandfather, Catcher, who had become the original ruler that brought Thalia together.

Grey went on. "He tested himself with transfusions, working all kinds of chemicals into his blood in order to kill off the disease, until one day, it actually worked. That was the start of the process we use to cure disease now, pulling blood and infusing the white cells with electrically generated force that makes them stronger than any known disease. When the blood is transfused back into your veins, it purifies the rest of you until your system is cleaner than a newborn's, free of any disease.

"When my grandfather met Laina, she tried to taste his fate, but his blood had become so muddied by all of his tests that he was rendered unreadable. After they had my father, they discovered that he, too, was unreadable by the hands of fate, since my grandfather's blood was pulsing through his veins."

I glanced down at Grey's mug as he gripped it with tight hands, his tension making my next question one I could already guess the answer to.

"That means your blood is unreadable, too."

He nodded.

"When my grandfather died unexpectedly, Thalia was suddenly dropped on my father's shoulders. It would have been Laina's responsibility, but my grandmother was so distraught by the loss of her husband that she ended up taking her own life.

"My dad was only fifteen at the time, and was suddenly expected to take on the role of ruler after having just lost both his parents. They say he took the loss in stride, driving all of his focus and energy into his father's work of ending diseases in Thalia—including diseased fates.

"That was why he sought out my mother," Grey went on, softly. "With Laina gone, he knew he needed another gypsy to aid him in his cause. My mother played her gypsy heritage off like such nonsense didn't exist. But the minute her family arrived on Thalia soil to join the growing population my grandfather had started, my father pursued her until she couldn't resist.

"By the time they married, he had finally convinced her to test her abilities, giving her a tiny taste of blood from a recent test. The fortune of the person's fate flew out of her as soon as the blood touched her tongue. It marked a huge breakthrough for my father's testing."

Grey's voice sounded pained as he spoke about his mother, and an expression of guilt passed across his face—one that I myself was all too familiar with, from Axel. I reached over to him this time, settling my hand on his and encouraging him gently to continue.

"Anyway, once he knew she really was a true gypsy, my dad began running tons of tests on my mother, connecting her to all kinds of wires and pods as she tasted vial after vial of blood," Grey went on. "He documented the fates as she spoke them, turning her brainwaves into coding as the unworldly magic took hold, pulling fortunes from a place of in-between conscious states and the wheel of destiny she was able to tap into.

"By the time she became pregnant, he had hundreds of fates documented, and he was sending Catcher marshals out to observe whether they were actually coming true. As they returned with news of truth to every word my mother had said, he began a hunt for more gypsies, pulling my aunt in from Vancity along with other females from bloodlines that were supposed to be connected to the gypsy legend.

"All that time, my mother was happy to help him, believing her newfound power was going to contribute to the greater good of Thalia. That is, until he finally cracked the code, creating a machine that could file the molecules of someone's blood into a code and then read the fate of any individual. At least, anyone who wasn't a direct descendent of my grandfather, Catcher."

Grey looked back toward me, pain still resting on his face. The palms of my hands became damp, my body knowing that the story was about to take a turn for the worse before he spoke his words.

"After my mother became pregnant, my father ended all testing on gypsies, partly because she begged him to, and partly because he already had what he needed. He allowed them to return to the general population on the condition that they keep their abilities and every-thing they had endured a Catcher-sealed secret. To make sure they kept their word, he promised them a cruel ending of their own fates, should word ever get out." The pain on Grey's face took on a slightly haunted look. "That was when his newfound power began to get out of hand.

"When my mother died the following state of the year—in spite of everything he'd done to cure and prevent disease—I think some deep part of him snapped. Even though he had first sought her out because she was a gypsy, he really did love her. Having everyone you love yanked away from you by fate, especially when you thought you had finally mastered the power to control it, would probably drive anyone mad.

"In the weeks following my mother's death, he began testing the blood of anyone who underwent portal fusions or any type of routine examination. If the coded fate of anyone's blood foretold of any kind of harm to Thalia or himself, he began ordering their deaths 'for the greater good of Thalia.'"

Grey quoted the last words with fingers, his pale face telling me what he really thought about his father's policy.

It was all becoming clear now. The sinister feeling I'd gotten from Donte's face when I researched his name. The secrets he kept from the general population. Even the twisted logic behind the sealing of fates.

Knowing that my name was on the kill list as "high priority," I couldn't help but fight for the idea that lives shouldn't be cut short because of what their blood said could happen. But in the next moment, a thought flashed across my mind, bringing the faces of those who were most important to me to my inner eye.

If I had lost my parents, Mina, my uncle, and even Grey to a fate I could have foreseen, could have prevented . . . what lengths would I go to, to protect whatever I had left, even after they were all gone?

"What is my fate, then?" I asked Grey slowly, unsure if I wanted to hear the answer. The thought of other lives being lost if I was given the chance to live made my ignorance a comforting blanket . . . one I didn't necessarily know that I was ready to give up. But I steadied myself, keeping my eyes on Grey's, and didn't retract the question. Too much was at stake.

I had to know.

Grey hesitated a moment, dropping his attention to the mug in his hands, away from my eyes. I could see the struggle going on inside him as he weighed the words he was about to say. Finally, he looked back up at me.

"Your fate showed the death of the Kingsley blood," he said.

CHAPTER 18
smoke signals – phoebe bridgers

"You mean . . . "

"Your fate showed the deaths of both me and my father," Grey confirmed.

The words hung in the air, soaking up the silence like a sponge. Grey looked at me steadily as I stared at him in shock.

"If I live . . . you die?" My voice cracked on the last words. My dreams had only just become true, the physical reality of them sitting across from me on a couch tucked away in the mountains, only to now find out that he would be ripped away from me by the death of either him or me.

My throat tightened. I felt like a fist had just sunk itself deep into my stomach. It wasn't fair. Fates changed every day, didn't they? There was no way we were somehow born with one solid path, given no free will to change it whenever we changed directions or made new decisions within the realms of our lives. There was no justification for sending a family off a bridge in the middle of the night. No justification for messing with the lives of children.

Specifically my brother's.

"We don't know that for sure," Grey answered slowly. "You've been alive all these years, after all, and nothing has happened."

"Nothing has happened *yet,*" I corrected, standing quickly and setting my mug down on the dark coffee table in the lounge area with a thud. I paced the floor, letting the truth of everything swallow my hope, my hands balling into tight fists laced with anger and frustration. Again I wondered: How accurate were these tests? Was it even safe for Grey to be around me?

"What if you're not safe here?" I demanded out loud. "What if I kill you?"

Grey laughed, which only deepened the anger I felt.

"It doesn't work like that. It's not like you're going to suddenly decide to wrap your hands around my throat and kill me out of sheer will. It's more circumstantial," he explained, trying to sound convincing.

I stopped pacing the lounge to turn and face him, frustration still bubbling in my voice.

"Is this why I have been dreaming of you my whole life?" I asked him. It was the only other question I didn't fully understand yet.

I saw him take a quiet breath before he answered.

"When I was six, I spent a weekend here with my aunt Ryka," he began. "She disliked my father as much as he disliked her, and her opinion of him only got worse after my mother passed. That weekend, she sat me down the morning I was supposed to head home and told me there was something my mother had wanted me to do. She had always spoken of my mother like she was still around, something I used to believe stemmed from my aunt missing her. But this time she told me it was something my mother had requested before she died.

"She handed me a small vial of blood and asked me to drink it. She was a gypsy, so drinking blood and casting spells were things she always told me about in tales, to help me sleep at night. This time, though, it was real. She said that if I drank the blood I would save the life of someone my mother cared about a lot, so I did it.

"I didn't feel any different afterward, and I went back to Terigon nearly forgetting that the entire thing had happened . . . until I went to sleep that night. My portal then was more advanced than most other kids my age, which was meant to keep me ahead in my advancements so that I would be prepared to take over Thalia one day. My dad had been busy that day with work and knew he would be getting home late. So he enlisted a marshal to direct me to bed in the penthouse tower of city hall, that night.

"The marshal he chose was your uncle."

I stopped dead in my tracks, having returned to my pacing as he explained the story to me.

Uncle Char? Grey had mentioned that they were friends, but I hadn't realized how long or how deep he had been in with the Catchers; enough that Donte felt comfortable trusting him with his only son, clearly.

"He updated my system that night before I went to bed, telling me he was adding more games so long as I didn't tell my father. He was always tweaking and updating my port with fun games that other kids my age had. It made life under the heavy eye of being the future heir a little more bearable."

I smiled at this, suddenly warmed by the idea that Grey and I unknowingly shared that same experience with my uncle growing up, without having known it.

"When I went to bed that night, I dreamt of my mother," Grey went on. "She was standing on the other side of a river, watching me. She smiled, and I heard a message from her enter my mind from across the stream. She told me to save you. And that's when you came walking out of the trees toward me."

My mind replayed the same dream from my own perspective, Grey looking across the water before shaking his head that it wasn't my time to go, and telling me to wake up. I looked back at Grey now, contrasting him now with the way I remembered him then. His features were the same, only older and more handsome: the lines of his strong arms, the softness of his sea-grey eyes that took me down like a shipwreck whenever they turned my way. He lifted them to mine now, anchoring my heart to his on cue.

"After that, I was able to sink into your dreams anytime I fell asleep at night. My temple port even started going off whenever your dreams were distressing, even though I could never actually get in, when that happened. Which, by the way, has been happening like crazy lately." He gave me a probing look and I nodded slightly, unable to form the words to talk about the horrible nightmares.

"I found I was able to move and manipulate your mind to make it experience whatever you wanted, and seeing the way it lit you up became the only thing I ever wanted to see. You became my great escape. Saving you saved me." His eyes fell back to his hands as they twisted around each other, the obvious discomfort of vulnerability making him look a little more like Hale and a little less like Grey. My heart back-flipped, moved by his words.

He really had saved me, and in more ways than one.

I crossed the lounge in three strides, falling into his lap before taking his face into my hands. I kissed him, harder than I had ever kissed him before. Our lips merged perfectly, like cream to coffee, my fingers lacing through his hair as if they had found home. I felt his hands waterfall their way to the small of my back, the subtle force of them pulling me in closer as he leaned us back into the couch.

When we finally broke for air, I felt three words flow their way to the tip of my tongue, but bit them back before they could leave it. I wanted him to know how much I loved him, how much I always had. The way he looked when he said my name, the flutter of my heart when I caught him staring at me, the sea of stars he lifted me to in my darkest hours. I wanted him imprinted on my heart, tattooed onto my soul, and laced into my bloodstream for every breath I had left on this earth. But I refrained from saying it.

The love I felt for him ran deeper than anything I had ever known, strong enough to pull me under and keep me afloat at the same time. It was the kind of love that ran like a current through my veins, seizing me and taking me to places I truly could only dream of.

This was the reason I couldn't say it. Saying it would only make everything harder. With the fate of my life hinging on his, and vice versa, I knew in a heartbeat what option I would choose.

"I'm sorry," I said instead, meaning it more than he could ever know. Our foreheads pressed together, and he nuzzled his nose against mine before planting another soft kiss on my lips.

"Me, too."

☾

We spent the next few hours going over more of the details that had led to the Catchers discovering where I was.

When he had decided to take me out, Grey wasn't sure whether to let me in on any of it or not, having no idea how much I already knew. Before he'd had time to decide what to do, a mandatory Catcher call went out, summoning all council members and marshals to an emergency meeting. After gathering at headquarters, Donte notified them that a fate from fourteen years ago had slipped through the cracks, and that they had gained access to my portal system software, allowing them to hack in anytime I went under. He wasn't sure exactly how they had hacked in, having left as soon as he could with the knowledge of their plan to send me to the tracks that night.

They had been looking for me since my Syncher file came to life, following false leads in cities all over Thalia before finally discovering that I had been in Terigon all along. Once my location was known, his father had demanded that my fate be terminated immediately.

My skin crawled when Grey mentioned that part.

"By the time I made it to the meeting, they had gained full access to your portal. They said you called them?"

I tried to jog my memory, replaying the details of what had happened just last night, even though it felt like a lifetime ago.

"When Christoph dropped me at Koze, I called a portal number that showed up on my screen after I regained access. I thought it was my uncle calling from a disguised line. The phone made a screeching sound before I hung up," I remembered.

Grey nodded, clicking together the substance of my information with what he knew, like colouring in empty pockets of his mind.

I stood up, unsure of where to go from here or what to do next. We were stuck in the in-between, fate having played its cards while we waited, hiding from the monsters that were no longer the shadows of a dream.

This time the fight for our lives was real.

I walked back and forth in front of the couch before finally turning to him again.

"So," I said, "what now?"

CHAPTER 19
blood bank – bon iver

"THIS IS NEVER GOING TO WORK," I said, securing the rubber band around my arm. Grey came back from the bathroom, a bag full of supplies in tow.

"Could you stop being so pessimistic for five seconds?" he asked sarcastically, plopping down on the couch beside me. When he gestured for my arm, I stuck it out in front of him, my vein popping up high through my skin.

Grey had proposed the idea last night: a blood transfusion. If we filtered his blood into mine, letting the unreadable blood of Catcher Kingsley course through my veins as well as his, we might just be able to muddy up the fate code, he had said. After all the messing Grey's grandfather had done with his own blood, he was able to somehow render his cells unreadable to gypsies. Even if the transfusion didn't break me from my fate, Grey was convinced at the very least that my fate would no longer be readable. If he could then get his father to have me retested, we might be able to convince him or at least his marshals not to follow through with the termination orders, since there would be no tangible proof for my fate needing to be terminated.

It was a long-shot plan, to say the least. But it was all we had.

Pulling a needle from the bag, Grey rolled back the cream-coloured sleeve of his sweater before turning to me.

Taking my arm, he angled the first needle toward the vein, my eyes darting away before he made contact. When I looked back, the needle—tied to cylinder tubing—hung from my arm, and Grey had begun examining his wrist, searching for the vein that connected to his artery.

From the minute Donte and the Catchers had become aware of my unsealed fate, Grey had been spending any spare time he had in the Yorker library, researching ways to break me of it. The subtle markings of pinpricks on his wrist suggested that he had practiced this routine on himself before, in preparation. He confirmed as much when I asked, saying that the radial artery could be tricky to find.

Handing me another needle, he rolled up the sleeve on his right arm a little higher, its vein popping up willingly. I steadied my trembling fingers as I pricked his warm skin, the needle sliding in smoothly. Finally, I flipped over my bare wrist, my confidence bolstered to see that Grey had found his own wrist artery on the first try.

Once everything was connected, we did our best to get comfortable, our eyes following the dark, thick liquids that began to slowly trace down the tubes, filtering his blood into my veins and mine into his.

I thought again about what a long shot this idea was, but Grey was right. What other choice did we have?

Sinking deeper into the couch, I laid my head against its backing, curious how much time it would take to transfer enough blood to complete the process. How long would we stay in this cabin before returning to Terigon?

I hoped we'd stay an extra night or two, despite the pressure weighing on us. In a way, the cabin felt like another dream with Grey—another nighttime escape from a waking world. Only now, surfaces had more substance and Grey looked crisper. We had lain awake in bed for most of last night, reminiscing on the little-kid dreams we'd spent having fun together before puberty hit and our friendship had turned into crushes, which had then turned into the love of our dreams.

If only I had known then that he was real.

"Why didn't you ever tell me who you actually were?" I asked now, genuinely curious as to what had made him keep quiet about it, all those years.

"I wanted to," Grey said, slowly leaning back beside me, careful not to detach the tubing that bridged the gaps between us. "After that first night, I was so confused. I thought maybe you had just been a dream of mine, too, but then you popped up again. The only thing I could connect it to was what my aunt had told me, so I waited to do anything until I saw her next.

"My dad didn't pass me off to her often, so a few months went by before I got to visit her again. I came back just after my seventh birthday. My dad had a mandatory meeting in Port Edward, so as usual, I jumped the air train and came here. When I told aunt Ryka about the blood and the dreams, she smiled and told me it was a gift. Something that I would understand one day, but had to keep a secret until then. I told her about seeing my mother that first night, right before you came, and she said the girl in my dreams would lead me back to her.

"Back then, the idea of my mom had always been such a mystery to me that, after catching that brief glimpse of her, I would have done anything to see her again," he finished.

"Did she ever come back into your dreams?" I wondered how often Grey had dreamt without me in it, an idea I had never had to think about before.

"No, and after a while I stopped waiting. You had become my muse instead," he turned his head to look at me, a soft smile on his lips. I returned it with my own.

"Why haven't I been dreaming of you lately?"

"Because you haven't been dreaming. You've been having nightmares. I haven't been able to get in," he reminded me, pointing out the obvious. "It hasn't helped that I haven't had as much portal service lately, either," he went on, an expression of remorse on his face. "The past few weeks, I've pretty much either been here setting up in case we ever needed to escape, or I've been at the terrace practicing this." He lifted his wrist, the past puncture wounds faintly visible in the soft morning light coming through the cabin's windows.

I had nearly forgotten that the cabin didn't have portal service, Grey's presence feeling so much like a dream that using my temple port hadn't even crossed my mind, my wrist hub lying untouched in the bedroom.

I nodded, my mind slowly starting to float like morning fog as our blood drained and replenished, cycling through our bodies like a river.

"How are you feeling?" Grey asked, and my eyes fluttered open. I hadn't even realized that I'd closed them.

"Good," I said, a faint smile curling up my lips again. My eyes felt like sandbags, threatening to close again with each blink.

"You can fall asleep," he said softly. "I'll be right here."

For the first time in my life, I happily closed my eyelids knowing I wouldn't find Grey on the other side. Instead, a sense of comfort flooded through my slipping mind as I leaned into him, his hands guiding me carefully as my head found his shoulder, falling asleep on Grey instead of into him.

☽

Hours later, I set the small dining-room table with utensils, resting them on either side of the empty plates Grey had told me to set out. It was weird setting things out before food had even graced the plate. Normally, portal food arrived before I even had the chance to grab a fork. Now, I stood behind Grey as he tossed vegetables in a pan, frying them with spices and seasonings as a large pot sat on another section of the old-world stove, boiling hot water with pasta inside.

I was impressed by how easily he moved around the kitchen,

185

tossing pieces of food in the air before catching them in his mouth. Before long, we had turned it into a game, lobbing handfuls of grapes at one another from the cooling system Grey called a refrigerator. They flew in the air as we laughed, trying to land them in our mouths. In the far corner of the cabin, Grey had turned on a record player— another old-world gadget I had only ever seen in antique books, or my dreams. It looked just like the one from the night we spent in the treehouse, making me wonder what other things Grey had shown me in my dreams over the years that might have been reflections of something he had known in real life. An album from BØRNS played as we danced around the kitchen, water boiling over onto the stove while we tossed grapes and twirled around to the beat.

After plating the food, Grey pulled two glasses from a cupboard and snatched a bottle of wine he had brought up during his visits to stock the place.

"I figured we might want to celebrate," he said, turning the bottle toward me.

Laughing, I raised an eyebrow at him as I took a seat at the table. "Might be a little early for celebration don't you think?" I pointed out, watching him uncork the bottle and then make his way back to the table, where he placed the glasses beside our plates. The steam swirling with the scents of rich sauce and vegetables made my stomach grumble. After the transfusion, we had both slept the day away, the entire process taking a toll on both of us. When we woke, it was near dinner, and we decided it was best to make the most filling thing the cabin had to offer.

"We're here, we're alive, we're together, and not to gloat, but we're about to eat some damn good food. I don't know about you, Carson Wallace, but that sounds like good enough reason to celebrate to me." He poured the first glass.

Looking down at my plate of pasta and then back up to Grey, I thought back to a time when a moment like this would have been all I could have ever hoped for. When I thought Grey had only been a character in my dreams. After Grey poured the second glass, I lifted mine to his, waiting for him to take a seat and do the same.

"To fate," I said, smiling wryly.

"To fate," he returned, clinking his glass with mine before taking a sip. Then, standing briefly, he leaned across the table and planted a kiss on my lips before settling back into his chair.

Picking up my fork, I twirled my first bite of pasta, deciding Grey was right. The simplicity of this moment alone was reason enough celebrate.

After dinner, we rinsed our plates and washed the dishes, reminiscing on more of our dreams over the years.

"Remember the time you dressed in that ridiculous plaid shirt and axed down a tree for firewood?" I laughed, recalling how oddly hot he had looked despite the way the checkered-print sweater had engulfed him whole.

"Hey, I made an amazing lumberjack and you know it."

"Lumberjack?"

"So little you know of the old world, young grasshopper," Grey teased, planting a dollop of bubbles on the edge of my nose before returning his attention to the pots in the sink. I had never washed dishes before; they were another mindless responsibility I usually left to portals. Between the time spent cooking, eating, and cleaning, my heart had grown full, the routine steps of our night making me wonder why we had ever taken such preparations and cleaning rituals away. If my parents and I had been forced to cook and clean together, port screens turned off—or better yet, out of service—would it have brought us any closer, I wondered?

"We should build another one, like in the dream," I said, feeling the urge to dive into another hands-on project despite my tired muscles from the transfusion. It didn't really matter what the project was; I just wanted to be doing anything with Grey. He made even the simplest tasks enjoyable.

"You want to build a fire?" he asked.

"If we can! Why not?" I asked, my head turning back to the lounge area to spot the empty fireplace that was built into the wall facing the couch. It looked like it hadn't been used in decades, but it sat in waiting nonetheless.

"We could potentially do that. Let me think, what could we burn . . . " Grey emptied the sink before wiping his hands on a towel. My hands swirled another towel around the last dish, absorbing the last drops of water before I placed it back in the cupboard.

"One second," Grey said, heading back into the bedroom. Returning, he held a jar of sticks with wicks on their ends, reminding me of the smaller set I had seen once before, on the date of my birthday.

"I remember Aunt Ryka making these for her gypsy rituals. I've never used one, but I'm sure it can't be hard," Grey said, setting the jar on the coffee table. Walking over, I picked them up, noting the rough patch that lined the side of the jar. I let out a breath.

"I think I know how," I said.

Grey returned to the cabin, his arms hugging bundles of wood that he had gathered from the forest. Laying them in a pile inside the pit of the fireplace, he looked to me, and I struck the match, a sense of déjà-vu sizzling through my fingertips as it caught. My eyes widened at the flame, lost in recent memories and dreams, before throwing it to the wood below.

At first, nothing happened. Then, slowly, the cracks and cradles of the wood began to catch, orange and yellow flames slowly eating their way across the bark.

We whooped in triumph, then settled back into the couch, Grey's arm slung over my shoulder as I nestled into him, watching the flame with hungry eyes, the destruction of its beautiful power captivating me.

"We have to head back tomorrow," Grey said quietly, pulling me from my fiery daze. A moment of silence fell between us, filled only by the snaps and cracks from the fireplace.

"How will we get back?" I asked.

"I have someone picking us up at the air-train station," he told me, his words hinting at some kind of surprise. "You might know him pretty well . . . "

I sat up, snapping my head in his direction.

"Uncle Char?" I demanded.

Grey laughed, amused by the fact that I was only piecing this together now.

"Wait—was he the one who brought us here?" I asked, trying to think back to the night we first arrived. I had fallen asleep, my body tired and pained from the fall on the tracks, only to wake up in bed inside the cabin. I hadn't thought to ask exactly how we had gotten from Terigon to his aunt's cabin, my mind still reeling from the newfound discovery of Grey's real-life existence.

"Yes. I told your uncle about my father's plans, so he secured us one of the trains and brought us back to Vancity before lifting us here.

My mind spun with the constant surprises my uncle kept bringing me. A few short weeks ago, he had been the quirky relative who kept me sane through years of awkward tension between my parents and me. Now he was also the uncle who had kept my existence a secret all these years, working on the inside to make sure my life was never discovered. He took my parents in after the fire, made my dreams of Yorker a reality, gave me a loft in the city of my dreams. Only . . .

"My loft . . . " I started, suddenly piecing together how my uncle had lent it to me in the first place.

"Well, technically, it's my loft," Grey smiled. I gaped at him for a moment, then smacked his chest.

"How come you didn't tell me?" I accused playfully, more pieces of the puzzle fusing together at this latest revelation. My uncle had mentioned that the loft was safe, seeing as it wasn't under his name. He'd promised they wouldn't go looking for me there.

"We've had plenty of information to go through. The loft seemed to fall at the bottom the list, in terms of importance," he pointed out, though he cracked another smile of triumph anyway. "I took the loft over after your cousin left, making sure that it was no longer traceable to your uncle after he told me his plan to bring you to Terigon."

My heart swelled at the thought of Grey and my uncle consulting over how to keep me safe . . . while I spent the entire time obsessing over the fire.

"Grey, did the Catchers set our loft on fire, or was it really me?" It was a question I had been putting off, not sure if I wanted to know the answer.

Grey shifted, obviously trying to buy time before finding a way to answer, leaving my heart sinking into what I had always known inside to be the truth.

"The day your Syncher account came to life, we were all notified of your existence. I was in the meeting when my dad ordered marshals to Vancity to terminate your fate. I called your uncle after to let him know what had happened and that they were after him, too. He promised to make sure nothing happened to you. When the marshals arrived the following day, they said your loft had already gone up in flames by the time they arrived.

"My dad was furious. He wanted to know whether or not you had made it out alive. No one was sure." He kept his gaze away from mine, afraid the confirmation that it wasn't the marshals would hit me hard. If he had seen the terrors of flames that had haunted me all those nights following the disaster, he would have understood why the information didn't surprise me.

"Why didn't they just come looking for us at my Uncle's?" I asked.

"Carson, your uncle Char is—was—a Catcher rebel on the inside. He knows better than to have his living premises on Catcher file. He worked the system years ago to ensure no portal locators could penetrate the firewall of his loft. His address on file is one on the other side of Vancity."

My eyebrows went up, dumbfounded by the ties and secrets of this world that had unknowingly encompassed me not only in my sleeping hours, but my waking ones, too.

"Do you think all of this is going to work?" I said finally. I didn't want to accept a fate where Grey and I couldn't be together. Too many working parts played into the fact that we were both still here now. That couldn't just be coincidence. Now that I knew Grey was real, I couldn't imagine my life without him.

I knew that, if it came down to it, I would die if it meant keeping him alive. But a selfish part of me wanted to have my cake and eat it too. It wanted the transfusion to work, or to at least conceal my fate, giving me years of time to tiptoe around on the fringes of civilization if I had to, being careful to hold on to my blessing without turning it into a curse.

Grey's hands took mine, pulling me toward him as he pressed his forehead to mine, the seriousness of what we were about to do encompassing us in the tiny cabin. Lifting his hands to my chin, he tilted my head up, kissing me softly like the early rays of a morning sun; warming my lips with his as the light of a new life lingered on the edge of our future tenuously, like hope. Pulling away, we stretched the moment out as long as it would go, our heads resting together again as our eyes collided in waves of blue and grey before he finally responded.

"We're in the hands of fate now," he said.

CHAPTER 20
breath — the ivy

THE SOUND OF BIRDS singing drifted through the window and my eyes fluttered open like butterfly wings, white walls filling my vision for the third morning in a row. Shifting in my spot, I felt the weight of Grey's arm as it lay across my torso, the press of his body up against mine as we slept tangled in the bed.

I rolled over as delicately as I could, turning on my right side so that I was facing him while he continued to sleep soundly. My eyes floated across his features: the long lashes that held shut the eyes I'd named him for; his angular cheek bones that turned into his sharp jawline; the scruff on his chin, which had grown thicker during the days we'd spent in the cabin. His face looked peaceful, his chiseled features gentle in the morning light, as soft as his breath.

I thought back to last night, when we had lain in this exact position, only painted in the darkness of the midnight hour instead of the sun, while we went over the plans we had for going home. Before long, the topic had slid into the future we planned to have if everything went according to plan: living out our days at Yorker, studying together on the terrace, finding a new place in the city, and eventually breaking the news to the world that he no longer needed to be equitted. I imagined the hellfire and fury that would await me from Temperance if I somehow managed to live through this, making me wonder which kind of death would be the worst way to go:

termination by Catchers or by cat claws? I didn't doubt that Temperance could give them a run for their money.

We had fallen asleep with our fingers laced together, my head on his chest as I listened to the sound of his heartbeat; something I had never been able to hear clearly, in dreams. In an instant, it had become my favourite song—the only thing that shooed my thoughts far enough away to give me peace—and I had let the beat soothe me into sleep.

Now, lying here, I could see it pumping from the subtle beating of his chest, and I promised myself I would do everything in my power for the rest of my days to make sure it never stopped because of me.

There was a time I thought the only place I wanted to be was in a field of dreams with the boy who made them. Waking up to Grey, I found a place in the real world that finally beat that of any dream.

I floated in the moment for a little longer, knowing very well that I was lingering in the calm before the storm. Smiling, I knew that no matter what happened today, these last few days with Grey had filled me with enough love and joy to last me a lifetime of the days I might lose. I could die knowing I had loved with my whole heart, and had been given that kind of love in return. And if I had to go out to keep that love alive, I would do so knowing that something this strong didn't just die when the heart stopped beating. Whatever we had—whatever force was at play that kept Grey and I together all these years—would float among the ripples of clouds, lap within the waves of seas, and burn upon the flames of passion that proved life was more than just waking and sleeping. It was living, breathing, and being in all the moments and things in between.

That would be the faith I carried with me today, no matter the ending to our story.

Lifting a hand, I carefully shifted the weight of Grey's arm off my body, slipping quietly from under the sheets until my feet found the floor. Taking soft steps, I made my way out of the bedroom and into the kitchen, where I started a pot of coffee like and old-worlder, just as Grey had shown me yesterday.

As I listened to the bubbling of the machine, burning up the water before filtering it through the grinds, my eyes were drawn to the world outside the kitchen window. I could just barely see the snow-capped mountains that fanned out across the skyline in the distance. From what I could make out, we seemed to be in one of those mountains ourselves, tucked away in thick clouds of trees that I could see in the far corners of both sides of the window. Morning dew stuck to the ground and branches, sparkling despite the soft, foggy haze between us and the rising sun.

The whole panorama brought me a sense of stillness and calm, and for a split second my brain wavered again, wondering if it was in a waking dream or another Grey setting. Smiling, I realized that, for the first time, it was both.

I made my way to the front door of the cabin, wanting to feel the fresh air on my face. Pulling it open, I walked barefoot out into the damp grass, my toes tingling at the sensation, goosebumps rising on my skin. I walked a few feet away from the cabin, taking in the view again with fresh, outdoor eyes.

Breathing in deeply, I filled my lungs with the clean, crisp air before releasing the breath, steam rolling from my mouth in the early morning temperature. The presence of calm and contentment enchanted me, and I walked hand in hand with them, allowing the moment to briefly sweep me up.

Crack.

The sound pulled me from my internal state of bliss, catching my attention from the left. Turning my head, I listened for anything else, unsure as to how close the sound had been. A sudden curiosity that seemed to come from nowhere pulled me toward the trees, my feet taking me farther from the cabin and into the brush. I floated my hands over the surfaces of thick barks and tree branches as I passed, clearing and feeling my way through the maze of trunks, until a glimmer caught my eye in the distance.

Go pick it up, I thought to myself, my feet already trekking toward the shiny object. As I neared, I saw the tangled image of trees reflecting across a metal blade, and bent down to investigate further.

It was a knife, which struck me as odd even as my hands picked it up without thought. Knives like these were something of the old world, its blade long and sharp enough to cut through skin and bone. I looked back at the cabin, which was still faintly visible despite the thicket of forest I had wandered into. The front door still sat ajar.

I tried to make my way back to it, but my feet wouldn't move. *Not yet*, I thought to myself, again unsure of where the words materialized from.

An unsettling feeling crept into my stomach, and a sudden urgency to get back inside the cabin made my heart lodge in my throat. Something wasn't right.

Channeling every ounce of focus and energy I had, I managed to get my right knee to lift just barely off the ground, and forced it to turn back in the direction of the cabin—just as my name pierced the air.

"Carson . . . " I recognized the voice before I heard branches cracking, and turned my head.

Uncle Char stepped from behind a thick cluster of trees.

I blinked in confusion. Uncle Char was supposed to pick us up today, but not for a few hours still. The unsettling feeling dug deeper into my gut, my mind urging me to race back to the cabin, but my muscles remained cemented in place.

Looking me over, Uncle Char's face fell.

"I'm so sorry," he said.

CHAPTER 21
embody me - novo amor

BEHIND MY UNCLE I caught the movement of more bodies as they came into view, dressed in black from head to toe. Two of them I didn't recognize, but the face of the third I knew instantly, and the sight of it sent a cocktail of anger and fear coursing through me at once. His dark eyes met mine, the malicious smile crossing his face looking much more genuine than the forced one he gave the public.

"Well, well, well. Hello there Miss Carson Wallace. It seems as though our introduction is long overdue," Donte's voice filled my ears. "Forgive the circumstances, I wasn't sure how willing you'd be to speak with me, had I just knocked on the door." His smile deepened.

Catching the subtle blue flash of his left temple, a sudden realization hit me with blunt force. The cabin must have been the only place safeguarded against portal service. My mind had fallen vulnerable the minute I stepped away from the front door.

I tried to speak, but my mouth wouldn't work. He held my tongue with an invisible fist, which only made my blood boil further.

"You kept us waiting quite some time, didn't you my dear?" Donte drawled on. "Was playing house with my son growing old on you?"

He clasped his hands behind his back as he neared me, the pungent smell of artificial evergreen oozing from him, offending the fresh trees around us. He narrowed his eyes down at my hands before planting himself in front of me, just a few feet from where I knelt. I caught my uncle's gaze, but his eyes darted to the ground in shame.

How could he?

"Ah yes, it seems as though you found my knife. Lovely thing, isn't it? Shame it can't be trusted in the hands of the common people any longer. I had it shined and sharpened especially for you." He met my eyes with his malicious ones, and the urge to spit in his face rocked me like a tidal wave held back by the dam of my hacked portal.

"Carson?" Grey's voice called from the cabin, catching the attention of everyone but Donte and me, our eyes still locked in a game of tug-of-war. His smile spread like wildfire, teeth glistening in the rays of sun breaking through the trees.

No.

Grey called my name again, this time sounding a little closer. I wanted to turn and scream at him to run, to tell him they had found us, my mind pressing hard against the cemented bones of my body.

"Over here, son," Donte called out, still staring me down with his sinister black eyes.

My heart lurched, my mind wanting to wrap Grey up; to shield him from the gutting reaction I knew hearing his father's voice would have. To save him from the dawning realization that our plan had spun out.

Moments ticked by like hours, with no movement from anyone, before I heard Grey's footsteps begin to carry him in our direction, my heart aching and racing with every step.

Finally, Grey came into view, just visible in my peripherals, his lean frame standing out against the greenery surrounding us.

"Dad, what are you doing?" His voice sounded cool and controlled, as if he were handling a flame that was threatening to catch the entire forest on fire.

"The real question here, son, is what exactly do you think *you're* doing? Hiding out with the very girl you know we've been hunting for weeks? I knew you to be an idiot, but this—" Donte's hand gestured toward me before his eyes finally set mine free, taking Grey's captive instead. "What is the meaning of this?" he demanded, coldly.

"Dad, you don't understand. She's no longer a threat, I swear it. Test her!" Grey's cool tone cracked a little, a hint of desperation creeping into it, and I could tell he wasn't as confident in our plan as he had made it seem the night before.

Donte laughed, a cruel, rumbling sound of amusement that rolled nastily into my ears. Pushing down my revulsion, I tried to cling to it, focusing on each of my senses, trying to get a sense of what I could control and what I couldn't.

"You really are a fool, aren't you boy?"

"I gave her my blood, we broke her fate. I swear if you just test her she—"

Donte laughed again, and this time the sound was ugly, his poised persona broken by Grey's words.

"You think giving this girl some of your blood will keep her from her destiny of killing us both?" he spat.

My eyes moved toward Grey, and I immediately set to figuring out if I had moved them or if it was part of the simulated control. I tried to break my focus away from their banter and direct it to my hands, to feeling the cool handle of the knife. Concentrating, I tried to release it, moving against a force much stronger than my own will.

Grey kept his eyes on his dad's, a power struggle settling into the air between them like the ramming horns of two bulls.

"Just retest her," Grey spat back, the words infused with distaste.

Donte remained still for a moment, pondering his next move like he would a game of a chess, before knitting his fingers behind his back again and turning toward the other Catchers.

"Let's get a second opinion, shall we?"

Focus, Carson, I thought to myself, trying my best not to soak in too much of the commotion around me, funnelling all the attention I had into breaking free of the invisible prison.

"Char, what do you think? Should we retest your sweet little niece?"

Grey's eyes turned wild, having not noticed my uncle until then. Uncle Char remained tucked behind the front lines, his shoulders sagging in guilt.

"Char, what are you—?"

"Ah yes, son, he turned you kids in. It was a good deal on his behalf. We granted him freedom from the punishment he would normally receive, after years of treason and deceit. We even agreed to let his daughter live.

"Although . . . " Donte spun back toward Grey, his expression filling with smug satisfaction at the sight of the shock and betrayal showing openly on his son's face. "I should have known you were hiding out here. Silly me to have assumed my only child went running off on a bender in the midst of a high-profile fate case. It seems I underestimated your need for my attention, something we can discuss once matters have been dealt with here. Now, where were we?"

Donte lifted an exaggerated hand to his chin, as if pondering lightly over what word he needed for a portal crossword puzzle.

"Ah, yes. Char, do you believe we should waste our time and resources retesting the girl?"

Uncle Char kept his eyes on the ground, mumbling out a barely audible response.

"Speak up, Charles!" Donte boomed. It was the only time I had ever heard my uncle called by his full name, as if being punished by a parent.

"I said fates are sealed unless intercepted."

"Meaning . . . ?" Donte prompted, knowing the sting of pain it was causing among the three of us.

"It would be a waste of time."

"You son of a bitch," Grey spat, charging at Uncle Char. One of the attending Catchers acted fast, sticking out his arm to stop Grey before he could attack my uncle.

"Now, now, Hale. Let's not get too hasty here," Donte tutted, circling back over to me. This time, he came inches from my face, making my skin crawl with hatred. I urged my arm to move. To lift the knife and sink it deep into Donte's leg, or better yet, his throat.

I felt a subtle jolt in my hand, and my breath caught. I had found a tiny crack in the simulation control, fuelled by my rage.

If Donte noticed, he pretended not to.

"It seems like you need to blow off some steam, son."

Donte circled behind me.

"Dad, what are you doing?" Grey's face filled with the first signs of fear, making my heart sink through new levels of despair.

"If it's a fight you're looking for, let's give you one. Carson, my dear, kill my son."

His words pushed my body into action before I fully understood what they meant.

I charged at Grey, my mind fighting every movement, but my body in a wild rage, beyond my control. The knife glistened in my hands as I raised it in the air, just missing the arm of the Catcher marshal as he released Grey.

"Carson, no!" Grey dodged the knife, jumping to the side, fast on his feet.

"This isn't you! They're controlling you," he pleaded, but his words were useless. I knew I didn't want to kill him, and I fought the compulsion to stab at him again with every millisecond I had between the first and second lunge, my heart screaming at me to stop even as my body utterly betrayed me.

Grey dove behind a tree, pleading with me again to wake up.

I am awake, Grey! I don't want to do this, I thought desperately, the knife slicing through the air again as I came closer, barely missing his back as he dodged away from me again.

"I don't understand it, boy," Donte began calmly from behind us as the fight raged on. "I gave you a life full of everything you could possibly want. I have dismissed your reckless behaviour without punishment, and prepared you to one day take power over a country that you haven't earned."

I lunged again, the tip of the knife nicking Grey's sleeve, leaving a small cut on his forearm as he ran back toward the Catchers.

I followed him like a wild cat, sinking low as I balanced on the balls of my feet, ready to pounce wherever he moved to next.

"What is it about this girl you feel the need to save?" Donte asked indolently.

Grey stopped moving, facing me before answering.

I lunged, despite the screams of thought fighting against the movement.

"I love her," he said.

The blade pierced his chest as the words drifted into the air.

CHAPTER 22
already gone – filous

I GASPED, the moment hitting me with the same force of the knife to Grey's chest. We fell to the ground, tangled in a mess as blood began to seep from the wound.

The moment slowed, a wave of emotion raking through my body, making my breath come in heavy pants. I looked to Grey's eyes, finding that he was already looking into mine, and my heart convulsed, choking me with a sense of shock that left me paralyzed. Tears welled in my eyes as Grey's softened, willing me to keep breathing.

"It's okay," he whispered as my hands began to shake.

"Grey . . . " I whispered back, suddenly aware that I was no longer under Donte's control.

"It's okay . . . " he breathed again, the words barely audible this time.

I looked him over, horrified by what I had done. *I stabbed him. I stabbed the boy who loved me.*

He was going to die just as destiny had stated, my life ending his.

"Grey I—" I choked.

"Run," he said, the word stronger than the ones before.

I stayed frozen, my body unwilling to leave his. I stared down at the wound, at the blood soaking through his shirt and mine.

"Well done, my dear," I heard Donte say from above. "Wells, collect Hale. Char . . . kill the girl."

My mind had ground to a stop, his words falling upon a numbed wall of horror and heartbreak.

"Carson." Grey's whisper broke me free of the chains that had begun to wrap around me. For a moment, the world melted away, and I was lost again in the clouds of smoke that rested around his pupils, dilating more with every second. Eyes I knew I'd never look into again.

"I love you, too," I whispered, regret from not having said it earlier washing over me.

A faint smile touched his lips before his face turned serious again. This time, he left no room for negotiation.

"Run."

Standing, I didn't dare look back before my feet took to the earth beneath me.

"What the—" Donte's words already sounded smaller behind me. "After her!"

Footsteps started charging toward me, but I refused to look back at who they came from. I pumped my legs harder, the stratospheric wave of powerful emotion breaking me free of any simulation control as my stiff muscles loosened to the movements like they usually did during the first moments of pounding the ground. Tears clouded my vision, making it harder to dodge branches and trunks as I looked for a pathway among the trees, but I didn't stop. I charged forward, ramming my feet into the ground below, allowing the pain to pound through the numbing sensation around my shattering heart.

My arms pumped viciously in the air, more tears staining my cheeks as I gasped for air, running not just from my pursuers, but from everything I had done. I ran from Grey, ran from his bleeding heart and dying eyes.

Run, I remembered his last word to me, my feet moving faster as my muscles burned. The air raced past my ears, the trees melting together all around me as I channeled my focus onto an inanimate point ahead of me. I ran faster, letting the lack of oxygen sear through my muscles, eating away at the ripping feeling that tore through my chest.

I killed him.

The tears fell harder now, making it nearly impossible to see. I reached out, my hands catching a tree as I spun around it, shifting my direction, unaware if the feet that followed were still behind me or not. My strides began to falter, the tidal wave of emotions beginning to crash down on me in earnest as my foot caught the root of a tree, sending me tumbling down a stretch of rocks and shrubs.

I felt the sting and scratch of sharp edges and branches and I ricocheted off the ground around me, falling to lower ground, until I finally sprawled out onto the earth.

Rolling painfully onto my back, I caught a piece of the sky above me through the thick canopy of pines, a single cloud floating slowly by, unaware of the commotion below.

"Carson . . . " a soft voice trailed into my consciousness.

I turned my head toward it, hardly caring what I saw. I didn't want to move, I didn't want to run. Whoever it was, they could have me.

I had nothing left.

Chestnut-coloured hair tumbled down around the figure in long waves, framing the face of what I thought might be an angel. Only, I had seen that face before.

Grey's mother stood in the distance, a pale figure amongst a blanket of trees, dressed in soft grey. Even from far away, I felt her familiar eyes settle into mine with ease.

"You did what had to be done," she said, a compassionate smile on her face, before a thundering crack of impact knocked me unconscious.

CHAPTER 23
see you when I see you – handsome ghost

I KICKED MY LEGS *off of the bed in my room in Vancity, planting my feet firmly on the dimly lit floor. Looking to the bed port, the hour read 0400. Right on time.*

I pulled open my nightstand drawer, the pack of matches resting in wait. Smiling, I picked it up, my eyes beginning to adjust to the late hour. I walked over to my bedroom window, tapping a demand into my temple to open it.

Portia was standing outside, just as I knew she would be.

As she smiled at me, I fell even deeper into a state of calm and ease, despite what I was about to do. I smiled back, happy to have her here as my guide.

"You know what to do," she said, her words falling gently upon my ears despite how far away from our loft she was standing. Her light grey tracksuit faded easily into the fencing that led to our neighbour's yard, her chestnut hair the only thing standing out against a wall of light shades, cast in moonlight.

"Do what needs to be done," she said, and without hesitation, I spun on my heels, heading toward my bedroom door. I made my way down the hallway and stairs, my feet leading me into the kitchen and lounge area as I navigated the pathway toward the couch. Turning the pack of matches over in my hand, I flipped open the cover, one match missing from the pack. I pulled another free, feeling the slim stick between

my fingers as I turned the square box over again. Catching the match across the back, a flame burst to life, making the room dance with subtle shadows cast upon stale white walls.

A moment passed, the smell of the match burning its way into my nose as a fleeting moment of panic crossed my mind.

Was I sure I wanted to do this?

"Do what needs to be done," I recalled Portia's voice in my head again, her calming grey eyes easing my sudden discomfort.

Flicking the match away from me, I watched it land on the couch before tearing the pack back open and lighting the next. This time, I torched the curtains.

Then the lounge-room chair.

Next, the dining-room table, our entire loft joining in a united flame as it sang a song and dance of fire.

Pleased with the view of flickering flames burning away the broken home that had housed me all these years, I turned to make my way back to my room—but stopped dead when I saw my parents standing at the foot of the stairs right in front of me.

"Good job, hun," my mother said, my dad's arm reaching up for my temple before everything faded to black.

🌙

My eyes flashed open, my chest rising and falling in quick breaths as I took in the space around me. In the corner, my dad sprung to his feet, crossing quickly to my bedside before calling for my mom.

"She's awake!"

"Wh-where am I?" I heard my own voice croak, my throat desperate for water. I tried to ask for some. "Wat—"

"Get her some water, Cortez," my father said, cutting me off from having to speak. Leaning down, he ran his hand over my hair, tucking it behind my ear before kissing the top of my head. "Don't worry Carson. You're safe now," he reassured me.

Confusion seized my pounding brain, my hand finding its way toward the source of the pain. When it got there, I felt a bandage wrapped securely around my head.

What was going on?

I tapped my temple, waiting for the date and time to flash to life. Nothing.

"Your portal is broken, sweetie," my dad said, responding to my action. "Your Uncle Char had to make sure it was out before bringing you here, in case they tracked you."

Uncle Char? I tried to sit up too fast, and a wave of fuzziness rushed through my head, leaving me dizzy.

"No. No. Uncle Char turned us in. It's all his fault," I managed, the details from before flooding into me all at once. "Grey's dead! It's his fault," I said again, knowing it was only half true. It wasn't just Uncle Char's fault that Grey was dead. It was mine, too.

"Who's Grey?" my dad asked as my mother returned to my bed, handing me a glass of water. I downed it in large gulps, feeling the hydration seep into my body, breaking the clouds swathing my mind. I tried sitting up again, this time with more success.

Four walls surrounded us, closing us into a perfect, windowless square. The soft, blue-grey paint looked dated, along with the chairs that rested in either corner of the room.

That was when I spotted Mina, suddenly rising from the chair my father had been blocking.

"I'm so glad you're okay," she said, walking to the other side of the bed I was in and taking my hand. Her face was pinched with worry, her purposely bushy eyebrows knitted together as she looked at me.

"Where are we?" I asked her, knowing that she was the most likely of the three to tell me the truth.

"A hospital," Mina answered, leaving several important details out, judging by the look that passed behind her eyes.

"Where?"

"Just outside of Vancity. You're safe here. The Catchers don't know this place exists," my mother said, looking over my dad's shoulder.

"You guys know about the Catchers?" I asked, extending the empty cup to indicate that I needed more water. This time my dad took it, leaving the room to fetch more.

"Yes, honey. We've known all along," my mother said.

I didn't think she understood what I meant. There was no way she knew about everything that had happened since I last saw her. Where did I even begin to explain?

"No, Mom. They kill people. They kill innocent people based on some fate test. They killed Axel!"

Again, the words were half true. I knew very well that it was because the Catchers had been pursuing me that Axel died, leaving me, too, at fault.

My mother's face grew soft, her eyes filling with tears. "We know, honey," she repeated again. "We know everything."

"But how . . . ?" My dad reentered the room, handing me water that I suddenly no longer needed. Behind him came my Uncle, his face full of apology and guilt.

"*YOU*." Venom slipped through my teeth, my body tensing as I tried to lunge forward.

Both Mina and my parents held me back, my uncle's head dropping lower as he rounded the end of the bed, making sure to stand the farthest from me.

"Carson, wait," Mina said, her words colliding with the protests of my mother and father.

"Hear us out," my dad chimed in.

I ignored them. "It's all your fault!" I shouted, my voice booming around the room louder than I had anticipated. Tears began to fall down my cheeks as the returning wave of realization that Grey was gone flooded through me.

"It was all part of the plan," my mother said, and my head whipped toward her, waiting for further explanation.

"He had to turn you in, Car. We couldn't risk bringing you both here. We weren't sure if Hale would turn and we knew very well that his father would go looking for him before long. Turning you in was the only way to make sure we could get you here without him."

I stared at her, dumbfounded by her words. I felt the ache of Grey's loss knife its way into my heart again, the agony of what she was saying burning the truth deeper into my veins.

It wasn't just my fault that Grey was dead, nor was it just my uncle's. It was my mother's, my father's—everyone's. Everything that had factored into what had happened . . . we all wore a piece of it. We had all taken on the decisions that led us here.

"Get out," I said, tears flooding my vision again. Reaching out my left hand, I grabbed Mina's, needing to feel the comfort of a friend as my heart broke into a million pieces.

They just stood there.

"I said, GET OUT!" I screamed at my parents and uncle, and my mother's shoulders flinched.

"Okay, Car. We'll give you some time . . . " my dad said, glancing over at Mina, who gave him a soft nod.

Mina perched herself on the edge of my bed as they filed out of the room and closed the door. I lifted a hand to my head again. The effort of yelling at my family had sent a new flood of pounding into my temples.

Mina waited patiently, knowing not to press down on the weight I was already feeling. Dropping my hands, I opened my eyes to her, feeling grateful for her presence after weeks of near-solitude that felt like a lifetime.

"How long have you known about all of this?" I asked. I had to admit, the shock of seeing Mina here and realizing she was somehow a part of all of this left me curious.

"I'm new," Mina said. "I only got involved after your parents told me the danger you were in. I'm so glad you're okay."

She leaned in, hugging me softly to ensure she didn't hurt me.

"You look like an absolute mess," she laughed, and a small smile touched the corner of my mouth, despite the horrible feeling still burning through my chest. A moment passed without words as I tried to process what I wanted to ask next.

"So, where are we really?" I asked, deciding to get the most important element out of the way.

"We're in the rebel headquarters," Mina responded, then paused, allowing me to process.

"Wait. Rebel headquarters?"

"It's one of the old bunkers that housed survivors from the world war, but it's been updated and firewalled so Catchers can't find it. Your uncle made sure it wasn't located on Catcher maps a long time ago, when Portia began gathering people for the rebellion."

"Portia . . . "

"Kingsley. She was married to Donte before she faked her death, leaving the Catchers behind after they ran all those experiments on her to create the fate testing."

"You mean, Portia is alive?" The shock hit me with sudden certainty as I remembered seeing her in the woods, remembered my dream of the fire.

Had it actually been a dream?

"Yes. She runs this place." Mina's hand gestured to the room around us, indicating that much more lay outside the door.

Alive. Portia was alive! My first impulse was that I had to tell Grey.

No sooner had I thought it than my stomach sank, the reality of his death hitting me like an air train for the third time since I had woken up.

"What happened out there?" Mina's voice was soft as she took my hand again, her gaze searching my face as I felt my eyes flood with tears again. I didn't know how to answer her, my heart having spent itself, unwilling to care about much else at this point.

I reined it in, using the little bit of energy I had left to mask the look on my face and breathe the next words into the air.

"I think I need some sleep," I said, not looking Mina in the eye. After a moment, she nodded, getting up from the bed.

"Okay," she murmured, releasing her hand from mine. "I have some duties to take care of, but I'm going to come back right afterward and check on you," she told me, rounding the bed. I nodded, still staring at the edge of the narrow mattress, holding back every emotion that threatened to spill over until I was alone.

Mina left the room quietly, looking back once before shutting the door softly behind her.

I waited a few moments, making sure that she had truly gone, before finally letting the current suck me under. Sobs bubbled up my throat and escaped as tears filled my vision, drowning me in a sadness so heavy I couldn't breathe. I cried for what felt like hours, letting the blue-grey walls lull me closer and closer to another deep oblivion, until my eyes finally closed again.

EPILOGUE
goodnight – shoffy

MY EYES BLINKED OPEN *to a sea of sky surrounding me in shades of pink, orange, and yellow, all of them blending together like the brush strokes of liquid paints. The cloud beneath me curved and curled around my body, holding me weightless in the setting sky.*

Standing, I walked to the edge of the cloud, taking in the rippling sea of foam beneath me as I breathed in the warm air laced with the final rays of the sun. The view was magnificent, rolling hills of condensation building up like mountains that rose around me.

"There you are."

Spinning, I saw him. Dark jeans, long black sleeves, and tousled hair—the perfection of an intentional mess.

"Grey!" I ran to him, jumping into his arms the minute I was close enough. Wrapping his arms around me, he spun, the two of us laughing as we fell back into the cloud below.

"You're here!" I exclaimed, joy flooding me like the sun itself.

"I am," he laughed, bending closer to kiss me. I felt the familiar tingle of peppered pinpricks as our lips collided, the sensation reminding me that this was all just a dream.

Pulling back, I stared into his silver eyes, brought to life by the golden hour of the sun. I wasn't sure if I would ever see those eyes again.

"How are you?" he asked, his hand finding mine before he began drawing circles into my palm. I looked down at our hands,

catching the movement with sad eyes.

"I'm all right," I lied, not wanting to puncture the moment with reality. My portal had been broken. I knew that any dream I was having now was truly one of my imagination. Nothing more.

"How are you?" I dared to ask back finally, not sure how else to redirect the conversation.

He laughed again. "I've definitely been better," he said, amusement filling his words. I smiled, not wanting to be rude.

He lifted his hand to my mouth, his thumb tracing over my bottom lip softly as he took me in with tired-looking but happy eyes. "God, it's only been a few days, but damn I miss you," he breathed.

"I know," I said, unsure of how much I wanted to say. One wrong move, a jostle of emotions, or a turn of phrase, and I might wake myself up, ripping myself away from someone I wasn't sure I'd ever see again.

"Carson."

I looked up at him, fighting the feeling of tears that swelled in my eyes. Knowing what it was like to hear my name fall from those lips in waking hours made this version feel like a tease. A cruel joke my mind was playing on me to torture me for what I had done.

I started crying, feeling Grey pull me into a tight embrace as my tears soaked through his shirt.

"I'm so sorry, Grey," I sobbed, wishing I had been given the chance to say it in real life.

"I know, I know. It's not your fault." There it was again: my mind playing more cruel tricks, trying to pretend I was off the hook for what I had done. I didn't answer, unsure I was even able to, at this point.

Grey brushed his hand over my hair, hushing me as I continued to sob. After a few minutes, I pulled myself together, deciding I wanted to make the most of this time I did have with him, even if he was imaginary.

"There we go," he smiled, letting me cry out the last of my tears. "Hey now, you're here, I'm here, that's—"

213

"Reason enough to celebrate," I finished his sentence, wiping the last of my tears away with my free hand.

Laughing, we hugged tighter, holding each other a moment longer as the silence fell again between us.

"Question," Grey said, the sky suddenly darkening into shades of lavender and periwinkle blue.

"What is it?" I asked, trying to burn the colours of the moment into my mind, still unable to shake the fear that I might never dream of Grey again.

"Want to go cloud surfing?"

I tilted my head up to him, a smile beaming on my face. Lifting one hand in the air, he gestured for mine with the other, taking my palm in his and lacing our fingers together.

We walked to the edge of the cloud before counting down.

Three . . . two . . . one . . .

We jumped, soaring through the air, our laughter catching us like wings as we tumbled down to the cloud below, rolling and bouncing on its spongy surface.

My giggles rippled through me, followed quickly by a sense of guilt for feeling so happy with someone I had so blatantly taken from the world.

At the thought, sobs ruptured through the giggles. It was no use. I could no longer hide behind the charades of dreams that kept me from the truth.

"Carson, it's all right!" I felt Grey's hands on my shoulders again, rubbing my arms until I was able to stop the wave of tears.

"I'm sorry," I apologized again, only this time I was sorry for wasting what little time we had left.

"I thought you said this was reason enough to celebrate?" He tilted his head toward me, that same smile that always sent my heart into a frenzy.

"I know, but you're gone, Grey. You're not really here," I said, averting my eyes from him to keep from crying again, turning them *instead toward the river of colours that had begun to cascade through the sky around us. Like the northern lights.*

"But I am," Grey said, his hand finding mine again as he laid his head beside mine, staring up at the sky with me.

It wasn't what I meant, but I didn't want to ruin the moment more than I already had, reminding myself again that this might be the last time I ever saw the show of lights with Grey. I couldn't spoil it.

Dancing above us, colours flashed from bright fuchsia pinks to smouldering purples, only to then dip into sea-foam greens and billowing blues. Each colour painted a new streak in the sky, making me wonder how many more of them I had before it was time to wake up. How much longer until my eyes opened again to face a new day, with every colour waiting for me, except the only one I wanted to see?

The sadness tugged at me, threatening to pull me back into a conscious state, so I pushed it away, letting my eyes dance with the colours until time did what it always did.

"Carson," Grey whispered. I peeled my gaze slowly away from the sky and focused it on eyes that had once brought me the only source of life I needed. Only now, they reminded me of everything I was going to miss.

"I need you to promise me something." His face was serious beneath the rainbow of colours playing over his skin.

I nodded, knowing that anything he said I would do, despite knowing it wasn't truly him.

"I need you to come and find me," Grey said, and my brows pinched together at his words. What did he mean?

"Carson, I'm alive."

☾

Acknowledgements

ONCE UPON A TIME, I was an eighteen-year-old, skipping classes and dealing with the heavy pressures of the ending of an era of my life while watching my family fall apart under the splitting of my parents. During a time when I have never felt more lost, I found myself floating amongst the clouds of this book, originally written as an assignment for my writer's-craft class in my final year. I still remember the look on Mr. Roberts's (my English teacher's) face when I handed him a nearly two-hundred-page book, so I guess I'll start by acknowledging him and his class. Writing was something I had always loved doing, but it wasn't until his class that I found confidence in my voice, a source of emotional expression through words, and a place of escape from the parts of the real world I couldn't change. If it weren't for his class, this book would have never come to life.

Thank you to Kyra Nicholson, my loving and inspiring sister who listened to the entire first version during those early days, front to back, as we drove up and down the highway to visit our grandmother in the hospital. Your excitement, interest, and approval affected me in ways I'm not sure I ever told you about. As you followed the journey while this book went from a high-school project called *Dreamcatcher* to the full-out novel *Catcher* has become today, your words of encouragement and support built the backbone of this book and of my life. I couldn't have asked for a better best friend, and

I now owe you years of listening and support for the amazing stories you have floating around in that magnificent brain of yours.

Dad, between calling me up randomly just to ask how the book was doing, to helping me roll through ideas of how to publish it, the best route to take, and the heights the book could grow to—your excitement for Catcher fused with the energy behind my own during the times when I lost sight of my ability to follow the project through. My entire life, you have constantly instilled the idea of chasing your dreams while living within your means in me, and if it weren't for your constant acceptance and support for every idea and endeavour that crossed my mind, not only would this book not exist, but I'm not sure I would be the person I am today, doing the things I love the most. Thank you for being the best father any girl could ask for.

Poppa, you may not be physically here to see this dream of mine flourish to life, but I felt your presence many times as I was putting these words to paper. There was one solid moment, sitting on my sixth-floor patio, when I looked up to the sky that had just been falling into night, stuck between the hurricane of my personal life and the stagnated motion on *Catcher*, and asked you to help me channel every single ounce of emotion and energy I had into this book. When a star streaked across the sky, I have never been brought to tears so fast and hard in my life—and that night was followed up by two straight weeks with my head-down and words spilling forth, your bright-yellow light a constant guide for me as I pushed everything I had into this, no matter how dark the night got.

Maggie Doherty, or rather, Mina. It was one of our routine mashed-potatoes-and-dance-party nights in our old, limestone apartment on Queen that we stumbled across the few chapters I had already written of *Dreamcatcher*, stuck in the depths of my email from high school. After reading over the words I had then, you helped me collect the confidence and motivation to rewrite the entire thing, start to finish, releasing it as a fun project. Thank you for being the Mina to my Carson no matter how much our lives change, time pulls us apart, or dreams keep us away.

Christine Luney, where do I even begin with you? Between asking for constant updates on the book or helping me realize how far the entire process had come whenever I felt like I wasn't doing well enough, you have metaphorically held my hand since the day of our kindergarten class photo. You've been my soul sister for twenty years now, and we've supported each other through all the boys, cries, laughs, loves, naps, snacks, and everything in between. Even though our usual "dude" and "maaaaan" protocol rarely calls for regular sappiness, with both of us snapping each other into the laughter of life whenever things get too real or mushy, know that you are one of the most incredible people I know and a sister by choice. Even when work and boys become our new loves, I know ultimately this life will end with us swaying back and forth in rocking chairs at Fairfield Manor, complaining about the quality of the green beans and wondering how much longer until morning bingo.

Larissa Newberry, you were the ultimate bow that helped me wrap this project together. I swear our souls knew each other in some other life. Thank you for being my sounding board and sense of sanity as the weighing stress and pressures of trying to publish my first-ever book (along with trying to adult on an overall level) had me on the verge of cracking. Your kind words, loving support, and ability to know exactly when it's time for a double "w" break are the only reason the *Catcher* progression bar went from nearly done to finished. I can't wait to see what other projects we conquer in this life, fueling each other with light, love, and laughter—along with the occasional "what the hell is life" memes—en route.

Katherine MacKenett, my lovely editor. A big shout-out to the Universe for colliding us together. You rolling up your sleeves and getting elbow-deep into this project is ultimately what brought the story and my characters to life. With clammy hands, I remember dialing into that first call after you had read Catcher for the first time, waiting for you to tell me it was horrendous and to never write a single word again. Instead, you convinced me that writing can be a thing of magic and made me feel like a magician, despite the fact that my days as an author have only just begun. I can still remember calling my dad afterward, close to tears from the amazing words you blessed me with. Thank you for highlighting the things missing I just couldn't put my finger on, tying up the loose ends I left flapping in the winds, and ultimately falling as in love with Carson and Grey as I am. You have been a true partner in crime on this project, and I feel truly blessed to have been able to work with you on it, sharing our potions and casting our spells to create a kind of magic that is made of dreams.

There are so many other names I want to list here, from souls I only just met in the final weeks of *Catcher* who infused me with so much light and synergy that fates no longer seemed to be something of fairytales, to Greg who, despite no longer having the ability to give you daily updates on the process, helped me bring it to life by being there through the last and final time I decided to rewrite the story, and to the friends and family who have been there from start to finish, asking questions and inquiring about the journey. I could fill pages with the names of all the people who helped inspire me and this book, and I fear that I haven't highlighted you enough; but know that your presence was not only felt, but greatly appreciated.

My only wish is that every hand that played a role in this dream coming to life be granted all the love and magic this world has to offer, bringing their dreams to life, too.

☽

About the Author

If DAYDREAMING were a paying job, Kalyn Nicholson would have found her niche. Thankfully, between spending most of her daytime hours creating videos and podcasts surrounding her everyday lifestyle to nighttime hours drifting upon seas of dreams, Kalyn has found herself a place in this world where what she loves and what she does for a living collide. With more than a million subscribers on her YouTube channel, Kalyn has built a community of fellow dreamers, connecting with all of them through her words of wisdom and personal trials and triumphs. Between dreaming and creating, she's constantly keeping busy, inspiring and encouraging others to chase their own clouds of calling. To see more of her whimsical world, check out her YouTube channel (www.youtube.com/kalynnicholson), Instagram (@kalynnicholson13), and website at www.kalynnicholson.com.

Made in the USA
Middletown, DE
17 September 2018